THICKERELLA

TANZANIA GLOVER

I dedicate this to all the Thickerellas in the world. Go where you are celebrated, not tolerated, and flourish. Wear what you want. Do what you want. Be as loud as you want. Learn to love yourself so much that it hurts. And tell anybody who doesn't like it to kiss your fat ass.

To my auntie Tracey/Big Mama/Red. No matter how many nicknames you get in this lifetime, just know that you'll always be the original Thickerella to me.

PREFACE

I know that most fairytales start with the whole "Once upon a time" thing, but I'll spare y'all because it's 2020 and you should already know the drill by now.

This series is an experimental project for me because I wanted to challenge myself to write faster and to be more concise and intentional with my words. The experiment kind of failed because the first book took over six months to complete and it's too long to be considered a novella, but I am still very happy with the results and I'll try to make the next two shorter.

If you're itching for a longer, slow burn novel after this then please check out *Music to My Ears* and *The Beat Goes On* from The Soundtrack Series because *toots my own horn for once* each book is literally hundreds of pages of satisfying build-up, realistically written dialogue, phenomenal character development and exceptional story building. Also, I decided to write one final installment to the series so don't be too far behind when it's released.

Back to this one though. My main two intentions for this particular fairytale were to shed light on collective black family dynamics when it comes to *loving* sons but *raising* daughters and most importantly to remind plus-sized black women that they deserve all the love this world has to give especially from themselves.

Lastly, please don't be fooled by the beautifully drawn artwork on the cover. That thick thigh is meant to be an explicit warning that this is **not** your grandmama's fairytale so don't go clutching your pearls when you get to *certain* parts and please **do not** let any children read this. Enjoy and don't forget to check out the carefully curated music playlist that complements this magical tale!

1

ONCE UPON A TIME

I still remembered it like it was yesterday. November 2, 1997. Seven-year-old me sat wide-eyed and glued to the television screen just like the other sixty million people who watched as Brandy Norwood became the first Black Cinderella. Our Cinderella. I bounced around excitedly for the entirety of the movie, commercial breaks included, not only because of my joy, but also because I had to pee like a racehorse. I just refused to move an inch because I was scared to miss even one second of the magic on my screen. You see until that day I'd never imagined that somebody who looked like me could be a *real* princess and for that reason I was sure that it meant more to me than it did to the rest of those people watching in their homes that same Sunday night.

I mean sure I had always been my daddy's princess, but it wasn't until he passed three years later when I realized that my life really did have all the ingredients to the classic fairytale. I didn't have an evil stepmother and stepsisters per se, but I sure as hell had a mother with a mean streak and a good-for-nothing brother who both seemed to make it their mission in life to keep my self-esteem in the gutter.

There was never a time that I remembered my mama being particularly warm with me, but she didn't start outright being mean until after my father Timothy Sr. died from prostate cancer. Before then she would always berate him for spoiling me too much, but of course he never listened and continued treating me like royalty anyway. And while Michelle never technically neglected me and did just enough to look like a good parent to outsiders, I could still always tell from her actions and her lack of patience with me that I wasn't adored as much as my rotten to the core brother TJ.

Without my dad in the picture I was left alone with them and my "free ride", as Michelle called it, was over and I was told that it was time for me to earn my keep and become a woman. Just shy of eleven I was taught how to care for the entire household while fourteen year old TJ got to play video games and kick his smelly feet up every day. I even had to learn how to do the outdoor work that my dad always took joy in because TJ's lazy behind refused to even do his only chore which was taking out the trash. Of course that eventually became my responsibility as well.

Yep in the blink of an eye my princess status was completely revoked just like my mother's driving privileges after her third DUI when I was around fifteen. I remembered being terrified to learn how to drive then, but she made me get my permit just so that I could drive her around and run her errands which mainly consisted of buying lottery tickets and reupping on cheap alcohol.

Michelle had always indulged socially, but once she became a single parent like the women she'd always looked down on, she turned into a full blown alcoholic. She also had a bit of a gambling problem that she was still to this day in denial about and survived off of scratch-offs until she could scrounge up enough to go to one of the nearest casinos. We lived on the south side of Chicago so unfortunately we had them in nearly every direction and she was a regular at all of them even driving to "The Boat" in Indiana to try her luck sometimes.

After somehow blowing through my dad's hefty insurance policy in just a few years, she started actively advertising my babysitting services around the neighborhood because at the time I wasn't old enough to get a real job yet. And as if robbing me without a gun for my little pocket change then wasn't bad enough, she began putting bills in my name after refusing to pay off her own. I legit had to do credit repair before I ever had a credit card of my own because she decided to make all the mistakes for me before I even got a chance to.

By the time I was sixteen and working more hours I'd gotten crafty enough to bypass her and just pay all the bills directly. I learned fast when our lights and gas were still turned off even after Michelle had taken my check from my after school job to cover it. Of course she wasn't happy that I'd cut her out as the middle man, but she didn't complain much because I got us caught back up and I still gave her what was left for her pocket. My brother on the other hand got to keep all of his money to buy the latest sneakers and to support the weed habit that Michelle pretended not to know about.

TJ was probably the only person on this earth who despised me more than my mother and no matter how long I racked my brain for a reason, I could never come up with one. I had never done a single thing to him and mostly just tried to stay out of his way yet his disdain for me ran rivers deep. I didn't get it. He was clearly the favorite and always free to do whatever he wanted while I was saddled with the restrictions of a Buddhist monk. I was forced on birth control the minute I got my first period despite Michelle only letting me out of her sight for school and later for work. Of course it came with all kinds of side effects including but not limited to the weight gain that she then began criticizing me for. After a while I actually did start to eat my feelings and it didn't take much for me to start tipping the scales because I'd inherited my dad's tall chubby genes.

I was treated like a heathen and called fast for having innocent childhood crushes while TJ didn't even bother sneaking girls in his room. He just walked them right in through the front door and even had them spending the night sometimes. He was her little heartbreaker though so she just gave him condoms which he obviously didn't wear because a little after his seventeenth birthday my niece Tiffa was born. I didn't mind her though because she was literally the only good thing that came from his existence. Still Michelle's efforts would have been better spent on him because if she had hounded him about sex half as much as she did me, then maybe he wouldn't have made her a grandma so damn young.

But as bad as Michelle and TJ were, and believe me they were absolute trash, I still had Diane. While technically just my paternal aunt, she was a fairy godmother to me in every way possible. I had always been a little bit taller than other kids my age, but it wasn't until middle school when I started actually praying to be smaller because I shot up like a beansprout seemingly overnight. I often dreamed of shrinking myself down like I'd seen on *Honey, I Shrunk The Kids* but every time I woke up disappointed that I still awkwardly stuck out like a sore thumb.

When Diane, a proud six-foot goddess, noticed me slouching one day she made me stand upright and sternly advised me to never shrink myself, figuratively and literally, for anybody.

Turn your nose up to the sky to make yourself even taller, Tilly. You'll be closer to God that way.

While I appreciated her words of encouragement then, it took years for them to actually sink into my head but never once did she stop affirming me. When the plus sized dresses from the mall weren't cutting it for prom and Michelle had gotten frustrated and gave up on finding anything, Diane was the one who took me to get a custom one made which began my love affair with having clothes tailored. It was like a light bulb moment because I suddenly realized that I no longer had to make my body fit into something it wasn't made for. I could make the clothes fit me and the rest was history.

Michelle made it clear that I had to be out of her house after I graduated high school because she reasoned that two grown women couldn't live under the same roof even though TJ was twenty-one at the time and still home. I didn't question her logic though because at the time I was just happy to be set free. After graduation I realized that the only thing missing from my fairytale happily ever after was my very own Prince Charming who looked like Usher, but I was in no rush to find him because I just wanted to have fun for the first time in my life.

At the time Atlanta was still being hailed as a mecca for black people so to Atlanta I went. I received a full ride to Spelman where I was promised another fairytale in the form of a Morehouse man and a degree. Let's just say that I got the degree. While I was there I took any internship paid and unpaid that would have me to avoid going home in the summers and by the time I'd finished my graphic design program at Georgia State, I knew that Atlanta would become my home for good.

Not returning to Chicago was the best decision that I had ever made and I had a great life in Atlanta and I was lucky enough to find the best friends that a girl could have. I wore my hair short now so I loved my barber like a play cousin, but my tailor Nicole had become like family for real and always had me looking good. We were cool back in college, but we became inseparable after I started making drop offs at her family's shop every week and she had even recommended me for the building we lived in when the unit opened up on her floor.

Once we were neighbors and I saw how talented she was at making her own everyday clothes and cosplay costumes, I started using my natural drawing skills to design clothes that I'd wanted but were too costly to buy or that didn't come in my size. We had been playing around with the idea for years now about starting a clothing line or opening a boutique, but we both worked full-time and could never find the time to get passed the idea phase. It was such a shame too because we were like yin and yang. Nicole was great with sewing, but she wasn't very creative whereas I was always coming up with new ideas, but I couldn't sew to save my own life.

I knew she was my sister from another mister for real though when she helped me get through leaving my ex-fiancé Bryan last year. I was a complete crying-and-listening-to-Deborah-Cox-on-repeat mess then, but I came out better on the other side thanks to her support. And as much as I was hurt by the end of that relationship, I didn't regret it one bit because I learned so much about myself that it was worth the heartbreak. I guess growing up the way that I did, I'd learned to think that way about every unsavory thing in life because even though being a part of my family wasn't easy, I'd survived it.

I learned to have a thick*ish* skin. I learned how to be resourceful and no nonsense. I had been perceived as an adult because of my height and curves long before I became one so I learned how sleazy most men were before my friends and knew how to navigate relationships better. Until Bryan. But overall I had a good life now. I still had things that I wanted to accomplish, but I was right on track for it all. I had savings and a plan and I didn't mind helping Michelle from a distance. I much preferred getting a phone call from her once or twice a month asking for something than having to see the look of disdain on her face that my general presence seemed to cause.

So now knowing all of this imagine my surprise last week when I got the phone call from Michelle saying that she needed me to come home immediately. Well first she asked for a very large amount of money, but then she told me, yes told me, that I would have to move back to help her save the house. The bank had given her a time frame and an amount to pay before the foreclosure process would begin and when I saw the total I was floored.

"Ma, why didn't you let me know it was this bad? And when were you gonna tell me you got laid

off?"

"You didn't birth me, Tilly. I brought you into this world. Now are you gon' help family like I raised you to or not?"

I swear mothers everywhere would've been proud of the way she effortlessly laid that guilt trip on me. She reminded me how much my father loved the house. How he spent every weekend working on something outside from cutting the grass or cleaning the gutters or gardening. How he would be so disappointed in us all if we let it go back to the bank.

Initially I said moving back was out of the question because I'd made a promise to myself that I would never live under her roof again and because keeping our distance was what made this family work. But I just couldn't help thinking about how much my dad loved that house and how he would hate knowing that it wasn't a part of our family anymore.

And like the walking ATM I was, I eventually agreed, but I refused to give up my Buckhead condo because my stay would not be permanent and Nicole came up with the idea to AirBnB my place while I was gone to bring in extra money. The thought of strangers in my house still made me uncomfortable, but it was necessary and I had to do it so I put my valuables in storage and planned on bleaching and Lysoling the place down when I got back.

After telling her that I had arranged to work at the Chicago branch of my company for the year, I expected Michelle to say thank you or at least have a little enthusiasm, but instead she just told me she'd had someone on the other line and didn't even bother calling back that night. I shouldn't have been too surprised though because just last month she hadn't even bothered to call me for my birthday, but now she was expecting me to drop everything and come running because she needed help. And I was doing it.

I'd been foolish for years thinking that if I just continued playing the role of her dutiful daughter that someday some words of appreciation might dance down her harsh tongue, but I should've known better by now because I couldn't think of a single instance in all of my twenty-nine years that she'd acknowledged just how much I did for her. I must have been a masochist because even though I knew I'd never get it, I still craved her approval.

My arm, the left one with the hard to miss childhood scar, got very tan on the quest home as I drove through Tennessee, Kentucky, and Indiana. The ride took me almost two extra hours because I kept making stops and contemplating turning around at every toll since I would dearly miss the place that I now regarded as home. In

Atlanta I was Tillar Reed, well-known graphic designer and wannabe socialite and fashionista, but in Chicago I was just Tilly the fat maid. I wanted to believe that all of that ugliness from my mother and brother would finally stay in the past especially since they needed me now, but I wasn't counting on it.

But even if they hadn't grown any since the last time I'd seen them, I would try my best not to let their antics get to me because although I had ninety-nine insecurities, my weight was no longer one. I was far more concerned about my potential and my place in the world. I spent my days working for a popular soda company because I stopped calling it pop when I got south. I got paid a respectable salary for what basically amounted to drawing all day. I was hired as a graphic designer, but the reason I was one of the highest paid in my field was because I built up a rapport with the advertising department and became something like a consultant as well. I made myself necessary to the company by becoming what was essentially their cultural and sensitivity filter. I was good at it, but my heart wasn't in it.

I wanted to do something more meaningful with my time. I knew fashion wasn't exactly curing cancer, and boy did I want to cure cancer, but it had been the biggest part of increasing my self-esteem over the years and I wanted to use it to do the same for other women. For me feeling cute was less about attracting somebody to sleep with and more about hyping myself up to get shit done. No one could tell me anything when I put on clothes that were made specifically for my body. Eventually I wanted to start a cute shoe line for women like me with big feet too because the struggle was real, but I wanted to focus on clothes for the time being.

I let myself imagine the endless possibilities for way too long though because I got sad when I realized that I was literally heading in the opposite direction of making my dreams come true.

When I was ninety miles outside of Chicago and making my last stop for gas, I'd sent my fifteen year old niece a text so I wasn't surprised to see her and my six and seven year old nephews waiting for me on the front porch when I pulled into the long driveway. She was the most excited to see me though and even beat the boys running to give me an enormous hug before I could get out of the car.

"Oh my god! You really brought your car with you? How long are you staying?!" Tiffa asked as she selfishly blocked her brothers Timare and

Timere from getting in on her auntie action. No doubt she was glad to have me here for more than a few days for a holiday especially because I hadn't been home in almost two years. She was overdoing it though since she'd just spent her spring break with me a few weeks ago because everybody had to work so I invited her down. She loved the south just as much as I did and fell for Spelman's campus before the tour could begin so I knew I had a future Jaguar on my hands.

"For a while," I answered vaguely because I didn't want her or anybody else expecting me to stay for the entire year that I'd been approved for. I would work ten jobs here if it got me back south in a month, but I knew outside of selling something that was probably a reach and I'd be here longer. Not that I had anything against that particular lifestyle though because while I wasn't selling anything, I certainly wasn't giving it away for free either.

But back to Tiffa. After loving on the boys for a minute, I went back to her because I shamelessly played favorites, not just because she was my twin, but because my mother and TJ favored his two boys over her. I still didn't know why her mother Sofia hadn't broken off her foot in one of their behinds by now, but I did my part to make her feel extra loved.

She was chubby, brown and tall and

basically me all over again because my maternal family's genes were unmatched. In fact she looked more like me than she did her own mama so people always assumed she was my daughter when we were all together. Nicole still lowkey believed that Tiffa was my secret kid that I had left at home after meeting her.

I loved it all because I knew that it ate TJ up inside that his daughter came out looking black and beautiful just like me because he had purposely chosen my childhood friend Sofia, a light brown Afro Latina, to get the opposite effect. You could tell he made sure that wouldn't happen again by looking at the boys' mama Cassie because they were about as clear as *Casper*.

"There's my favorite niece!" Diane exclaimed as I finally stepped inside before Tiffa huffed. "Fix your face. You are my favorite *great*-niece. Tillar is my favorite niece."

"But we're your only nieces," I corrected her.

"All the more reason to be my favorites! Now let me get a look at you!" she said as she spun me around and complimented me. "Are you still giving those southern men hell?"

"Of course. Just like you taught me to. Where's Jordan and the babies?" I asked about her daughter and grandchildren because I'd been expecting to see them here. She explained that one of the babies had an ear infection so they were at the emergency room getting checked out.

"Anyway I'm late meeting the professor for dinner, but I wasn't going anywhere without seeing my Tilly Willy first!" she said before hugging me tightly one last time then making me promise to stop by her gallery for lunch soon. I heard TJ from the living room calling me *Free Willy* under his breath like he always did when we were kids, but I ignored him and walked her out.

Just like every other time that I was here, he was watching TV on the big screen while the boys ran wild. If I didn't know any better I would swear that he'd been in the same spot for twenty years because besides the kids and his criminal record there was no proof that he'd done anything else. He bounced back and forth from Sofia and Cassie to whatever other naïve woman that would have him to avoid paying anybody rent not that Michelle would ever charge him anyway. And speaking of the devil...

"Tilly, is that you?" Michelle asked after I knocked twice on her bedroom door. I knew that she heard all the commotion from Diane and the kids, but she'd been waiting for me to come to her.

"Yes I'm here. Are you decent?" I asked and she assured me she was before I let myself in. From the nice dress draped over her bedpost and Diane's attire I could tell that they were coming back from some church function that ran late, but she had changed into her favorite little green house duster to whip up something for Sunday dinner. I was shocked that the thing was still holding up because I had vivid memories of her wearing it from as far back as I could remember.

"How was the drive up?" she asked, but I just took in the sight before me.

Even though she was finally beginning to look worn down from all the drinking, she was still so pretty and I wished that I could look half as good at her age. But as pleasing to the eye as she was, she just didn't look happy and I guess there was no cure for that. I suspected that it was because her latest fling Ronald had ran off recently, but I didn't ask about him as I hated discussing men with her.

She didn't start actively dating until I left for college, but it wasn't until much later when I realized that it wasn't out of protection. It was out of misguided jealousy. I didn't recognize it back then because she made me believe that I was hideous since she was always comparing me to my cousin Jordan and her friends' skinny daughters. I swear I didn't know how I had managed to leave this house in my right mind, but clearly I still wasn't right in the head to be back now and especially under these circumstances.

"The drive wasn't too bad. I'm pretty hungry though so do you think we could order a couple pizzas? You look like you could use some rest anyway."

"Pizza for Sunday dinner? No I'm just fine. I'm making meatloaf so it won't take long and it certainly won't kill you to wait a little while to eat. You look like you gained weight since I saw you last," she remarked even though I had maintained my current weight for years. Despite carrying more weight than my doctor would have liked, I still wore it well and I had a clean bill of health because I hiked all around Georgia every weekend with Nicole since she was outdoorsy and always looking for a new trail.

"Just a few pounds," I said lowly instead of defending myself with the truth because it wasn't worth the hassle and she would continue to see what she wanted to see.

While Michelle got started cooking, Tiffa and I began bringing in my things and of course TJ's worthless behind didn't offer to help with anything. He really didn't deserve to have the same name as my daddy because I was much more kind like him. Michelle put down the potatoes she was peeling to come haul ass and redirect me to my old room when she saw us bringing things to the guest room. She claimed that one of the boys had recently peed in the bed, but I knew she just didn't want me in there because it was her pride and joy.

I hadn't stepped foot in my room in years since I always stayed in a hotel when I visited for the holidays. When I opened the door my eyes were pulled in every direction at the mess that lie in front of me. It looked like a disaster area with the kids' toys and clothes thrown about so haphazardly. The only things that were intact were my old posters, but I suppose that was just because they weren't tall enough to reach them yet.

I just sighed and promised that I would make the best of it and part of that was accepting these people for who they were and trying to stay positive. I cleared some space and stacked my boxes because I wasn't unpacking anything until I got this place cleaned up first.

I gave the boys rags to clean their crayon marks from the walls while Tiffa and I went through what little clothes of mine that could fit in the closet. The plan was to only bring clothes for work and a few nice *just in case* dresses, but of course I failed miserably and stuffed my car to the max. I was having Nicole ship what wouldn't fit because I knew I wouldn't be able to function without my full wardrobe here. I didn't know where I was going to put everything in this tiny closet, but my biggest fear was looking for a specific blouse or pair of shoes then remembering that I'd left them at home.

"I see you still got that dyke haircut," TJ said from my doorway when he finally decided to acknowledge my presence. I sighed because I knew instantly that he wasn't gonna try to make this whole thing easy.

"So do you," I countered with a pleasant smile to which he frowned as he sat on the bed. Me being a secret lesbian had been a running joke between Michelle and TJ for years because I went to an all-girls school for college and because I'd opted to stay in Atlanta after graduating instead of returning home. Well that and the fact that I never let them meet any of my boyfriends until Bryan, but it was honestly just because I didn't want anybody except my at-the-time future husband seeing what kind of dysfunction I came from and even then it was sparingly.

"And please don't talk like that in front of your kids. We wouldn't want them to grow up ignorant like you," I scolded him. "But speaking of my hair, I could really use a cut before I start work next week. Where's the shop that you work at so I can stop by and support you?" I asked trying to relate to him the only way I knew how to.

The few times that Michelle and I had spoken over the last six months, she wouldn't stop bragging about how nice the barbershop was.

You would have thought he owned it instead of just working there as a condition for his probation. I was admittedly a little jealous of all the praise he was getting because despite all of the accolades and awards I'd received for my career, she had never once said anything celebratory about me. Her only interest was my salary and that was just so she could determine how much she could ask me for.

"That's not happening. You ain't coming to my job with your titties out and shit," he spat bitterly and I rolled my eyes.

"Would it kill you to try to be nice to me for once in your life?"

"For what? I'm not about to kiss your ass like Mama just because you came back. You supposed to help out like I do," he said as he stood to his feet to leave showing that he did indeed still have that chip on his shoulder. And if by helping he meant draining her savings and eating her out of a house and a home, then he could keep that kind of help.

"What exactly do you help her with?" I asked smugly as I stood up as well and easily towered over his five-foot-seven frame.

"You know outside of all that blubber, your mouth is exactly why your 'successful' ass ain't got no man now," he said trying to deflect away from him having no tangible ways in which he added anything to Michelle's life. And as much as I hated to admit it, his words cut me deeply.

I was confident and I loved myself dearly, but in the back of my mind I always wondered if maybe my weight was why I hadn't found my Prince Charming yet. I had no shortage of attention, but sometimes it wasn't always the kind that I wanted because I preferred quality over quantity.

And I didn't know why he was so bitter towards me for making something of myself just because he didn't. At one point he was actually better than me at drawing, but he peaked in middle school and wouldn't stay out of trouble once our dad died. He barely had a GED now, but I knew that his second baby mama Cassie had done some scam to help him pass.

"No it's why I don't have a weak man like you and I use the word 'man' very loosely."

"Dinner's ready!" Michelle hollered out and it was right on time because I decided that I was all out of positivity for TJ for now and I'd worked up quite an appetite while moving and unpacking.

"I've really missed your food, Ma," I complimented as I made my way into the kitchen and took a seat at the table. Even though she was being a little pissy with me before, I decided to accept the meal as her olive branch because it was my favorite. I'd gotten authentic soul food in

Georgia so her cooking wasn't as pleasing to my palette as it once was, but anything would do after the terrible fast food I had on the road.

"You won't be getting too much of it. Look at them hips. You're already wide enough," she said and I let it fall off my shoulders because she was always criticizing me for one thing or the other.

"You mean these hips that I got from you, Ma?" I asked holding up a mirror to her shade, but she rebuffed it.

"You got them from your daddy's people. You built up tall and hippy just like Diane and Jordan. They just got sense enough not to eat so much," she said matter-of-factly once again reminding me that I may have gotten my physical beauty from her, but the inside was all from my daddy. It was just who she was though and I decided to not let it bother me anymore because she didn't even seem to mean any harm by it. She just had no filter and always said what was on her mind.

"Whatever you say."

I watched as she made a big plate for TJ and the boys then took a seat like she was waiting for me to serve her and Tiffa. I sighed before getting up to fix their plates then finally to make my own. Instead of enjoying her meal like everybody else, she was watching me like a hawk as I scooped up mashed potatoes and green beans for myself. I waited for her to comment on the portion size which was normal for any adult, but she thought that all women should eat like birds how she did.

"Leave enough for TJ's lunch tomorrow," she said predictably even though my plate was far from full and there was plenty left.

"Why? Aren't you worried about his hips?" I asked because I felt like being petty and getting him back for his previous comments. He ignored me, but I knew it bothered him because he didn't only look like us, but he was also shaped like us. His childbearing hips were the reason why he worked out hard and tried to bulk up so they wouldn't be as noticeable, but they still were.

"Leave my baby alone. He's still the man of this house," she said not even realizing the incestuous implication that came from those two combined statements especially since he wasn't contributing to anything to be considered the man of anything. And not to mention her most used lines since I'd left Bryan was that I wasn't getting any younger and that my degrees wouldn't keep me warm at night. They certainly kept me cool in the hot summers though and they were about to be keeping this roof over all of our heads now.

"Actually I'm your baby," I said reminding her that TJ was three years my senior, "and you didn't hear what he said to me before you called us in here. And besides I thought you cooked this for me because it's my favorite."

"Since when is this your favorite? You don't even like meatloaf," she said to my surprise and I wondered why she would make something that she thought I disliked anyway.

"Yes I do. This is grandma's recipe that daddy used to make for me all the time," I told her trying to reminisce on something positive, but she had no interest in it.

"Well I can't keep up with all of your favorites. Seems like most food is your favorite by the look of you if you ask me," she said causing TJ to drop his fork and laugh out loud.

"Alright that's enough," I said before pushing away from the table then carefully sitting the plate down on the counter. Even though I was upset I still didn't want to make a mess, but after how long it took me to truly love all of myself nobody was gonna make me look at my body and frown.

"Where you going? I know you're not about to leave this here."

"Wrap it up for your baby."

"You still so damn sensitive!" she shouted at my back as I grabbed my keys from the hook then swiftly headed back to my car. I saw Tiffa get up and watch me from the window, but one of them must have told her to sit back down because she was back seated just as quickly as she had gotten up.

If I had any sense I would have loaded my car right back up and went back to my real home, but who was I fooling? That exchange was nothing compared to how low Michelle could go. Still I just saw it as a preview of what was to come and I figured if I left early in the morning I could be home by sunset in Georgia and it would be like I'd never left at all.

I sat in an empty parking lot and cried while eating from the local fast food restaurant that I used to work at the summer before leaving for college. It was a place where grease came to be celebrated, but it was my only option because there was nothing else open this late around here. I stayed and listened to music for a while before working up the courage to go back then prayed that Michelle had gone to bed because I was about to cart my belongings right back out of her house: it hadn't been my father's in a long time. And the house wasn't nearly as important as the memories anyway because it stopped being a home for me the moment he died so I was letting myself off the hook for it. They were grown and resourceful not to mention disrespectful so they could figure it out for themselves.

God must've heard my cries loud and clear

tonight because when I got back in, the house was pitch black and no one was awake. I immediately started repacking the boxes that I had emptied just a few hours ago because my plan was to sneak out like a thief in the night that was until Tiffa burst into my room and startled me.

"Dammit. I need to put a bell around your neck girl!" I said as I clutched my now fast-beating heart. "You scared me half to death."

"I'm sorry," she sadly said before I turned on the lights to see tears in her big brown eyes, my father's eyes. Aside from his height they were the most prominent physical trait that he'd passed down to us and I would be damned if I wasn't looking at him or even myself when her tears fell and she begged me not to go.

I walked over to give her a hug and explain why I had to leave, but she became inconsolable when she saw the half full box that we'd unloaded earlier. It honestly surprised me that they hadn't knocked the emotions out of her yet like they'd done to me by her age, but I credited Sofia for that since she had always been a good person. I knew Michelle was less mean to Tiffa because she was TJ's daughter, but I also knew that she still saw all younger women as some kind of competition and had to belittle them to keep them in their place so I didn't have to guess what their relationship was like since she'd started developing.

And I might've just been having a sugar rush from the milkshake I'd had, but I swear it felt like my dad was in here with us and communicating with me through Tiffa because he wanted me here for some currently unknowable reason. Maybe he was tired of seeing me so disconnected from everything and everyone here and was using this as an opportunity to bring us back together once and for all. If that was true then the last thing I wanted to do was disappoint him and since I couldn't be sure that that wasn't what was happening I decided to stick around for a bit and help for as long as I could stand it.

"Shh. I'm not leaving yet. She's gonna have to try a lot harder than that to keep me from kicking your butt at volleyball all summer, okay?" I assured Tiffa as I rubbed her back for comfort. I hadn't rocked her to sleep in over a decade, but it was just as easy now as it always was back then.

When she was sound asleep I looked around once more at all the old posters on my wall and landed on one of my favorite musicals *The Wiz*. I laughed ironically to myself about the good sis Dorothy having a point. There really was no place like home, but to me it was just another four letter word because there was no place like hell either.

I didn't necessarily believe in fairytales anymore, but I really did hope that this situation would quickly turn into one because in those stories no matter how bad things began, everything would always somehow work out in the end. After tonight I knew I couldn't see myself staying the full year that I'd signed on for, but I decided to give it six months. Surely my mother would find a good job by then and maybe I'd even somehow convince TJ to finally get his act together and help out more. Then I could leave guilt free and get back to living happily ever solo as the Georgia peach that I was forever meant to be.

2

THE ROYAL TREATMENT

I spent my entire first week in Chicago getting my room set up just the way I wanted. Even though my stay would only be temporary, I still needed a baseline level of comfort before I could truly settle and live here. I was frustrated beyond belief, but I tried to look on the bright side for a peace of mind and because redecorating and remodeling the room and bathroom gave me more time to spend with Tiffa. Her volleyball season ended months ago and this gave her something to do other than babysitting her rotten brothers after school. And since this would sort of be her room again when I went back home, I let her help me pick out the color palette and some of the décor for our low budget DIY project.

We even managed to convince TJ and Michelle to help us out after they saw us putting in so much work and having fun. After six and a half days, we were finished and the little room almost felt livable except for the twin bed that Michelle refused to let me replace. I hadn't bought sheets that small since my freshman year at college because I made sure to live off campus every year after that. I had it decorated nicely, but it still just looked like a nice dorm room.

After raiding Target, Home Goods, and Home Depot, my emergency savings were officially depleted and I would be back to living paycheck to paycheck like the rest of America. I'd been out of this cycle for the last couple years when I gave up my insanely expensive weave habit. That five hundred that I was spending every six to eight weeks had been put up instead and given me a nice little cushion to fall back on for a rainy day. Unfortunately for me it had been storming here in Chicago and Michelle needed almost all of it before they would even agree to let her save the house. She had refinanced so many times that they didn't want to talk anything but money when it came to the house and I didn't blame them after going over all the paperwork that she had been hiding from me.

Even though I didn't start work until my second week back, I had still been getting up early the last few days to take TJ to work since his car had literally been repoed the day before I arrived. I didn't know what these people were doing up here with their money, but I didn't even bother asking and just figured giving him a ride was the least I could do for him because he did so much of the grunt work for the bathroom. And we had actually been somewhat cordial to each other after he saw that I was ignoring his usual pettiness towards me. My daddy had always told me that bullies loved attention and once you starved them of it, they wouldn't have an incentive to bother you anymore. He had also told me to punch anybody in the mouth who talked sideways to his baby girl, but that wasn't appropriate for TJ just yet because we were doing alright for now. And if anybody was happy to see him actually going to work it was me.

But as astonished as I was that my brother had been holding down a job for so long, I still hadn't actually stepped inside the shop yet. All week I'd been looking a mess and draped in paint and frustration so every time he tried to be funny and introduce me to his boss and coworkers, I would wave then speed off like the fuzz. I hadn't gotten a real good look at any of them yet, but from the quick glimpse I saw of his boss's side profile I could tell that he was a major cutie. That was why I planned on showing up with bells on when my appointment with TJ finally rolled around on Saturday. Even if I didn't necessarily want any of the men there, I did want to rub it in TJ's face when his coworkers would undoubtedly drool over me.

I had also been putting off meeting with

Jordan until I was at my best which for me meant a fresh haircut and digging out a cute dress from the heap of clothes that I'd brought with me. I knew if I saw her looking any less than perfect, Michelle would be nitpicking about me growing my hair back out and of course losing weight. She was in some weird one-sided competition with Diane when it came to us and so far Jordan had lapped me several times just on the strength of her being thinner, having longer hair and being married with babies.

I was finally ready to get it all over with when I unzipped a garment bag to find something casual, well as casual as I got because I was the queen of being overdressed. The mustard wrap dress that I settled on had more cleavage than a little bit, but I went with it because I always looked amazing in it and why the hell not? Any shade of yellow was my color because it looked amazing against my rich, deep brown skin, but this one in particular always made me look like a walking tall sunflower on heels and that's what I exuded as I headed for the barbershop a little sooner than I'd planned.

TJ hadn't come home last night and he still wasn't returning my texts, but I still went ahead with my plans hoping that he was there because he'd already gotten me to pay him early. Traffic was unusually light heading up north and I made it to Fade, an apt name for a barbershop, about ten minutes before my appointment time. I figured that I would be out of place with already done up hair and makeup, but there were almost as many women as men and the other women in there looked about the same. I wondered if landing a barber was what was hot in Chicago since I'd left. Or maybe they figured since this location was different from the ones deep in the hood that the men in here would be a higher caliber, I thought as I cased the joint. It was a nice little setup and they were packed on a Saturday so it looked legit. It wasn't small, but it wasn't too big either and it was surprisingly inviting. I had only gone to a male barber once before, but I walked out halfway through because he kept purposely putting his dick on my arm. I was glad I wouldn't have that problem with my brother except I was worried that he might fuck up the cut on purpose.

I counted six big booths with countertop vanities and I knew immediately which one belonged to TJ because it was messy and of course all the others had barbers and customers. I wished that being around so many other men all day would make TJ grow up and leave his childish ways behind, but who was I kidding? Men came to barbershops to be childish and a lot of the barbers weren't any better. I sighed as I took the only available seat near the receptionist area, but there wasn't anyone there when I took a seat and listened to the music playing.

This for my new chick tryin' get fit
Say she too thick
Ain't no such thing as too thick
What you wanna be a toothpick

It was J. Cole so it wasn't the worst, but even he would let a few unsavory words about women slip from time to time. I had never heard that song before though so I Shazam'd it because it was about to be my summer anthem. I was sitting with a couple other women and texting TJ, hoping that he hadn't faked me out while I finished listening. Ten minutes went by and a couple chairs opened up, but the women next to me all remained seated because they weren't amongst the few men and the one boy that were called up for their scheduled appointment.

"All of y'all are here for a walk-in with Cam?" the pretty young receptionist asked as she walked by with a cup of water. The other women all confirmed her suspicion with their own version of yes and she sighed like she was deeply bothered. "Y'all are gonna be waiting a while then. He's full today."

"Every time I come in here she always worried about his customers," the woman next to me said to no one in particular but loud enough so that the receptionist could hear and another woman echoed her sentiment.

"My job is to be worried about the customers and it would be a lot easier if y'all would accept the fact that some barbers can't do a billion walk-ins every day," she said with more attitude than was appropriate for work and I could tell by both women's body language that things were about to get heated so in typical Tillar fashion I knew I had to pipe in to diffuse the situation.

"Actually, I have a noon appointment with TJ," I said speaking up as she took a seat behind her desk.

"Name, please?" she asked sounding a little more pleasant with me than she was with the other women.

"Tillar."

"I don't see that name here. Did you make the appointment online or by phone?"

"Neither. He's my brother so he said he would make it for me."

"Oh you're TJ's sister?" she said as she looked me up and down.

"Unfortunately," I said before she laughed.

"Well that explains why it's not written here. And as you can see he's running late anyway so just sit tight with the rest of them," she warned me before turning to the only female barber whose booth was the closest to her. "Told you his good attendance streak wouldn't last, Reese," she said and the butch woman chuckled with her. "Can you take his noon so this girl can get out of here before menopause?" Reese quickly looked over at me and told her that she was booked full for the next two hours then suggested that she go ask somebody named Cam to fit me in since I was TJ's family.

I guess she didn't want to yell over the music even though it wasn't very loud at all because she got up and walked back to the last booth to ask the Cam dude if he could take me. Apparently he'd agreed because a minute later she was back at her desk and being pleasant with me.

"I got him to squeeze you in now before his next appointment shows up. And good thing too because no shade to your brother, but Cam's a lot better with feminine cuts. He does mine," she said confidently as she spun around so I could see her hair from all angles. Even though it wasn't fresh, it did still look good and I could tell that Mr. Cam knew what he was doing.

"Thanks for the heads up because there's nothing I want less than to walk out of here looking like Lil' Boosie," I said and she cracked up laughing at me like she had seen it happen in here before.

"It's nothing. You're Fade Family Gang," she said to me warmly, but I could tell that she just wanted to one up the other walk-in women who had called her out before. "I'm Lauren or Lo. It's nice to meet you."

"You too."

"Where'd you get that necklace? It's so pretty."

"It's from one of those new janky Instagram boutiques. I'll find it and give it to you on my way out."

"Thanks sis," she said genuinely and I was surprised she'd asked because she looked cute and comfortable in her little sweatsuit and sneakers, but I was always happy to convert women like her to the dark side of heels and cheap, but gorgeous jewelry that you only wore once.

For the next twenty minutes or so we sat there and discussed how trifling TJ was, where she got her nails done at because I would need a new set soon, and celebrity gossip until she suddenly sat up and fixed her posture. I didn't notice that it was because of the heavy footsteps that had approached her desk because I was still searching through e-mails trying to find the name of the boutique. House of something.

"All walk-ins?" a deep voice asked her from behind me.

"Of course. All for you," she said with a

playful lilt that she didn't have with the customers.

"Y'all know better. Make appointments people," he said to everybody in the waiting area in a heavy northeastern accent.

"Well I tried to, but apparently there's just not enough of you to go around, Cam," one woman said flirtatiously even though she had her teenaged son sitting with her. I still wasn't paying much attention, but I heard him dap up the kid and tell him that he was about to run grab some food from up the street then come right back.

"Wait Cam, you're supposed to fit TJ's sister in before your break," Lauren reminded him before he sighed heavily. I finally turned around to see that the voice was coming from the same man that I had been avoiding for the past week. The boss. He looked much different now though and I attributed it to his glasses that made him look like a basketball player with some sense. He also seemed even taller than I remembered from my seated position.

"Uh actually it's fine. He's already really busy so I'll just come back some other time if I can ever actually get an appointment," I joked because even though I could use a touch up, I wasn't in dire need of one and I really didn't want to make somebody do something that they clearly didn't want to do.

"Hold up. *You're* TJ's sister?" he asked in disbelief as he dropped his hand from the doorknob then walked back around to me. He adjusted his glasses like he was trying to see the resemblance as he took all of me in.

"Unfortunately," I repeated before doing the same to him, but my eyes caught his on the way back up and I wasn't expecting him to have a full on smile.

"I've been tryna meet you for a minute, but you always pulled off before I could even speak to you."

"Sorry about that. I was in a hurry then, all week actually," I said as I finally remembered the name of the boutique for Lauren. I quickly scribbled it on a card from my bag then slid it over to her, but she seemed more interested in what Cam was doing at the moment.

"Well if you're not in a hurry now, I could fit you in," he said as he nodded towards his booth.

"Are you sure?" I asked because I'd heard the amount of annoyance in that sigh, but I had a feeling that it'd all suddenly dissipated when he saw the cleavage peeking out from my dress.

"Yeah you're fam here," he said before reaching his hand out to help me up and he seemed surprised by my full height when I stood to my feet. I hardly ever had to look up to anybody especially with heels on and I guessed his height to at least be six-eight.

I turned my attention back to Lauren for a second to thank her once again, but she flat out rolled her eyes when she saw Cam put his hand on my lower back to walk me back to his booth. I guess that was the grand opening and the grand closing of me being her *sis*. It suddenly felt like I was back in Atlanta for a minute because that was the only place I'd seen women be so openly competitive for even broke and unattractive men's attention. And don't get me wrong, Cam was definitely a sight for sore eyes, but no amount of fine called for instant animosity.

I may have gotten ahead of myself, but I could have actually seen us hanging out and becoming friends while I was here because I'd lost touch with just about everybody from high school. I could only take Jordan in small doses and Sofia was always working so I really could have used one good girl friend, but I sighed because such was life.

When we passed her booth, the other barber from before Reese, gave him a knowing look after speaking to me.

"Ay I thought you were starving a minute ago. What happened?" she asked in a thick New York accent similar to his.

"I'm a'ight. I forgot I had a big breakfast," he

said evenly before Reese started laughing. They weren't being very subtle so it didn't take much to deduce that there was some inside joke playing out, but it was none of my concern.

His booth was the last one and a little bigger than the others though they all had a semi-private feel since there was a good amount of distance and a half wall separating them. I wasn't surprised to see TJ's booth was next to his just like a misbehaving kid who needed to be monitored by the teacher. I was about to sit in his chair when Cam stopped me then cleaned it off first. I was glad because I didn't need any accidental Bigen remnants getting on me before I had the chance to really be seen for the day.

He took my bag and sat it down on the counter before helping me sit down. At first I thought that he'd raised the chair up so high to accommodate my long legs, but I realized that he'd done it for his own benefit because otherwise he would have to slouch to reach my head. He made sure that I was comfortable then offered me something to drink before we got started, already earning him an A+ for customer service.

"No thanks. I'm going to lunch right after this and I am not trying to fill up first," I joked and he smiled big again. I noticed that his cheekbones moved his glasses a little, but I didn't want him to think I was trying to make unnecessarily long eye contact so I looked at my phone. "Do you have any pictures of your cuts on women? I'm going for almost a pixie fade kinda look so I want soft lines but still pretty clean and just leave my babyhairs alone please," I said as I showed him an older picture I had found earlier to show TJ.

"A woman who knows what she wants," he teased before taking my phone to study the picture.

"Yeah I really don't want a boxy, masculine cut," I said even though I'd already seen the job he'd done on Lauren.

"With that pretty face? Nah. Nothing could look masculine on you," he said trying to charm me like it was an absurd thought, but I was sure he did it to all the women to get repeat customers hence the full waiting area, a couple even without seats now.

"Well thank you, but I still wanna see pictures of your work. I don't trust just anybody with my hair."

"You can trust me with anything. I'm the best and I've never left a customer unsatisfied," he said confidently, but I wasn't sure that he was actually flirting until he added, "Plus I'm just a trustworthy guy in general."

"Yeah I can tell because it's written all over your face. Especially near your jawline right there. It's written in all caps," I cracked on him and he laughed like it was the funniest thing he'd heard.

"Oh so you're one of those funny girls, huh?"

"It's easy to be when the jokes write themselves."

"I'm a joke to you?" he asked acting offended, but I shrugged nonchalantly.

"I haven't decided yet, but please don't clown up my hair. I start my new job in the morning and I'm nervous enough so I at least need to look the part."

"Don't worry. You're in good hands," he assured me as he returned my phone then handed over his portfolio. I almost told him he sounded like my car insurance company but decided against further bantering with him. Instead I flipped through the book and complimented what I saw. He came over and awkwardly stood over my shoulder and looked with me like he hadn't seen his work before.

"Do you have any product in your hair?" he seemed to ask just because we hadn't said anything in a minute.

"Just leave-in conditioner from my twists last night. Is that a problem?" I asked because my barber back home never had an issue even when I used styling products.

"Nah. As long as it's not gel, I can work with it," he said before running his fingers through my hair without my permission. It was always so weird letting a stranger touch me so intimately especially because scalp massages were my thing. If he were any other man he would have surely pulled back a nub, but I let him touch it as he studied the shape of my head.

An explicit version of a new rap song came on and brought me out of my self-centered thoughts and I cringed at the misogynistic lyrics that were missing from the clean version. He must have seen the look on my face because he quickly picked up the remote to change the music which garnered groans from the other booths.

"You like Sade?" he asked me directly as he walked over to the aux and plugged his phone in, ignoring the men telling him to put the record back on.

"I don't wanna kill the fun. You can play whatever," I said even though I didn't want to hear anything else like what was just playing. Not that long ago I used to listen to that kind of rowdy stuff religiously, but I knew I had officially aged out of it when I started skipping every other song on the radio. All of the new stuff seemed to be vulgar just for the sake of being vulgar and had nothing on spelling I-N-D-E-P-E-N-D-E-N-T a dozen times in a party like I had done during my clubbing days.

"Ladies' choice," he offered once more then

tried to give me his phone to choose something I liked. A++.

"Sade is cool then. Thanks."

He walked back over and said something to me right as Ms. Adu began to sing about washing an unworthy man away from her skin. I wasn't paying attention though because I hadn't heard the song in ages and I was too busy relating to the lyrics. I must've taken a billion and one showers since the end of my relationship, but I still couldn't get the stain of Bryan off of me.

"Say that again?" I asked him because I had been in a trance, but I wanted to quickly shake off any thoughts of Bryan. Also I was trying to remember which album this particular song was from because I always got her newer stuff mixed up. I knew the old albums from beginning to end because Sade was my dad's favorite singer and we listened to her nonstop in the car.

"You said you were starting a new job and I asked what you do?"

"I'm an artist."

"Oh that's wassup. You paint or something?" he asked as his eyes widened with genuine interest.

"I draw," I said purposefully being vague. I always undersold my career title when I was discussing it with men because there would always be dudes out there that saw women as a potential comeup. I weeded them out by making myself out to be a starving artist rather than the superstar that I was in my field so they knew out the gate that they would be footing the bill for everything.

"So yeah I want my cut to be simple. No lines or other designs just yet. I want to see what the environment is like before I walk up in there with those white people trying to be myself, you know?" I asked expecting another laugh from him, but he didn't give me a response. I knew that my comedic timing was perfect so I looked up to see why.

Through the mirror I saw him looking down at my breasts as he took his time putting the black cape around me. I lightly cleared my throat to wake him out of whatever daydream he had fallen into and our eyes met in the mirror.

"Damn. My bad," he said genuinely and seemed embarrassed that he had been so fixated on them seemingly against his own will.

"It's cool. I find myself getting mesmerized sometimes too," I said lightheartedly before repeating what I wanted since the cape was on and he could focus now.

It wasn't a big deal to me anymore. People had been staring at them ever since they first sprouted at eleven so I was used to it. When I was younger I would wear turtlenecks and sweatpants in even the hottest weather to avoid the looks, but I grew tired of hiding my body and now I tastefully flaunted it every chance I got. "So this is your place, right?" I asked trying to throw him a bone to make things less awkward after he got caught gawking at me.

"Yeah. I'm Cameron by the way. Everybody just calls me Cam though," he said as he reached out for my hand.

"Tillar."

"What kind of name is that?" he asked before I narrowed my eyes at him. "No, it's not bad. It's just different."

"That's what my dad was going for, I guess. It's the name of the town he was born in down in Arkansas."

"Oh ok. I like it. Tillar," he said as he let it fall off his lips once more.

After that he finally dropped the small talk and got to work. I noticed immediately that he was a lefty because his tools looked a little different. I almost hesitated before he expertly used the corner of his blade to cut the semicircle above my ear at an angle to get the blend right just like my barber at home always did. I had gotten used to her small, feminine hands and although his were rough and large, he still managed to have a light touch. And I didn't have a small head by anybody's standards, but it still practically fit in his palm.

"Don't worry. I'mma protect them baby hairs," he ribbed me with his thumb right above my nose and between my eyes as he carefully touched my forehead because of my makeup. Our eyes continued to sync up in the mirror every now and then, but I tried to focus on my phone while he made small talk about music and some movie he had just seen with his cousin Reese.

Just when I thought he was done with me, he pulled out a razor and gave me a light cleanup. I was glad that he was being so precise because I wanted it to be perfect, but I really did have to go soon because I figured Jordan would be getting to the restaurant any minute now and I still didn't know how to get there. Right when I was about to tell him it was good enough, he grabbed the green barber's alcohol and wiped me down with it. It felt tingly along my hairline, but I ignored it as I admired the cut which looked even better than the one I'd shown him on the guide picture.

"Are you satisfied?" he asked as he handed me a small mirror to inspect the back.

"I am. Thank you," I said pointlessly because I was all smiles.

He brushed all the hair off of me with his duster then laughed when I jumped as he ran it over my face and ears. I was terribly ticklish and never quite got used to that part of the shop experience, but he let me know that he thought it was cute. Hm.

After that I removed the cape and stood to my feet. There was no hair on me or my dress, but I still instinctively brushed some imaginary dirt off of my shoulder before I played around with the top of my hair and fluffed it up some more. *I look damn good*, I thought as I inspected myself in the mirror from the waist up. I was adjusting my breasts and smoothing out my shapewear before I remembered where I was and of course he was just standing there stuck and watching me. There was no way that he could hide the way he licked his lips after checking out my backside so he didn't even try to.

"If you know when you wanna come back for a touch up, book the appointment on your way out. As you can see my spots fill up fast and I can rarely get to all the walk-ins," he said like he was trying to be helpful when I could tell that he just wanted to know when he would get to see me again.

I knew when men were flirting with me. I had long stopped asking myself why because I knew the reason. I was fly and my confidence, that I had faked until I made it, oozed naturally from my pores now. I kept myself up, wore natural looking makeup and clothes that fit and accentuated my shape. I worked on my posture until it was perfect and my head was always high. At five-foot-eleven and thicker than a Snicker I was already hard to miss, but I was hardly ever seen without heels so I made sure to command attention in every room I walked into.

I didn't know what kind of charm I had about me the last few years though, but men like him who probably swore they would never go near a fat girl were always in my face trying to see what was up. He hadn't done anything in particular to strike me as the type, but I just had a feeling he was *one of those*. The men with mommy issues who ultimately just wanted to lay their heads on my breasts while I told them everything would be okay. I'd had one too many of those in Bryan so I definitely wasn't interested in another one even the gorgeous one standing behind me.

"See I was trying to wait to see how many compliments I got first before making you my official barber. I'm not that easy," I teased him as I grabbed my purse then turned to look at him directly.

"I think it looks good."

"I think you might be a little biased," I said as my phone alerted me of a text message that I would bet was from Jordan. "Hey do you know where Wells on Wells is? The streets over in this area always did confuse me and my gps is useless."

"Like six blocks down on your left. You can walk if you already got parking down this way," he said like he was familiar with the spot.

"Thanks. I think I'll do that," I said before he lifted my chin to inspect his work once more.

"Yeah it's perfect," he said obviously complimenting the cut, but I also felt like he was talking about my face on the low. "I'm glad I outdid myself. I got you looking nice for your little lunch date so your man is gonna love it," he said as he looked down at me over his glasses and scribbled my total down on a yellow slip.

I fought the urge to roll my eyes because I saw exactly where this was going, but again I didn't mind because I liked to keep my flirting muscles in shape. And as unfeminist as it was I did enjoy getting hit on sometimes by men who were respectful and could take no for an answer in stride. He definitely seemed like the type because he clearly had other options.

"Actually it's not a date. I'm meeting a friend."

"A female friend?" he asked as he handed me the bill and I laughed at his forwardness. I thought with how attentive and flirtatious he'd been that he might offer me a freebie, but I understood that this was still his place of business after all. He just definitely wouldn't be getting my number now. Thems the rules.

"Dang you're in my business," I said pretending to be annoyed with a small grin as I prepared to walk away, but he put his arm out to stop me.

"Hold up. Do you uh...you wanna go do something sometime? Like dinner or drinks or an art show. Whatever you're into," he said trying to sound cool, but I could tell he thought I might reject him and his next statement proved me right. "You can say no by the way. I promise not to mess up your taper next time or nothing," he added with a nervous chuckle. It was cute.

"Hm," I said pretending to seriously think about his offer. "Well I know you're gainfully employed so before I answer, do you have a criminal record that I should know about?"

"Nope. I've never even been stopped and frisked," he said quickly, "and that's a feat for niggas from Harlem." I had already guessed that he was from somewhere in New York from the accent, but I didn't know which borough and it mattered because my old roommate was from upstate and always told me to avoid men from the Bronx.

"Okay. Wife or girlfriend? Kids? Do you smoke or do any drugs?"

"None of the above," he said confidently and I rolled my eyes. "You?"

"No, but this is about you now. And I know

that there has to be something unsavory about you so just tell me now."

"I already told you that I was trustworthy, didn't I?"

"You did, but I was hoping for something easy to disqualify you because I know you must hit on every woman that sits in your chair."

"Nah, I like to keep this space as professional as possible," he said sounding honest, but I knew it was a line.

"So why are you being so unprofessional with me then?"

"Because there's a first time for everything, Tillar."

"That was way too smooth to be your first time so I'll pass," I said before giving him another full once-over. "But you are cute though so you can definitely introduce me to an uncle or your daddy."

"You date older men?" he asked surprised then wrinkled his brow.

"Not yet, but there's a first time for everything, right?" I said causing him to smile again.

"Good one. But I don't have any uncles for you and my old man actually passed a few months ago," he said before looking down at his feet and I knew I'd unintentionally touched on a sensitive subject.

"Damn. I'm sorry. I didn't mean to be so rude."

"I know. But you still made me sad so to cheer me up you definitely owe me that date now. What day is good for you because I'm free whenever?" he asked like it would actually be that simple.

"Nice try, but I don't owe you for anything but this fresh cut you just gave me, Cameron," I said holding up the slip. He was nice to look at and would probably be good for a fun ride, but I wouldn't mess around with somebody who worked with TJ because I liked to do my dirt where nobody could find it.

"You can call me Cam and you don't even owe me for that. It's on the house for my new favorite customer." I looked down at my total to see that it was zero dollars and that he'd already written his phone number at the bottom.

"Even if I don't accept the date?" I challenged the authenticity of his generosity.

"*Especially* if you don't accept the date. You like the cut so you'll be back and I can try again. And I'mma be dressed better then because you caught me off guard today," he said pointing to his almost fitted white t-shirt and grey sweatpants. I looked him up and down and thought he was still fine in his super laid back clothes, but I believed him when he said he could do better. "Yeah I'm Clark Kent with the specs on, but wait til you see Superman next time," he joked as he took off his glasses and stood with his hands on his waist and looked off to the side with the iconic hero's pose . Okay he was funny too. A+++.

"Well I guess that's why they say you should stay ready so you don't have to get ready, Superman," I ribbed him.

"Nah. Trust me. Nothing I could've done would have prepared me for you walking up in here today, Tillar," he said casually as he cleaned his glasses then put them back on. I leaned my head to the side at how effortlessly he'd delivered that top notch line. He was good.

"My next appointment will be in three weeks so I guess we'll see then, huh?"

"Which day so I can get ready?" he asked after I took a few steps away from him.

"You weren't listening, Cam. Just stay ready. You have a good day."

"Impossible not to now," he said now shamelessly watching me walk away.

"Oh my God. Bye."

I must have been smiling too big when I walked over and gave the slip to Lauren because she immediately looked me up and down to size me up again how I had just done to Cam. I could tell she knew he wasn't giving me preferential treatment just because of TJ especially when she noticed his phone number on there. Despite us initially hitting it off, all of a sudden she felt the need to try to put me in the hot seat before I left.

"Hey Cam, when did we start giving out free cuts in here? I didn't know I was working for *that* type of establishment, boss," she remarked while holding eye contact with me. I just rolled my eyes as everybody laughed at her joke then noted to myself that I wouldn't be coming back here because I would hate to have to A-town stomp her over a man that didn't belong to either one of us.

A male customer jokingly complained about coming to Cam for three years and how he'd never given him so much as a discount before Reese chimed in about how he lacked certain physical assets to be eligible. I felt embarrassed at being put on the spot, but I took it in stride and strutted towards the door. From behind me I heard Cam's voice getting closer.

"Look what you started, Lo. Alright, everybody chill out. Tillar's about to be my wife soon and I can't tell our kids that I charged their mother the first time we met," he said before he called up the kid from before. I was sure I had all eyes on me at that comment, but I put my shades on to leave the building because I didn't want him to think I was flattered by his cheap words. After Bryan, getting saddled with a ring and kids was no longer my idea of happiness. In fact it sounded more like a lifetime prison sentence so him saying that actually turned me off some. C-.

Before I could get out the door Lauren decided to prolong the joke by asking if I wanted to book another appointment. I didn't feel like being nice, but I still politely told her no thanks.

"Here's your receipt then," she said smugly as she came from behind the desk to give it to me.

"I don't need it, *sis*. Keep it for yourself or throw it away."

From the corner of my eye I saw Cam watching our exchange, but I paid it no mind as I left his establishment and followed his directions to the restaurant.

In just a couple of minutes I made it on foot to Jordan sitting on the outdoor patio tables. Even from behind I could tell that I had gotten dressed up for nothing because she looked so…pedestrian. This was yet another reason why kids were out of the equation for me until I could afford to not look like that after having them.

I couldn't wrap my mind around her looking so homely because Diane had always been the blueprint of what being a great mom who didn't lose herself in the role should look like. She was truly the mother I always wanted and being at her house back in the day was like the complete opposite of mine. It was always peaceful and on the off chance that it was loud it was with joy from a special occasion. And of course I never needed a reason to spend time with my only auntie, but I just figured it would make more sense if I was close with Jordan who was only a year older than me. She wasn't anywhere near as sweet as Diane, but anything was a cake walk compared to my home life so I was with them whenever I could get away from Michelle.

Jordan and I were actually pretty tight until she left for college, but the first time she came home to visit I knew it was a wrap from then on because she was like a different person and even had a whole new voice curtesy of her PWI. After graduating she fell in love with a blerd, became a proud stay-at-home mom, and devoted her life to her family. On the flipside, and much to the chagrin of Michelle, I got more grounded in my roots from attending an HBCU, I was now beasting at my corporate job, and I could codeswitch with the best of them. It was a shame that our unique experiences had made us into very different people, but such was life.

I was tempted to be phony and run up and hug her, but she was breastfeeding Bailey as I approached. Her cheeks formed something like a smile when she saw me and she instinctively thought to get up.

"No sit. You have a full load, hunny. I'll hug you later when your boobs are put up," I ribbed her as I took a seat.

"I could say the same about you," she said getting me right back and we laughed as I smooched her cheek then little Blake's. "I can't believe Auntie Michelle let you leave the house like that," she quickly added in a less playful tone, but I ignored it because I could sense that there was a little resentment. Diane kept me in the loop and told me that Jordan had basically let herself go because her husband was just wasted space and she was doing everything on her own since he'd been laid off.

"Girl, I'm grown and Michelle cannot tell me what to wear."

"She must not have been there when you left."

"You already know. Anyway sorry I'm late. I just left the barbershop and I had to wait for somebody else to do my cut since TJ was a no show, blah blah blah."

"That's alright. We don't have to get to Gymboree until three and I already ordered for us," she said just as a waiter approached and sat two house salads in front of us. Before he got too far, I asked him to bring me out a menu because I was actually craving steak instead. And now I was definitely gonna get dessert just to bother Jordan because I knew what her little passive aggressive behind was trying to say by getting this for me.

"I didn't mean to offend you," she said acting guilty when I hadn't even said anything to her yet. "You know I'm still trying to lose this baby weight and I thought we could eat healthy together today, you know?"

"Yeah I'm not trying to lose anything at the moment and why deprive myself when I can eat whatever I want and still look this good?" I said because nobody could tell me I wasn't wearing the hell out of this dress. Of course she couldn't deny it so she just sat there and picked over her food.

We quickly changed the subject back to the kids to keep things pleasant, but before I knew it we were already back to laughing and bringing up fond old memories from back in the day. She was practically salivating over my steak so I let her have a couple bites before she worked up the nerve to just get one for herself. I was looking over the dessert menu while she went to change the baby in the bathroom when I suddenly felt somebody standing behind me.

"Wassup Tillar?" I heard a male voice call out before I looked over my shoulder to see that it was Cam from the barbershop coming out of the restaurant and he had a few takeout bags like he was getting food for more than just himself. "You got started on the kids without me already?" he joked about the double stroller at the table and all the other baby stuff that Jordan had with her.

"Funny. Did you follow me here?"

"No. I'm on my break just picking up some lunch. Oh that's right. You did say you were coming here, right?" he said to be cute and I cut my eyes at him. "Okay I wanted to come apologize for what Lauren did. She was out of line and I told her that after you left."

"It's fine," I said with a neutral face, but I was glad that she had been checked for her unprofessional behavior even though his was just as bad if I was being honest.

"It's not. I know that's why you didn't make another appointment and I wasn't about to let that little thing stop you from feeling welcome in my shop."

"Wow you're really serious about getting repeat customers, huh?" I asked sarcastically calling him out on his actual reason which was getting to see my panties on his bedroom floor.

"Business is good, but I am serious about getting to spend some time with you," he said before he stepped aside to let a man from the table in front of me through the narrow walkway. From my seated position his crotch was now directly in my face and under the bright sunlight I made out the outline of a long and generous helping of dick that made my mouth water more than the dessert menu I had just been looking over. I looked away when I realized that I was staring, but I must have been more obvious that I'd thought because he smiled down at me. "Ay Tillar, my eyes are up here."

"N-no. I wasn't looking at you like that. I was--"

"You were and now we're even," he said as he let his eyes fall back to my breasts but with no remorse this time. "How about you let me take you out tomorrow night to celebrate your new job?"

"I really can't. You work with my brother," I said then realized that TJ still hadn't shown up at the shop even after I'd left.

"Your brother works for me," he said correcting me. "And probably not that much longer since he's always late, but what difference does that make? We're all grown." He was right and there was obviously chemistry there, but he was still coming on a little strong. I liked for a man to pursue me not to hunt me down like he was doing. "You're not from around here, are you?" he asked seemingly out of nowhere.

"I live in Atlanta now, but I was raised here." I wondered if he'd asked because after living in the south for over a decade, that inner Mississippi and Arkansas that I'd inherited from Michelle and my dad respectively slipped out more frequently.

"I've never been, but I always hear about all

the beautiful women down there and I see they weren't lying."

"Wow you just won't quit, will you Cam?"

"Nope and I really don't wanna wait three weeks to see you again either," he said with more charm than a little bit.

I sighed hard because he was coming off even smoother than I initially thought he was and since I'd already been caught looking below the belt once, I shamelessly looked down at it again. He was definitely a shower because there was no way that thing could get any bigger and it was curved at almost the same angle as my favorite G-spot toy. I didn't know what I had done right in my past life to deserve being offered this, but damn it I was gonna enjoy it the first chance I got to. I gave him my number and watched as he stored it in his phone with a triumphant look on his face.

He asked again if it would be alright if he took me out tomorrow night and I hurried and accepted his invitation because I saw Jordan on her way back over to the table. He told me goodbye then said hello to her as he left the area with his lunch. She gave him a tight-lipped smile instead of speaking before putting Bailey down in her stroller.

"Who was that?" Jordan asked with a deep scowl that reminded me of Michelle. She really should have been her daughter and lord knows I would have traded her for Auntie Diane with the quickness.

"My new barber."

"Why did it look like he was trying to get your number?"

"Because he was. I just gave it to him."

"Don't do it, cuz," she said trying to sound down and I laughed at her. "What? I know you're still getting over Bryan, but that guy seriously looks like a drug dealer," she said without a hint of humor, but I couldn't help but burst into even more obnoxious laughter.

"Jordan, how does he look like a drug dealer with those Poindexter ass glasses on?" I exaggerated because the black frames were actually pretty attractive on him.

"Well nobody said drug dealers had perfect vision, Tilly. And he could be using the barbershop as a front to launder money. I've seen that kind of thing on *Dateline*," she said before pointing out that he had on an expensive watch.

"Well I hope he's not because I'm definitely gonna let the barber hit it from the back tomorrow night. Did you see his dick in those sweats? *Black Snake Moan* realness," I joked trying to bring out a little of the old Jordan, but she insisted on keeping that stick up her ass in place as she covered the kids' ears like they could understand what I was saying.

"Now I know you've gone crazy. When did you start talking like this?"

"When did you get so uptight? I used to be the scary one."

"Getting married and having kids changes you. You'll see if it ever happens for you," she said innocently, but I had clocked her shade again with the use of *if*.

Stressing about finances changes you too, I thought wanting to return her shade, but I couldn't because I wasn't supposed to know about her household's money problems plus I currently had too many of my own for it to hit the same.

When both of our broke asses were getting ready to argue about who would pay for the meal, the waiter chimed in from the side to let us know that a local businessman had already taken care of it by putting it and the tip on his tab. The look on Jordan's face when she realized he was talking about Cam was priceless.

"Drug dealer," she warned in a sing-song voice as we got up to go our separate ways.

"Dick slinger," I sang back before hugging her goodbye.

3

SIZE QUEEN

I woke up that morning desperately wanting to play hooky for my first day, but just thinking about staying in the little uncomfortable bed a second longer than I had to be there got me up and on my feet. I picked out a simple work appropriate black dress and blazer then listened to a motivational podcast as I sat bumper to bumper in some of the worst traffic I'd seen in years. Atlanta wasn't much better in that department either, but at the very least I could always find little open pockets here and there to make it where I was going on time. I'd planned on getting in a half hour early to set up my office, but I noticed that I only had five minutes to spare when I grabbed the box of trinkets and pictures to decorate my desk with.

I was happy to see that my reputation had preceded me because upon arrival the Chicago office had the red carpet laid out and paraded me around introducing me to everybody from the top down. I shook more hands than a politician in an election year and was surprised that no one brought out a baby for me to kiss. I was pretty disappointed to see that there were only two other black women here because we were practically running things in the Atlanta office, but I was just glad that I wasn't alone even though I'd peeped that the older of the two seemed to give off that *there can only be one* vibe.

By the time I was finally left to my own devices it was lunch time so I got settled then did a test run to make sure I'd be able to video chat for the team meetings back home since I would still be working closely with them for a new campaign that I was spearheading. I honestly could've worked remotely for the time that I was here if I wanted, but I got much more done in an office setting because I was somebody that needed structure and boundaries. Without the hustle and bustle of my coworkers surely I would be at home saying "You are not the father!" right along with Maury and calling people crackheads with Judge Mathis. Plus it wasn't like I could get anything done if Michelle or the boys were there during the day anyway.

I decided to brown-bag it for the first day because I knew spending so much on extravagant lunches how I usually did was out of the question until I figured out how to make more money while I was here. Just when I was about to bite into my turkey on rye, my purse began to vibrate in my open bottom drawer because I wouldn't dare put it on the floor as broke as I already was. Figuring that it was Nicole calling to ask about how everything was going, I answered on my AirPods and was surprised to hear a man's voice greet me cheerfully.

"Hey Tillar. Are you as excited as I am about tonight? Because I already got my outfit lying on the bed just waiting on that confirmation for you."

"Excuse me. Who is this?" I asked even though I'd recognized his voice immediately.

"Oh my fault. I guess I'm probably just another unsaved number waiting in line for you huh, Tillar?"

"Is this Cameron?"

"It's just Cam," he playfully complained. "I should've never told you my whole name--" he began before I cut him off as I suddenly came to a hilarious realization.

"Wait a minute. Your name is Cameron and you're from Harlem like the rapper Cam'Ron from Harlem?" I asked laughing and he sighed like he had gotten that many times before.

"I can't believe you're even old enough to remember him."

"Please you cannot be that much older than me. I grew up on Dipset. *'You tryna get down with*

Dipset/First you gotta get your lips wet'. Something like that right?" I asked trying to do my best impression of Jim Jones, but he was more interested in me than old song lyrics.

"How old are you anyway?"

"I just turned twenty-nine last month. You?"

"I'll be thirty-one at the end of November."

Astrology wasn't really my thing, but I was curious about how our respective Aries and Sagittarius sexual chemistry would mix.

"You couldn't just say thirty, could you?" I teased him before noticing the time. My hour break was nearly over after spending too much time Skyping with my Atlanta coworkers and I still hadn't eaten so I began rushing him off the line.

"Hold up. I didn't get a confirmation for dinner yet. We're still on, right?"

"That depends on if you have any grown man clothes. You were dressed like a gym teacher the last time I saw you and I don't go places where sneakers are allowed on dates," I said letting my bougie flag fly because you had to set the standard early with men these days or you would be eating at Chili's for every special occasion.

"Listen I had something in mind, but I'll wear whatever you want me to if it means I get to see you tonight. What, you want me in some nice slacks? You want my ankles out? 'Cause I'll let 'em out if you give me the go, Tillar," he joked and I couldn't stop smiling at how silly he was being.

"Only let them out if you're familiar with lotion. I won't be seen with your ashy behind in public."

"Noted. Me and my well-moisturized ankles will see you later on so now you can get back to work, beautiful," he said before ending the call.

Even though I really didn't want to do this whole song and dance with him, it was pretty refreshing to hear a man be upfront and enthusiastic about going on a date. These days it seemed like most just wanted to do everything but properly court a woman so it was a shame that he was basically wasting his good game on me since we were probably both on the same page about just wanting sex.

The rest of the work day went fine after realizing that maybe things wouldn't be so bad here after all. Work would be work as usual, but I had already snagged a cute new supplier without even having to go near a trashy dating app.

Despite it being my first day, I rushed home from work and beat everybody out that mug as soon as the clock struck five because I'd spent the last few hours daydreaming about letting Cam lust after me during dinner and drinks for foreplay before hopefully going back to his place and enjoying him for dessert. I hadn't had sex since my birthday and even then it wasn't anything to write home about because me and the old ex of mine that I'd summoned for the occasion had both gotten a little too tipsy to even enjoy it.

I had never been so disappointed in my life than when I made it home and saw a big cloud of smoke coming from the kitchen. Michelle's car was missing from the driveway and no one else should've been home so I cautiously entered, startling Tiffa who was using an old, outdated extinguisher to put out a fire. That thing had been down there for ages and sounded the part as it wheezed and barely got the job done before sputtering out the last of its contents.

"What is going on in here? Why would you do this?" I asked her after seeing that the culprit was her trying to heat up Pop-Tarts while they were still in the foil.

"I didn't. I just came to get my mouthguard then I saw them in there watching TV and smelled something burning," she said as she coughed and pointed to her already borderline delinquent brothers who were peeking out at us from the living room. I could tell that they were trying to gauge how much trouble they were in for the small fire, but lucky for them I would not be their disciplinarian today because I had hot feet and I was about to hit the streets.

"Who's supposed to be watching y'all?" I asked them before Timere informed me that apparently *I* was supposed to be babysitting after I got off of work. "The hell I am. Tiffa, I have a date that I need to get ready for so you have to stay with them."

"I can't. I have practice. And a date with who?" she asked nosily before putting the extinguisher back under the sink and opening up the windows.

"Nobody you know and isn't your season over with now?" I asked before wondering how much it would take to bribe her and praying that it wouldn't be much because I was low on cash.

"Yeah, but if I want to get lots of scholarships like the best auntie in the world, then I should probably be working hard for them every day, right?" she asked trying to butter me up, but there was no need to because after giving it some thought I wouldn't dare burden her with babysitting kids like I had been at her age.

"Fine. Go," I told her and watched her grab her backpack and sprint towards the door before I changed my mind. "And let this be a reminder not to have sex before you can afford a real sitter and upkeep for fire extinguishers," I yelled after her. I turned my back to have a talk with the boys when she suddenly peeked her head back in the door.

"Hey can I take your car since you're not

gonna be using it?" she asked and I was tempted to run after her, but the look I gave her made her scurry away.

The two little monsters didn't exactly need the extra sugar, but I went over to the toaster to show them how to make Pop Tarts the right way so they wouldn't try the microwave again. I was praying that their afternoon snack would be my only responsibility until I got ahold of Michelle or TJ to come get them soon, but my bad luck streak wouldn't let up yet. Neither was answering their phones which meant that I wouldn't be getting the happy ending I was expecting after all.

After questioning the boys about which adult had been here last and how long they had been alone, I was flabbergasted at their answers because they had no problem throwing TJ and Michelle under the bus because apparently this was their routine.

I lost track of time trying to give them something constructive to do and giving them an impromptu lesson about fire safety, but I called Cam to let him know about the change of plans the second I remembered him. Of course he sounded disappointed that he wouldn't get to see me, but he sounded even more bothered by the fact that TJ had left his kids in the house alone.

"Damn. He acts like he's father of the year at the shop. That's why I don't really trip about him being late or leaving early because he always claims that it's for the kids," he said and I felt like maybe I shouldn't have been running my mouth to his boss.

"Yeah it seems like he puts up a good imitation of a decent guy for just about everybody but me," I said doubling down instead. I'd been raised to keep all family business in house, but I didn't feel any loyalty to TJ since he had never shown any towards me.

I thought after I gave him the news that we would end the call, but apparently he still wanted to talk even though we couldn't go out. I kept the focus on him and asked pretty surface level questions while I made dinner for the boys and put them to sleep early for what was probably the first time in their lives.

When a tipsy Michelle made it in later that night with not a care in the world about her house nearly burning down earlier, I knew that she'd probably had one of her rare good nights at the casino. It was usually never more than a few hundred that had nothing on what she'd put in on her previous trips, but to her a win was a win. I didn't fuss at her about going and instead decided that her getting here before midnight was a win for me so I quickly called Cam to see if he was still up for hanging out. To my surprise he had already been asleep and he obviously didn't catch my drift because he went on to say that everything was closed since it was so late.

"Well what about your place then? It's still open, right?" I asked trying to drive home the point because I didn't care about having dinner in a restaurant when I was trying to give him a late night snack in bed.

"Nah. My Gram always says that the only thing open after midnight is legs," he said through a tired yawn.

"Your grandmother sounds like a wise woman and she is correct. Do you have a problem with that?" I asked but the line went quiet for a couple seconds.

"Damn quit acting fast, Tillar," he joked even though I could tell that I'd caught him off guard with the offer for sex. "I'mma take you out somewhere nice tomorrow night and we're gonna get to know each other first. Alright?" he asked with authority and if it wasn't for me being so turned on by that sudden extra bass in his voice, I would have hung up on him for wasting my time so I just sighed.

"Whatever you say, *Cameron*. I'll see you tomorrow."

I pouted in bed for a while before accepting that I and I alone would be in charge of getting myself off tonight. I hadn't done it since being back home because I knew that masturbating in my old bed would feel weird, but I looked up at *Confessions* era Usher Raymond IV on the wall and got the job done in no time then fell fast asleep.

The next night when TJ passed the open door to my room, he stopped in his tracks and inquired about where I was going because I hadn't really been much of anywhere since getting here.

"Out to dinner with your boss," I said honestly because with the way men gossiped I was sure he had heard about Cam flirting with me in front of the whole shop even though he hadn't brought it up to me yet.

"Yeah right. Ay you got twenty dollars?"

"Twenty dollars for what?" I asked even though I knew I wasn't giving it to him, but I wanted to see which lie he was using these days to get weed money.

"To pay Cassie's cousin for watching the boys today. You gotta help if you can't keep them sometimes," he said as if his responsibilities were somehow mine just because I was home.

"Sorry, but I'm childless so I don't pay for babysitters," I said as I put on more mascara. He just kissed his teeth before slamming my door shut behind him. I didn't care because I knew he must have wanted something to come by my room anyway after I'd chewed out both him and Michelle before leaving for work that morning. I wasn't about to be putting up money for a house that might soon be burned to the ground so they needed a permanent sitter for the boys.

I made myself temporarily forget about all the chaos around me because I was determined to get what I wanted out of Cam soon. Usually I would have been dressed to the nines for date night, but tonight I wore minimal makeup and simple clothes, but admittedly even my dressing down was more effort than some folks when they tried. Still I wasn't trying to wow him because I just wanted to fuck. I saw through his attempt at being different by not letting me come over the night before and it just made me have tunnel vision about my latest goal.

He'd texted me earlier to let me know he was taking an Uber and offered to send me one as well, but I declined because I wanted to be able to leave immediately if I wanted to. I also had a quick errand to make on the way there.

The second I walked inside the restaurant I spotted him at the bar enjoying the music. Even from behind I could tell he had done his best to impress me with his grown man clothes that were appropriate for the venue. I'd chosen Buddy Guy's Legends because along with the live band being a nice touch, it was still a chill spot where you wouldn't look out of place in anything you wore. I tapped his shoulder to get his attention and his eyes lit up like a Christmas tree when he turned around and saw me.

"Hey beautiful," he said like it was my name as he stood and embraced me. "For a minute I thought you were standing me up."

"Nope. I'm here," I said simply because I couldn't exactly tell him that I was late because I'd went to three different drugstores before I found the brand and type of condoms that I preferred. Chicago was severely lacking in that department so I would be ordering some online soon if tonight went well.

When we were seated he instinctively pulled out my chair, intent on showing me that he was a gentleman, but I wanted to cut to the chase. I wanted dick and his in particular. I was only gonna be here for a year, hopefully less, so I wasn't looking for anything serious and especially not with somebody who knew TJ. He was funny and seemed cool so far so I wasn't opposed to making him a friend with benefits until I left the city for good, but that was as far as it would go. The moment I opened my mouth to relay all of that to him was cut short because instead he said that he had something he wanted to address me about.

"Now don't get me wrong. You look amazing, Tillar, but I thought we were doing the grown up thing tonight. As promised, I got my ankles right and exposed for you yet you walked in here looking mad comfortable. What's up?" he pressed me in a fake tough guy voice and I laughed at him as I looked down at my black leisurewear ensemble.

"I'm protesting. You know I didn't actually want a date."

"What you want then?" he asked me directly as he closed the menu and sat it down.

"I'm a lady so I won't say it out loud, but I have a feeling that you know exactly what I want, Cam." He grinned sheepishly then lowered his head.

"Nah. You ain't ready for that yet."

"Excuse me?"

"I didn't stutter. I can't give you that too fast 'cause you might get hooked and start bugging out on me. You'll be busting out the shop windows and shit and my insurance is already high as hell."

"Is that supposed to be a deterrent because it's not?" I asked because I had always been curious about the kind of D that made women lose their minds. I would never want to own one for obvious reasons, but a good sample never hurt anybody.

"Yeah and it's for your own good so let's take it slow," he said as he put his hand on top of mine. I didn't want to be rude, but I slipped it away because that wasn't something that I was interested in from him.

"Look you seem like a great guy and all, but I'm not in the whole 'dating and getting to know somebody' space right now. I won't be here for long and I just want to have a little 'no strings attached' fun before I head back south, okay?" I asked straightforwardly, but he looked like he wasn't buying it.

"Nah 'cause you're not that type of girl."

"Says who?"

"Says everything about you. You're too good for something like that."

"How about you let me decide that?"

"But what if I say I'm looking for something real with you? What then?"

"What does 'something real' mean to you? Because what I'm talking about is something real. It's very real." I grinned as I ran my foot up to his thigh under the table. He looked down at it then back up to my eyes as he politely put my foot back on the ground. I almost frowned before he went on.

"I mean what if I want the strings attached?"

"Well that would be too bad because as much as I want to sample your product, I'm just not in the market to buy right now. My bad for making you waste your time and letting your ankles breathe for nothing tonight," I said pretending like I was about to get up and leave when really I just wanted him to drop his nice guy act.

I knew that he would have loved nothing more than to have my ankles over his shoulders at the end of the night, but he wanted it on his terms because a lot of men were sick creatures and would much rather feel like they were tricking women into something than just accepting a situation like the one I was suggesting.

"So that's it then?" he asked predictably as he stopped me. "Wow I can't believe I'm really being pressured to have sex right now. I never thought I'd see the day," he said sounding amused at me.

"I am not pressuring you. Am I?" I asked as I joined in on his laughter.

"You are and you're pretty good at it too."

"I'll stop then. You obviously don't want to so for real you and your ankles can enjoy the rest of your PG night in peace without me," I said attempting to pump fake him again.

"Wait. No. Tillar, I want to. Trust me on that," he assured me before licking his lips and proving that he was susceptible to reverse psychology. "I just really want to get to know you outside of that first. That buildup from waiting makes it worth it, don't you think?" he asked trying to persuade me, but I wasn't budging on what I wanted right now so I shook my head no. He smiled at my persistence then sat back in his chair and thought about it for a minute or two too long.

"Okay now I'm pressuring you. You tryin' to be down with Dipset or what?" I questioned playfully. Finally he sighed then nodded his head towards the door as he opened his wallet and put some cash on the table.

"Let's go."

"You're serious?"

"Yeah. I don't know what you're doing to me tonight, but I went brick as soon as you put your foot on my leg," he admitted candidly and I appreciated what I was sure was his first honest statement thus far.

"Well wait a second because you've got me in here smelling all of this good Cajun food so now I want some."

"Get it to go then," he said in the same tone that he'd used with me on the phone last night, like he wasn't playing any more games with me and I couldn't have been more happy with the quick turn of events. And see how fast his *taking it slow* shtick went out the window? That's why I never believed men when they spoke because most just liked to hear themselves talk.

After we had been served our food in a to-go bag, I waited for him to make the first move to leave before I remembered that he'd pitched a tent and it was more than likely straining against the fabric of his pants. He nodded his appreciation as I got up and casually stood in front of him, but I couldn't help looking back at it first. He wasn't lying. It was still hard as a rock and although the pants he wore were black, they were clearly not made to hide such a monster. Whew.

With a hand on my waist, he stood close behind me to conceal it until we got out to my car. He had gotten an Uber there so I drove a little over the speed limit as he gave me directions to his place which luckily wasn't too far away. I didn't know if he was embarrassed or what because he didn't speak at all unless he was telling me which way to turn, but it wasn't a bad quiet. It was more like a dark and sexy one. Like he was picturing all the things he was about to do to me. Or maybe it was just me.

When we got to his place in Old Town he let me go in first then turned on the lights but immediately dimmed them some as I took in the big modern studio apartment. It was a man's place so there was no real décor, but it was simple and neat and he had a lot of live plants. All the greenery made the place look like a little jungle and I liked the vibe that I got because it seemed like him. And I knew he had to have some money to afford living in this part of the city because he was probably paying about the same as I did for my two bedroom condo in Buckhead.

Even though we had already awkwardly swapped our most recent test results while we waited for our food to be done, I still let him know that we would use protection and gave him the just purchased three-pack from my purse. He had no objections as he studied the label, but we stood there for a minute not really knowing what to do next until he offered me something to drink. I accepted then finally left the spot that I was glued to in order to watch him make it because I wasn't a fool and he could still be crazy. For some reason that made my stupid pussy jump around in my pants, but I guess that this was pretty exciting for me. For once I had seen something I wanted and went after it. This had to be how men felt all the time.

"You staying over?" he asked wondering how much alcohol to give me in case I wanted to drive home when we were finished.

"Depends on if it's good enough for me to want more in the morning," I said honestly as I stepped out of my shoes.

"Yeah you're staying then," he remarked with confidence as he poured extra D'usse in my glass.

"Not too much. I still have to get up for work." I wasn't much of a drinker, but I figured a few sips would loosen me up a little.

The lights were low but not completely dark, but he still lit a few candles before going over to his record player and putting on an oldies type song that I'd heard before. I wasn't familiar enough with it to know the title or the artist, but it was very slow and sensual.

"This is how you like to set the mood, huh?" I asked before I took a sip of the drink, but he didn't say anything back as he began unbuttoning his shirt. He was a little more on the thinner side than I'd first thought but still pretty solid to be so tall. Slim thick. As I studied his body, he threw his drink back in one gulp then walked over to me.

With every step he took, I noticed more and more that his eyes were overflowing with lust. He was about to take what was his because for tonight at least I would belong to him. I wouldn't dare try to stop him after seeing that unmistakable gleam of sex veiled behind his eyes that I was sure mirrored my own.

I knew there was officially no turning back when he took the glass from me then brought both of his hands up to hold the sides of my face as our lips touched for the first time. The gentle kiss was much sweeter than I expected it to be because I assumed that it would match the hunger that was coming from inside of him. I knew instantly that I didn't want to do that too much because I was always a sucker for a good kisser and I didn't plan on being a sucker anymore.

Right when I was about to put an end to it, he slowly sucked my full bottom lip into his mouth and I shivered down to my bones when I thought about him doing the same to my clit soon. He was amused at my strong reaction for a second, but I didn't let that deter me from taking off his shirt and working on freeing him from his pants. Standing in just his underwear, I was pleased to see that he hadn't ruined his pretty dark skin with any tattoos because it was gorgeous enough on its own.

He tried to latch onto my lips again, but I kissed his jaw instead and trailed from his neck down to his chest then let my tongue flick over his nipple. Instead of the slight sound of pleasure I thought I'd hear from him, he laughed at me like I had told a joke.

"What was that?" he asked as he defiantly brought my lips back up to his.

"That's an erogenous zone for some men too," I told him through the kiss that I swore I didn't want but was loving all the same as he backed me into the arm of his sofa.

"Not for me. And if you don't mind, I would prefer to do that to you."

"I'm sure you would," I said full of sarcasm

while internally hoping that I hadn't made a mistake and picked a basic, missionary-only loving dude.

I wasn't into anything too crazy myself, but I definitely needed my spot hit repeatedly like yesterday and I had a feeling I wouldn't get it from the guy who thought getting his nipple licked was funny. I wasn't giving up on him yet though because I did not come to play. Even if he just laid there I could still have a lot of fun on top as long as he could keep that big thing up.

I hadn't set out to wow him with my casual clothes, but I knew he would be impressed when he saw what I had on underneath them since I had come prepared in some of my finest lingerie. I had almost left that stuff in Georgia but decided at the last minute to bring it just in case and seeing his eyes widen let me know that I'd made the right decision. Once he had gotten an eyeful of how well I filled out my sexy undergarments, I didn't waste any time reaching behind to unhook my bra because the way he got caught looking at them the day we met let me know that he was indeed a breast man.

The gentle pleasure of having them free and released lasted only a second because they were quickly picked up by his big hands. He just stood there and admired them for a long while like he had never seen a woman before.

"Damn Tillar," he said appreciatively as he weighed them. He finally tore his eyes away to ask if he could taste them so I nodded then threw my head back in anticipation. His warm, wet tongue didn't disappoint one bit as he greedily sucked my full areola in his mouth.

"You know there are other parts of me that need attention from your mouth too, Cam?" I boldly informed him after I realized that he was in heaven and wasn't planning on stopping his back and forth attack on my nipples anytime soon. I could only enjoy that for so long though and I was ready to get down to business after feeling his stiffness pressed up against me and how quick his tongue was.

"Is that right?" he asked as he suddenly got down on his knees like he was about to worship me. He didn't ask for my permission this time as he brazenly yanked my panties down in one hard jerk. I liked it though. He could save his good manners for the dinner table because I wanted him to enjoy this meal as sloppily as he wanted to. Especially because I was sure that it was more than his usual serving size.

"Yeah I don't know if you could tell or not, but there's a lot more here than just those." He grinned then asked me in a role-playing tone where I wanted to be licked now. His face was so close to my pussy that they could've been Siamese twins so I had no doubt that he was intentionally teasing me. "Wherever you want to," I whispered, trying my best to get him as hot as he had gotten me.

"I want you to tell me where and be specific," he said with authority as he ran his tongue up my thigh then traced the trail with his warm breath. I nearly fell back on the couch before he caught me. "Better yet, come over here and show me where."

I could have gotten things popping right where we were, but he led me over to his bed then helped me sit. It was one of those modern looking low floor beds so I didn't know how exactly I would be getting up, but that was none of my concern at the moment. I knew this was about to be one hell of an experience so I was spread-eagled and showing instead of telling before he could even get back on his knees.

He quickly pushed my fingers out of the way but not before sucking on them first so as not to waste a drop of my already running juices. The second his tongue left his mouth and made contact with my body again, I lost control of everything and the delighted look in his eyes let me know that he knew it. He grazed my clit with the tip of his tongue and continued watching me watch him. I whined when I realized that he was holding back because he wanted me to beg him for it. He seemed to get off on how he was now in charge of how I would feel pleasure and how much of it I would feel and how long I would feel it.

"Cam, that's enough. Please suck it," I pleaded with him with no shame and he laughed again.

"Watch your mouth."

"I can't. I'm watching yours."

"Open wider," he demanded as he put his face back between my thighs. I felt a little exposed, but I pushed them to the limit like he'd asked as he had his first kiss with my clit as well. "Mm. I knew you would taste good," he moaned complimenting me, but I didn't know how to respond to that.

He finally went to work and used his full lips and teeth to grip it then repeatedly flicked his tongue over it. I was glad he had just enough hair to grab onto because I locked my fingers in it as I squirmed about in pure euphoria. He really was a good kisser and great with those lips too. Before long my hips were lifting off of the bed and his mouth continued to mimic my wild movements and never stopped lapping at me. Even when I shuddered my way into a second orgasm and instinctively tried to close my legs, he kept them pried open and further explored until I pushed his head away because I couldn't take it anymore.

He asked me a question, but my mind honestly couldn't make sense of words at that point so I just kept my eyes on him while he got up to get a condom. I heard him opening it after he got back in bed but before he could enter me I reached down and double checked that he'd actually put it on. *Trust but verify*, I thought as I let him finally push his way inside of me.

I continued to watch his face because I knew that the confidence he was wearing from making me come so hard was about to disappear and I was right. All of a sudden he got an almost panicked look on his face before he pulled back out in a hurry.

"What's wrong?" I asked and tried not to sound too patronizing. I was still recovering from his mouth, but I smugly smiled to myself because I knew he wasn't expecting it to be like that.

"Nothing. Just making sure this is on right," he lied as he pointlessly checked the condom again. Lucky for me, he wasn't a quitter so he quickly got his bearings together and dove in again only this time he had to admit just how good I felt out loud.

"I know, but you better not be trifling and use that as an excuse to finish first." He chuckled then moaned when I wrapped my legs around him and pulled him in some more. I wasn't going for any of that *just put the head in* mess. I wanted as much of him as I could take since he'd gotten me wet enough to take a good amount.

After a little while of getting adjusted, he finally showed me what he was working with and I was relieved to see that he had a nice rhythm to his stroke because he almost had me worried for a minute. I definitely wasn't trying to make too much direct eye contact with him, but after a while I just had to see his face because it sounded like he was really enjoying himself up there. I mean I was too, but he wasn't the least bit shy about moaning and wasn't even trying to hold back like I was. I liked that. His uninhibited moans and the obscene sounds our bodies were making as we purposely collided with each other were making me wetter than I had ever been. He must have noticed it too.

"Mm. You always this wet or just for me?" he asked like we were having a casual conversation and not in the middle of fucking the living daylights out of each other.

"Do you always moan this much or just for me?" I quipped back because I didn't want him to know that he was doing so good until I had at least finished one more time.

"What, you want me to be on silent mode?"

"If you don't mind," I said before encouraging him to get back acquainted with my breasts and I certainly didn't have to tell him twice.

I closed my eyes and got back focused on the way that he was stroking me. He was curved at the perfect angle like he was made for my body and he was going the perfect speed. Not too fast, but not too slow either. Usually I would have to reach down to my clit to help finish myself off, but his pelvic bone kept rhythmically hitting it every time our bodies connected and it was making every nerve inside of me tingle as my hips suddenly lifted again. He came back up and sucked on my lips some more as I came again.

"Open your eyes and look at me, Tillar," he begged me, but I couldn't. They were crossed and going in different directions anyway so it was much better this way.

He didn't let me have my moment alone for long because not long after he was ready to finish too. He had probably been holding it because he seemed so relieved to finally let go. His orgasm seemed to start in his shaking legs then quickly shot through the rest of his body. He buried his face in my neck as he groaned loudly and gave me those last few good thrusts before he shouted my name.

I was completely shook because I had never been with a man that came that aggressively and I was literally stuck when he practically passed out on top of me gasping for air. Finally after a minute of trembling he rolled over and just laid there staring up at the ceiling like he didn't know what to do with himself. When he was stable enough to coherently speak again, he looked over at me like I had two heads or something.

"You deadass could have warned me about that," he said in all seriousness, but I couldn't help but laugh at how dramatic he'd just acted over a single nut when I had kept my composure through a few.

"Well nothing I said could've prepared you, right?" I joked reminding him of what he'd said the other day in the shop. He agreed as he cuddled up next to me and kissed me again. Shit. He was really trying to make this be more than what it was so I decided to use my sense of humor to take the focus off of how close he was to me now. "Are you alright though? It looked like you weren't gonna make it at the end and I was worried because I haven't done CPR in years."

"I know you're not talking. You looked like you were really feeling it too," he bragged.

"Meh. It was okay."

"Just okay?" he asked like he actually believed my act, but before I could answer truthfully he had already reached under the sheets and found my clit with his thumb and pushed his two longest fingers inside of me. They were just as big as they were long and almost as filling as his dick was, I noted as I arched my back and accepted them. He was back in control and being super precise so of course I was coming again in no time. And I didn't know if it was just because I wasn't expecting that one or what, but to his delight I couldn't suppress my moans anymore as I officially tapped out of this round. He won. All the As and all the plusses.

He looked very pleased as he pulled his drenched arm up and mannishly inspected the mess I'd just made on his hand.

"See Tillar, your pussy wants the strings and I'mma make you want 'em too," he said as he got up and finally went to flush the condom. I breathlessly looked after him and noticed for the first time just how cute his butt was as I sat up in bed. I did my best to wrap myself up in the sheets because after all of that I really had to pee. My legs were still weak though and I realized that I couldn't get up from so low without some assistance.

"A little help here please?" I asked as he came back out. I was impressed by his strength because he bent and lifted me up with almost no effort making me feel as light as a feather. I could definitely get used to that.

"You good?" he asked looking down at me with a markedly intense gaze, but I looked away as it was finally dawning on me what I had just done. He sensed it and called me out on it when he saw me covering myself up.

"Tillar, I know you're not acting shy after where I just had my tongue. Shit we go together now," he joked as he put his boxer briefs back on. "You hungry yet?"

"I'm famished."

"Because of me, right?" he asked fishing for me to tell him how good his sex was.

"Because I haven't eaten since breakfast actually," I said matter-of-factly.

"C'mon. Just admit you liked it," he said playfully after me, but I grabbed my big purse and scurried over to the bathroom instead.

I didn't want to get my handy dandy overnight bag out of the trunk and have him think I was automatically spending the night before. But as a rule I stayed ready though so I had military rolled some cute pajamas and a few toiletries in there earlier for this very reason. He had kindly left towels out for me so I took a bird bath then dressed in my pjs because he was right. I wasn't leaving and I would definitely want more again in the morning or even later if another round wouldn't kill him. My nipples were still hard thinking about him doing just half of that again.

When I came out he was already eating his food and had a plate waiting for me on the bed next to him. He was about to get up to help me, but I was fine because going down was a piece of cake. It was the getting up that was hard.

"You are satisfied, right?" he asked again in the same way he had done when he cut my hair and I liked that he was so eager to please me. He was already turning out to be the perfect guy for the setup that I wanted.

"Yeah everything tastes great. Thanks for asking," I quipped and he nudged me because I knew he wasn't talking about the food. "You mean you really can't tell?"

"You seemed into it, but there are women who fake it so it'll be over sooner."

"Not me. I actually could've gone longer."

"You saying I came too quick?" he asked with a cute grin.

"No. Trust me I would've been gone already if it was bad. I just wanted to mess with you before. Oh fuck," I said before he worriedly inquired about what was wrong. It wasn't anything major though. The restaurant had just forgotten to put a cornbread muffin in my to-go box. He had already taken a bite of his, but he still reached over and gave me the rest of it. "You're a people pleaser, aren't you Cam?" I asked him before taking a bite, but he shrugged nonchalantly.

"Certain people."

"Well I'm glad that I'm in that category because this is so good."

"It's a'ight. I can make them better."

"Where on earth did you learn how to cook cornbread better than this?"

"From my Gram."

"Not from your mama?" I asked then immediately wished that I'd just taken another bite of the muffin instead. I was just so used to feeling envious when I heard people talk about cooking with their mom because I had never experienced it. Michelle never wanted me in the kitchen because she always said that I would probably mess something up and I guess I had internalized it because til this day I still wasn't much of a cook. I was an expert at cleaning the dishes though.

"Nah. She passed when I was a kid and I barely remember her. If it weren't for pictures, I wouldn't even know what she looked like," he said pretty evenly considering what he was talking about. And even though he was sitting there half-naked, I still wasn't expecting him to reveal something so personal.

"I'm sorry to hear that. I sort of understand because I lost my dad when I was ten. I always felt like he left me too soon, but I guess I should be more grateful because I still remember everything about him."

From the silence that followed I knew that he had more to say just like I did about our respective fallen parents, but we both just sat there and finished eating because despite what we'd just done we were still very much strangers. I was glad because I really didn't want to trauma bond with him anyway. I just wanted sex and maybe one more cornbread muffin.

When we were done and he'd put our plates in the sink, he asked if I wanted anything else to drink. I declined him, but it was only ten and I wasn't quite ready to go to sleep yet so I looked around his place wondering if he had one of those cool hidden TVs somewhere.

"Have you got any Netflix to go with that chill, Cam?" I asked and he smiled at my wordplay.

"My bad. I don't have a TV," he said then watched me closely to see my reaction.

"How is that possible? What do you do all day?"

"Uh…I work out sometimes, I run the shop, and I guess I read a lot," he said after shrugging, but I was sure he was leaving out the parts about having sleepovers with female customers like now.

"Like real, actual books?" I asked and I hoped that I didn't offend him even though I meant what I'd said. His look screamed fuckboy on stilts that considered reading tweets on Twitter as literature.

"Yeah real, actual books," he said as he gestured over to his tall bookshelf in the corner. I hadn't even noticed it before, what with my eyes rolling back into my head so many times since I'd been here.

"Sorry. It's just you don't look like the type. Recommend something for me."

I reached up for him like a baby as he came to my rescue and saved me from the ground again. He smiled down at me then nicked my lips once more which quickly turned into more than just the quick one he'd intended on giving me. His manners must've returned because he apologized then let me know that he just really liked kissing me as if I couldn't already tell.

"That's alright. But for future reference, I prefer my kisses down low," I told him being only half serious as he led me over to the shelf that was filled with books of all sizes.

He stood behind me with one hand absentmindedly on my stomach as he scanned the higher shelves with the other. I didn't say anything about him invading my personal space or touching me in a place that I'd worked on being less self-conscious about because he didn't make a big deal out of it so I wasn't going to either. It was nice though, feeling the coolness of his palm on my warm belly. He had the typical tall people cold hands thing going on that I'd had to get used to with all the men I'd dated. I had them too, but it wasn't as bad.

I recognized a few of the authors, but I could honestly say that I hadn't read even one of them. As a child and teen I loved getting lost in a good book more than anything, but reading so much in college had singlehandedly ruined that relationship so I wasn't quite up on the latest stuff like he seemed to be. After a few minutes of picking one up then putting it back, he finally found one that he deemed worthy and handed me a purple book called *Cheaters*. It was by an author named Eric Jerome Dickey and I knew of him because my Auntie Diane used to read all of his stuff back in the day. Jordan and I would sneak and read the sex parts, but I'd never actually read anything in full by him so I was curious.

"This is deadass my favorite so you better give it a chance. I think you'll like it though."

"Don't just assume because I'm a woman that I'll be into romance novels."

"I didn't. I just thought you could use some romance in your life," he said with loaded words and I didn't have a comeback because he wasn't exactly wrong. I could have used some, but since romance from men came with a whole heap of expectations and other bullshit I decided to forego it for the time being.

"Touché," I said before sitting the book down next to my belongings so I wouldn't forget it before I left in the morning. "Okay now that the library is closed, what are we gonna do now?"

"Well I usually read until I fall asleep, but we could always talk or is that too much like a date to you?" he quipped before I rolled my eyes. "Where'd you get this?" he asked suddenly about the big scar on my left arm. I guess it was his first time noticing it because he had only seen me in long sleeves so far and I was currently showing more skin than a little bit.

"TJ got my arm caught in the let-out couch in our basement when we were kids. I swear brothers are sent from hell." I remembered foolishly thinking that I would lose my whole arm when the large patch of skin ripped off, but it just left a distorted almost embossed butterfly shaped scar.

"They're not that bad."

"You have any?"

"Two younger. Chris and Chase. It's just you and TJ?"

"Yeah. Apparently my mama wanted more kids, but she didn't want to chance having another girl like me so she stopped trying."

"She actually told you that?" he asked in disbelief and I was reminded of why I didn't talk about her too much. I saw how uncomfortable it made Nicole and other friends when I used to bring up our relationship so I'd learned to keep my mommy issues to myself.

"In so many words, yeah," I said before changing the subject back to my scar. "It used to cover half my arm, but the bigger I got, the smaller it seemed. Where'd you get yours?" I asked about the shallow but still indented scar on his lower abdomen. It was where you'd expect to see an appendix scar, but it looked like a small chunk was missing instead of a surgical scar.

He looked down at it then quickly said it was a long story which just made me more curious because he could have just said what it was if it was no big deal.

"There's no TV so we have all the time in the world."

"Yeah, but I would rather get some sleep. I'm stuffed and you know you just wore me out," he said before bringing me back over to the bed. He was about to turn off the record player, but I told him to leave it on so I could at least fall asleep to the low instrumental music.

♕

I kept my phone right next to me when I slept so when the first alarm went off, I quickly snoozed it because I wasn't ready to get up just yet. I'd assumed I was at home in my bed until I felt somebody roll over and put their arm around me. Before I panicked I thought back to last night and remembered where I was and who I was with. Cam. I should've known better anyway because I wasn't in the uncomfortable twin bed I'd been getting used to at my mother's house.

Careful not to wake him, I slowly removed his hand from my stomach and sat up. I groaned when I realized again just how low his damn bed was. I mean yeah it was comfortable, but it was just another reminder that I was getting old and that my knees weren't what they used to be because it was a struggle for me to get up.

"You leaving already?" Cam yawned out after I had successfully pushed myself up from off the bed without his help.

"Yeah I gotta get back to the plantation."

"But I thought you said you wanted more?" he asked as he rubbed my side of the bed then invited me back down with him. I would have loved to stay for another round or two, but it was only my third day and even though I was working independently I was still very much on the clock so I didn't want to be late.

"Next time I'll set my alarm earlier," I assured him not even pretending that I wouldn't be back. He didn't talk much and he fed and fucked me well and that was all I really needed in this life of sin.

"You got time for breakfast or coffee then?"

"No. I still have to get home to get dressed first," I said more hurriedly than I'd intended, but he didn't seem to mind.

"I thought you said you stayed ready," he teased me with a cute grin as he got up.

"I usually do, but I wasn't bringing my work clothes here."

"You better next time," he told me as he walked passed me over to the bathroom.

Still putting on his gentleman front, he got up and walked me down to my car. It was still pretty dark out so I did really appreciate it because I wasn't familiar with this part of town even though it was a nice neighborhood. When we got to the front door, he reminded me to read the book then kissed me one more time. It was a little awkward with the first signs of the sun light starting to push through and his neighbor coming in with two big dogs. Ultimately I was just glad that he was thoughtful enough to have brushed his teeth first though since he seemed set on using his tongue every time we kissed even this early.

"What time are you free later?" he asked when it was just us in the hall again.

"Why? I already got what I needed out of you to get me through the week," I said in a joking tone even though I was serious. He half-heartedly chuckled along.

"If you want it to get you through every week while you're here you better at least call me then. I still wanna take you out for real."

"Yeah I'll see how heavy my schedule is looking and I'll let you know," I said lying because it would literally be the same every week. I just wasn't interested in doing that kind of stuff with him. I guess I didn't hide it as well as I thought I did because he was whining about it soon after.

"Really Tillar?" he asked calling my name like we were more familiar than we actually were. "That's the best you can do?"

"What? We had fun, right?" I asked as I kissed his cheek and he reluctantly nodded and sighed. "Right so we don't have to do all of that extra stuff. I can just come through here whenever I get time, okay?" I said thinking that it would be the end of the conversation, but he stopped me from reaching for the doorknob.

"You're that jaded? Why is it so hard to believe that I want to get to know you?" he asked sounding offended and I frowned as he continued. "I don't know what kind of niggas you're used to, but I don't sleep with just anybody," he said like he wasn't a willing participant in the last ten hours we'd spent together.

"Oh please. Don't do that, Cam." I could

have tried to explain that I had a lot on my plate or how I was stressed out of my mind, but I didn't have to explain myself to anybody let alone some man I'd just met. My reasons for wanting dick sans dating was my business, not his. "Look it's nothing personal. I laid everything on the table for you last night so if you can't handle this, then that's fine and we don't have to see each other again."

I waited around a second to see if he would change his mind how I'd gotten him to do last night, but instead he stood there looking like he was waiting for me to do the same except I wasn't. And I was about to be running late soon so I just turned and let myself out because some goodbyes didn't need to be verbalized.

I had just gotten situated in my car when I heard a light tapping on my window. I didn't even bother looking as I pressed the button to let it down because I knew who it was and I was proven right when he bent so that I could see his face as he spoke.

"Can you just give me one chance to get this right, Tillar? One real date," he said almost pleading with me, but instead of being endearing like he'd probably hoped I was just annoyed that he wasn't respecting the boundaries that I had clearly set.

Maybe I had given him the wrong idea or

confused him by staying over and cuddling before we fell asleep when I should've just left. I was just about to take the blame when I reminded myself that men always did think that their dicks were more magical than they actually were and he'd probably figured I would be sprung after sex with him. I sighed hard because he had already ruined what could've been a beautiful and simple situation.

He needed to grow up.

"I have to go. I'll see you around, Cam."

After getting to work late my day was instantly off to a bad start. I'd forgotten to bring in an important USB and missed an important conference call because of a mix up with the time difference. I couldn't help but to blame how I'd left things with Cam for throwing me off of my game because fussing around with him had put me in a funk before the day even began. By quitting time all I wanted to do was soak in a hot bath then get some shut eye, but the second I walked through the door Michelle began to question me about where I was the night before like I was a child.

"Out," I said shortly because I really wasn't in the mood to be lectured by her. She was making dinner, but I grabbed an apple and a water bottle then headed to my room because with the way I was feeling, one sideways comment from her would have me taking my frustrations out on her.

"I hope you got something other than a wet ass. Don't be bruising your back for nothing when we got bills to pay," she said after me, but I didn't have the energy to respond to her. Me shutting my door and staying in my room until she went to bed said it all.

Later that night I finally tracked down Nicole and explained why I had missed her call last night. I hadn't seen her face in weeks so I made her Facetime me so it could feel like I was there with her as we talked. A man-eater in every sense of the word, she was surprisingly on Cam's side about everything.

"Why are you so mad that he wants to go on a date with you?" she asked as she sectioned off her hair to detangle it. I remembered thinking that my hair was long and thick until I met her years ago and watched it fall passed her thighs when she shook it loose from a big bun. Her wash days were insane, but her beautiful kinky mane was worth the extra effort it took to maintain it all. I was always in awe of how she was able to disguise it or incorporate it into her cosplay brand since she had first gone viral way back.

"First off I'm not mad. I'm annoyed that he won't just respect what I said I wanted from him. And if he really wanted to date he wouldn't have had sex with me so fast in the first place."

"So let me get this straight," she began before sitting her wide-toothed comb down, "You bullied him into fucking and now you're using it against him? Tillar, you really are a nigga now and I think my work here is done."

"Please. Nobody bullied that man into doing anything that he didn't want to do. You know men just act out when you treat them how they thought they were about to treat you. If anything he's trying to bully me into being more with him when he knows he doesn't even want it himself."

"Well what makes you say that? He already beat so he actually could be for real."

"He's not. I know his type."

"You think you might be already assuming the worst about him because you're still scared of getting back out there after Bryan?" she asked in the wannabe therapist tone that she often used with me. I hated it even though I knew it was necessary at times. "I'm not saying this new dude is 'the one', but shit it's about time you try somebody new. I'm sick of that nigga being your last ex."

"You and me both," I told her honestly even though I wasn't going anywhere near the question that she'd asked. "But I'm getting sleepy so I'll leave you to tend to all of that hair, Rapunzel, and you can let me deal with my boy problems on my own."

Just before she hung up I remembered to ask her if she had gotten any new updates from her latest private detective and just like I'd expected she hadn't. She went through them like Michelle went through bottles of wine because she was obsessed with finding her birth parents, but each PI seemed to only be able to find information that she already knew. I guess I understood the plight of wanting to know where you came from, but sometimes I wanted nothing more than to just completely ghost my family one day. I'd already sort of done it for college, but being roped back in how I was now was not exactly part of the plan.

I couldn't sleep after getting into bed, but there wasn't anything on TV that was interesting enough to hold my attention and I had already spoken to everybody that I cared to talk to for the day. I sketched for a while before glancing over and seeing the edge of the purple book peeking out of the bag I'd thrown on the chair when I got home that morning. I reached over and thumbed through it for a second before deciding to give it a shot since I didn't have anything better to do.

I flipped back to the first page to see that Cam had gotten it signed by the author and there was even a short inscription that mentioned an insightful remark he'd made about the book's characters. All of a sudden I was intrigued then surprised that he would even loan me such a personal copy. I likened it to me lending a stranger my favorite little black dress, which was blasphemous because the odds of getting it back would be slim. That thought led me to the next one which figured out that he really must've assumed we'd be seeing each other again. I almost felt remorse for being so cold to him before I turned the page because that's when I got lost and then found myself again in those first few chapters.

4

FIT FOR A QUEEN

The next few weeks at work were rough. My load was the exact same as before so it had nothing to do with the actual work part. It was the people. The first few days it seemed like the Chicago office was happy to have me and of course I was being treated well by the higher ups, but as much as I hated to admit it, I wasn't really cutting it socially with everybody else and that had the power to make the day enjoyable or barely bearable.

People who claimed to only come to work to make money not friends were being disingenuous. If you had to spend a third of your day somewhere then you should bare minimum not hate the people, but it seemed like everybody was already cliqued up and since they knew I wouldn't be around long they found no need to fake an interest in me. I immediately missed the southern hospitality from my home office because being close with my coworkers made the days pass faster.

And it also probably didn't help matters that a lot of the men were constantly in my face and being overly helpful about getting me adjusted to the new office. I was polite as always, but I made sure to never do anything to make anybody think that I was interested in the least bit. But ever since I'd made the mistake of bringing in donuts for everybody during my second week, some of the women officially had it out for me because the head of accounting made an off the cuff remark about trading in his work wife for me. Apparently she was well-loved here so me "stepping on her toes" was a nono.

I definitely wasn't trying to be *that* girl here, but there was nothing I could really do to quell the real issue that some of them had with me because I knew where it was coming from. Most seemed to dress in anything that fit or maybe not because a lot of it didn't fit very well at all. Except for a few, they were all dowdy and matronly in their boring business casual white tops and dark slacks. As for me, every occasion demanded a put together look and work was no exception because it was an opportunity to pull out my beautiful blouses and tailored three-piece suits which was what I loved most about work fashion in Atlanta.

There, there was no such thing as being overdressed ever. I had major culture shock and felt like I had travelled to a different universe when I got there for college because where I had grown up it wasn't unusual to see simple clothes at the grocery store or bank. But there every walkway outside of your house was treated like a runway. There were no dingy pajamas worn to class on campus like there was in the movies. Everybody was fashionable and when I decided to be an Atlien, I also decided that I would be fashionable too because after getting away from Michelle, I was finally tired of shrinking myself in height and width trying to fit in or at least fly under the radar. I didn't just want to be the cute but fat girl fading into the background anymore. I wanted to stand out.

Lucky for me I was roomed with three other girly girls who I still referred to as my fashion fairy godsisters because they got me together real quick and taught me how to dress for my size and body type. They spent up most of my first little refund check on stylish clothes and shoes that made me go from fat and frumpy to fat and fine and I hadn't looked back since. While I was studying for my classes I also made time to study fabrics and proper undergarments and everything else my mother had neglected to pass down to me.

I guess I couldn't blame her too much though because she honestly didn't need half the effort that I had to put in to turn heads. I had inherited her pretty face and figure, but since I came in a larger package I couldn't ever afford to be lax with my appearance. I had to be on at all times because it seemed that some people couldn't wait to catch me slipping on an off day, but as long as I had a say that day would never come so those old office bitties would just have to stay mad.

By week three I had completely given up on making friends. The other younger black woman Erica who did always speak to me seemed to stay out of office politics and in her own cubicle so I left her alone so she wouldn't start getting treated differently too. I spent my lunch breaks alone in my office talking to Nicole or rereading the latest chapter of the book I'd gotten from Cam. I had bought the digital version because I preferred my iPad for when I had long documents for work and because I didn't want to mess up his signed hardcover in any way.

I found myself reading very slowly, even going over some pages several times because I really didn't want the book to ever end. I'd learned more than a few lessons and I wasn't even halfway done so I knew that I would be going through the author's back catalog to see what other gems I'd missed out on. That is if I ever got more than a few minutes to myself which wasn't very often these days between Michelle and TJ's bad kids working my nerves because they were officially out of school for the summer.

Since I'd gotten home Michelle had been slacking off on housework because she expected me to do it just like old times, but I could've sworn that my peasant girl days were long behind me. In Atlanta I had a cleaning service come through whenever I needed and I laundered everything that didn't have to go to the dry cleaners. Still, Michelle saw nothing wrong with putting yet another burden on me and I finally worked up the courage to tell her about herself after clocking out for the day.

"Ma, some things are gonna have to change around here. I don't mind doing a load or two of laundry for you, but I'm not going near TJ's skid row looking underwear anymore," I warned her because I swore it seemed like he bypassed wiping his ass altogether because he knew I was responsible for the laundry again. "And you could make him do the dishes sometimes too. Do you know how much my nails cost?"

"If they cost so damn much then learn to do them at home like I do," she suggested haughtily like she wasn't still shopping at overpriced Whole Foods like she didn't almost not have a whole place to live in. "And you know my baby doesn't need to be messing up his clothes trying to learn laundry rules at his big age. It'll be quicker to just do it for him."

"You said it right. His big age. He's a whole grown man, not a baby so you can do it if you want it done."

"Well you know I'm getting up in age too, Tilly and I can't keep this big house clean all by myself and work all the time. Something's gotta give," she said convincingly even though she had literally just started her new job a day ago. I just rolled my eyes behind her back because this was coming from the same woman who wouldn't even let Tiffa call her Grandma in public.

Between my work and home life being equally stressful and boring and the superb sex scenes in the book, I had been thinking of Cam a lot lately. He'd called me once the day after I left his place weeks ago, but I didn't respond because I knew I was done with him and all the services that came with him including his cuts. I figured that he would be too clingy for my taste and there was nothing worse than a man who didn't know or wouldn't accept his given role. I was positive that he had a nice rotation of women in and out of his shop so the fact that he put on a show about not sleeping around with just anybody was very laughable.

But it wasn't until I finished the book when I realized that I at least had to see him once more to return it and I just so happened to be due for a touch up anyway. I'd been meaning to look for a new barber before now, but the past three weeks had gone by faster than I thought they would. I could've asked TJ to do it, but after seeing pictures of his work on his social media pages I saw that Lauren was right about him not cutting women's hair very femininely. And speaking of her, I knew I didn't want any attitude or funny business out of her when I made my appointment so I did it online to avoid speaking with her.

Cam wasn't lying about being booked because he only had two slots left for this upcoming weekend and they were both in the AM when the shop first opened. He didn't strike me as the grudge holding type so I hoped that he would still be professional, but even if he was upset about me not returning his call then I would just offer him one last romp because I could certainly go for some more too. I might've even humored him for a little while if it meant I had regular access to that beautiful piece of art swinging between his legs.

By the time Saturday rolled around I was so tired that I didn't even bother trying to top my last appearance in the shop. I wore a cute hat and simple matching workout clothes even though I wasn't headed to anybody's gym this morning. When I finished there, I would be climbing right back into bed where I had spent my last few weekends because I was too broke and sleepy to really do anything else. I was running a couple minutes late because I'd decided to treat myself to my favorite coffee shop Bean, but I knew my time slot was safe when I walked in and there were only a couple other customers in there this early.

I must've really gotten under Lauren's skin last time because it was immediately clear to me she'd tried to dress up for the occasion since she knew I was coming. Now I was no hater and I could admit that she was actually a very cute girl, but the clothes were wearing her and the expensive shoes were much too big for her small feet so I knew she'd most likely borrowed them to try to show off for me. Even though I was dressed down and wasn't wearing any makeup I still managed to look more put together because of the fit of my clothes alone. Yes I was extra enough to get my gym clothes and even my pajamas tailored too because it made a world of difference and I wanted to exude perfection whenever possible. If she were nicer, I would have told her that she actually looked more comfortable and approachable in her athleisure, but she got a C+ for effort today.

I didn't see Cam anywhere so I approached Lauren to check in first, but before I could even give her a phony greeting she smugly let me know that I would be getting cut by Reese instead of

Cam today. I studied her face for a second and sensed that she was more than happy to relay that news to me. I was just about ask why when out of the corner of my eye I saw Cam come out of his office and as expected he wasn't working on anybody because it was my appointment time. I left her standing there while I excused myself over to him.

"Hey Stranger," I said playfully from behind him, but he didn't seem too amused when he turned and saw it was me.

"Wassup?" he asked dryly as he picked up a brush and went over his beard in the mirror. It was already perfect so I could tell he was just doing it to keep his hands preoccupied.

"Not much. I finished the book the other day and you were right. I liked it a lot," I said as I took it out of my bag and placed it on his counter. "Can you fit your favorite customer in for a quick touch up? I made the appointment with you, but the receptionist must've written it down wrong or something from online," I said pretending that I didn't know her name.

"Reese can take care of you when she gets here. I'm busy," he said in a faraway tone and continued to play with the hair on his chin.

"I'll just wait then because I want you to do it," I said before it finally dawned on me why he was being so short with me. "Wow and I could have sworn you said that I would be the one bugging out on you. You are really something else, *Cameron*," I said putting plenty of spice on his name.

"Ay Tillar, I don't allow any drama here so either let Reese take you or you can take your business somewhere else," he said matter-of-factly.

"Are you really that hard up for a date?" I asked him with a slightly raised voice and he cut his eyes at me when a few people looked in our direction.

"Get out of my shop," he growled lowly behind severely clenched teeth and I suddenly gathered that he was more pissed than I thought.

"And if I don't?" I challenged him as I took a seat in his chair and folded my arms across my chest, daring him to do something about it. I should've been heading for the door, but something inside of me wouldn't just let me walk away. Maybe Nicole was right. Maybe I really was turning into a bully after all. He stared me down for a few seconds then rolled his eyes when he saw that I wasn't going anywhere.

"I don't got time for this shit," he said before tossing the brush down and going back to his office.

I sat there for a minute contemplating what I wanted to do before I got up and followed after him. I knew the other barbers and customers had been listening in on our exchange and if for no other reason than to spite Lauren, I was gonna get this man to cut my hair come hell or high water. I knocked as I entered then carefully closed the heavy wooden door behind me so that he would know I wasn't slamming it. He never even looked up from the paperwork that he pretended to be so focused on reading so I walked over and leaned on his desk like my name was Fran Fine.

"You know you are way too tall to be letting me hurt your feelings from down here," I said to make him laugh, but his scowl didn't move a centimeter. I sighed hard because he was behaving like a baby when he should have just been grateful I let him use my titties as pacifiers for that one night and let it go. "Cam, you knew what I wanted from the start so--"

"And you got it so what are you really here for?" he asked impatiently, but he did finally put his stack of papers down so I decided to try to smooth things over.

"Just a touch up I swear. I even planned on paying this time and I always tip my barber really well," I said honestly, but it didn't make a difference.

"I don't want your money, Tillar."

"What do you want then?" I asked even though I already knew the answer. I was met with silence though so I sighed again then dropped my arms from their crossed position after remembering Nicole's words about me being scared to get back out there. "Look whatever. If it means that much to you then I'll let you take me out on a real date and I'll even wear a dress this time."

"Are you really that hard up for a haircut?" he asked mocking me and I chuckled before I knew he was still being serious. "I'm good. I don't beg for shit so don't do me no favors with your little pity date."

"No, it wouldn't be like that. I mean yeah, you're petty as hell and I'm seeing red flags everywhere, but I really do need a good barber while I'm here and I could really use a regular good dick supplier too. You're my two for one special, Killa Cam," I joked then felt victorious because he blushed but tried to hide it. "If your terms mean that I have to let you wine and dine me to get unlimited access to both, then I'll do it. But I'm warning you that I'm an expensive date and I invented the word spoiled. I don't compromise. It's my way or no way. All I care about is looking good, feeling good, and keeping my credit good so if you wanna spend all your money on me, who am I to stop you?" I asked purposely trying to insult him, but all he seemed to hear was that he was getting his way.

"For real?" he asked sounding surprised so I nodded then stood on my tip toes to kiss his cheek for good measure. It still felt so weird being with somebody so much taller than me especially now because I was in flat sneakers. "A'ight bet, but I'm still not cutting your hair today," he said just to be difficult.

"Then I'm not letting you play with your two new friends anymore," I said referring to my breasts and he finally grinned as he leaned on and looked down at me.

"You've got a smart ass mouth, Tillar, but I like that about you. You're lucky that you're so pretty and got good pussy or else I would've put you out of here for real. And you better not ignore me when I call you again," he said as he bent down to kiss me on the lips. He must have let all the aggressiveness out in his words because his kiss was soft and sweet. "Go back to my chair. I'll be out in a minute."

I smiled sneakily to myself as I left because I was getting my way too. I saw Lauren closely watching the door to his office when I came out of it. I contemplated sticking my tongue out, but I wouldn't be that childish even though it would serve her right for our last encounter. His demeanor had changed when he came back out. Of course he wasn't giddy or anything, but I could tell that our little exchange had relieved some tension that he had probably been carrying around for the last few weeks.

He made so much eye contact in the mirror that I was sure he would make a mistake, but he was an expert and did me right again. Towards the end, he remembered to ask me about how work was and if I was allowed to play around more with my hair. I let him do a couple small parts on the sides, but I still kept it pretty conservative. When he was finished he insisted on walking me out and as we were leaving a customer that was coming in asked if he was leaving for the day because she had an appointment.

"I'll be right back. I'm just walking my girl to her car," he said casually and I immediately turned to see Lauren's face to make sure she'd caught it. She had and I reveled in it for a minute until we got outside where I decided to correct him.

"Why did you do that? I don't want this to be a thing in there because of TJ."

"You made it a thing first by getting loud with me. And your brother is grown. He's not gonna care," he said as he put his hands on the hood and used his body to press me onto the door to my car. "I'mma see you tonight, right?"

"I didn't say I was available tonight," I said playing hard to get for show because I had nothing planned except for watching Michelle while she watched *Wheel of Fortune*.

"But I did."

I didn't know why I was fighting it. I was about to bae him real quick and get spoiled until it was time to head back south because I deserved it. I knew I'd slept with him too soon for him to actually take me seriously and I definitely wasn't trying to turn this into something so I would just go with the flow until he stopped the charade or until I got bored.

"Tillar?" TJ's voice said my name from behind me and he sounded eerily just like my dad's. His ears must've been ringing not just from the car that dropped him off blasting a trap beat, but also because we had literally just talked him up. It wasn't until I looked behind me to see the boys' mama Cassie sitting in the driver's seat. She didn't speak to me so I kept my lips zipped too. "What you doing here?"

"Hey. I was just in the neighborhood and I decided to get a quick cut."

"I got clippers at home," he said simply and I could tell he was trying to behave in public because he needed his job, but this wasn't some big brother protection thing because he couldn't care less about me. He just didn't want me to be a part of his life in any way especially at work.

"Thanks, but Cam already took care of me,"

I said trying not to rub the whole thing in his face too much.

"You're late again, Teej," Cam said with no hurriedness in his voice at the situation and it turned me on seeing him not try to explain his arm being draped around my waist. It just was what it was.

"Yeah I had an emergency with my sister. You understand," he said sarcastically.

"Get to work man," Cam chuckled out as he followed after TJ, but before he went in he looked back at me. "I'll make reservations for seven."

My plans of lying around all day had been foiled, but I wasn't even mad about it because it gave me an excuse to get extra dolled up for the first time since I'd been in town. Like the mama's boy he had always been, TJ had gone running to Michelle about what he'd seen so by the time I made it home she was awake and going off on me about embarrassing him at work. I didn't even argue back. I just agreed with her and let her fuss while I waited for Tiffa to come over and help me get ready. She wasn't allowed to wear makeup yet, but I figured it was never too early to learn the proper techniques and Sofia wasn't interested in most girly things.

Cam asked me to meet him at his house so I assumed that I would be driving, but when I got there he had a car with a driver waiting for us. He helped me out of my seat and I saw the appreciation behind his eyes at how great I looked because Date Night Tillar was a whole different animal than just regular everyday Tillar. I had dressed with a purpose and the girls were on tasteful display to tease him who also looked great in his well-fit dark suit.

We had a short ride downtown so I figured that we would be dining at one of the typical places, but instead the driver pulled up to a big abandoned looking warehouse on Clark. If it wasn't for me seeing another couple hand their keys over to the valet, I swear I would've gotten the hell out of there because the outside looked like a prime spot for sketchiness. It must've been done purposely because when we stepped inside the only word that came to mind was opulence. And we definitely stood out because not only were we the tallest patrons in there, but there weren't too many other melanated people either.

I knew that I'd told him that I was expensive, but still a nice steakhouse would have sufficed and I wondered how he had even gotten reservations here on such short notice. Regardless I thanked heavens that my penchant for overdressing had finally come in handy because this black dress was made for occasions like this. When we were being seated, I felt like everybody was looking at us or me rather. I even saw another man give Cam an appreciative nod in my direction. He nodded back then smiled at me while helping me sit.

"You got me feeling like the man in here," he said as he leaned over and whispered in my ear. "I promised I was gonna prove this was more than sex by holding out on you, but I can't wait to take this dress off of you later."

"That's if I let you. Don't be presumptuous," I said pointlessly because I'd definitely came prepared to have a good time.

"I forgot you're the boss here right?"

I noticed the waitress slyly flirting with him when she took our drink orders, but I didn't care. I learned a long time ago to never let stuff like that bother me because it was the man's job to nip things like that in the bud. Plus when he noticed it he made it known in a not so mean way that he was taken and held onto my hand as he looked over the menu.

"How'd you find this place? I've never heard of it before," I asked when we were alone again.

"I know about a few low key spots like this. I had to do a lot of digging when I got here because I missed all the good food from back home."

"It's not hard to find good food in Chicago."

"Harder than it is in New York. It's harder to find bad food actually," he bragged.

"Please New York cuisine is so overrated," I

said just to play argue with him because I had only been once to see KeKe Palmer as Cinderella on Broadway and I enjoyed every single thing I had. "And my maître d' sounding like DMX definitely didn't add to the experience."

"You're funny, but nah. Even when it comes to the street food, y'all ain't got no bodegas, no chopped cheese. The bagels and hot dogs taste funny here and don't even get me started on the pizza," he said like he was tired of holding all that in and was glad to finally get it off of his chest.

"You're a liar and the truth ain't in you," I retorted, making sure that I kept the volume of my voice in check because this conversation was not what you would expect in such a nice restaurant. "We've got plenty of your beloved Timberlands though and a few rats. That should keep you feeling at home plenty."

"Yeah Timbs, rats, and maybe something else now," he said as he intertwined our fingers. His wide palm and extra-long fingers made mine look like a child's hand next to his.

"Something?" I questioned because I would not be referred to as an object.

"Somebody," he corrected himself before looking in my eyes. "You got *somebody* waiting on you in Atlanta?" he inquired all of a sudden and I detected a hint of jealousy.

"No. Just me, myself, and I," I told him

honestly because Bryan wasn't even worth mentioning anymore. Still just thinking about him put a sour taste in my mouth so I started talking again to get him off of my mind. "So how'd you end up in Chicago anyway if you hate it so much?"

"I don't hate it here and that…that's kind of a long story," he said before letting go of my hand and trying to focus on the menu. I wasn't in a rush to hear his entire backstory yet because I certainly wouldn't be sharing mine anytime soon, but I still wanted to tease him.

"That's your excuse for everything, huh? How are we ever gonna *get to know each other* if you won't answer my questions?" I said as I perused my menu. There weren't any visible prices so I was trying to get what sounded the most reasonable. Usually I didn't care about running up a bill, but this place was on another level.

"I guess I just needed a change of scenery but not too different and I always heard Chicago was like a smaller version of New York. And my cousin Reese was already here and--" he remarked then like he was reading my mind he said, "I'm not a broke nigga, Tillar. Order whatever you want." I smiled to myself then slipped in something I'd been curious about since our first "date".

"Why don't you have a car then?" Usually that would be a dealbreaker for me, but I wanted to hear his reasoning since he owned a business and lived in a very nice area.

"I've got my license, but I'm from Harlem. We either walk or get on the subway and Fade is in walking distance so it's not like I really need one."

"Well what about when you go other places?"

"That's the thing. I'm a homebody and I don't go too many other places. I get my groceries delivered and there's a gym in the basement. That's pretty much it for me."

"So what, you just Uber or get a driver when you go out on dates?" I asked because I wanted to know how he navigated even though it was obvious that he was fine enough to get women to bend to his will. I was proof of that.

"I've been cool on that for a minute. And since my dad died I've just been trying to get used to living without him, you know?"

"Is this your first date since then?" I asked then instantly felt bad when he nodded yes. He was really putting himself out there after a big loss and it was all for my game playing behind. The waitress coming back was a welcome interruption because for the first time probably ever I didn't know what to say to a man.

Luckily for me after she took our orders he picked the conversation back up and effortlessly carried it over the nice meal. We laughed a lot and continued our city comparison war, but it was all in jest. I was surprised that he adapted so well to the environment because my first impression of him was completely off the mark. I figured he was the kind of guy who was only good for one thing, but so far he was showing me to trust that old adage about not judging a book by its cover or its big dick print.

By the time the fancy dessert cart had come out, I was close to my limit on food and wine so I declined, but he insisted thinking I was trying to be cute for him when that couldn't be further from the truth.

"Did you not just see me devour the past three courses? I'm not about to pop out of my spanx trying to prove something to you, Harlem World," I said playfully.

"Do you mind if I get something or are you ready to go?" he asked politely as he eyed a slice of chocolate cake.

"No, of course not. I don't have a curfew."

"Lucky me," he said before putting a small bite up to my lips.

"What are you thinking about right now?" I asked after seeing *that* look in his eyes when I licked the frosting that'd gotten on my lips.

"You don't want to know what I'm thinking about."

"I thought you said you weren't gonna think about that."

"Look at you. I can't help but to think about it. Especially when I'm not supposed to be thinking about it." He ate some then finally revealed it to me. "I'm thinking about how much better this would taste eating it off of you."

"Eating it off of where exactly?" I asked with my head slightly tilted because my curiosity had been piqued.

"Your place or mine?" he asked instead of directly answering my question.

"Yours. Always yours," I said hurriedly.

"I like the sound of that, but I have to ask why. You got roommates?"

"Something like that," I said vaguely then elaborated after remembering him sharing about his dad. "Well actually nothing like that. I gave up my beautiful condo in Buckhead for the year to come here and help my mama save the family house and in the meantime I'm sleeping in my too small childhood bed and staring up at old posters of Usher while talking myself out of killing her or TJ or both of them."

"My place it is," he said with a small grin as he placed his hand on top of mine. "But wait Usher though? I know you heard about--" he began before I cut him off.

"Shush! We have no way of knowing if those rumors are true!"

"Tell me that's not why you moved to the A."

"I promise it's not! But I did meet him once a couple years ago."

"Uh oh."

"Nothing happened. It was at a Waffle House with some friends and he just told me I was beautiful and complimented my style. He's really tiny though so it could never work."

"Among other reasons," he said making us both laugh a little too loud. I wouldn't stand for the Usher slander much longer though so I asked for his celebrity crush from back in the day. I was more than sure that it was somebody typical like Janet Jackson or maybe Lil' Kim since he was from New York. "You remember *America's Next Top Model*?" he asked to my surprise.

"Of course. You liked Tyra Banks, huh?"

"Tyra's cool, but I had a thing for one of the models on there. Tocarra something."

"Tocarra Jones," I told him because I was more than familiar with her as I had seen her in all the plus-sized shows for Atlanta Fashion Week over the years. His affinity for me suddenly made a whole lot of sense. Although we didn't look anything alike, we did share a few undeniable similarities because she was tall, dark brown, and *blessed* in certain areas just like me.

"Yeah her. She really changed the game for me."

"So I was right then. You do prefer…let's say more full-figured women?" Obviously he did a little bit because he was interested in me, but I didn't want to just assume because like Tocarra, I too had some men switching up their whole type after seeing me.

"I'll put it like this. I can appreciate beauty in women of all shapes and sizes, but I don't think my old man was lying when he used to say that bones are for dogs and meat is for men," he said before leaning on his elbow and waiting for my reaction.

Just when I was about to respond, the waitress suddenly appeared and passive aggressively put the bill on my side of the table instead of in front of Cam. He didn't notice it and just picked it up and quickly looked it over before going for his wallet.

"You better not tip her," I said when she was out of earshot again.

"Why? It's bad enough that she knows she's not the prettiest woman in here anymore because of you. Now you want me to stiff her on the tip too?" he asked in a teasing tone letting me know that he had indeed noticed her microaggressions towards me throughout the meal.

"Yep. Nothing over twenty percent."

"How about this instead? You want me to cause a scene for you because I will? I'll flip over every table in here in your name, Tillar. Just say the word," he said making me laugh and I realized that his thick accent really made his brand of dry humor even funnier.

"Please don't because both of our black asses will be in jail for the rest of the weekend," I said then leaned over to make sure he obeyed me about the tip, but it wasn't until I saw him sign the check that I realized all this time I didn't even know his last name. Cameron Logan. I quickly pushed the fact that I had slept with a man without knowing his full name to the back of my mind. It wasn't hard because like a high school girl with a pen and notebook, I mentally scribbled my first name down next to his last name to see how it would fit. Tillar Logan. Not bad.

"You need to go home to get clothes? Or you could just wear nothing. I'm cool either way," he said after the driver let us out in front of his building, but I just led him over to my car then popped the trunk.

"No. I always keep a weekender bag in here just in case something comes up."

"So that's what you kids are calling it these days, huh? Back in my day that was called a hoe bag," he ribbed me.

"Semantics, but you don't have permission to call it that," I said before he took and carried said hoe bag inside for me. His new high bed was the first thing I noticed because that was where he sat it down. "When did you get this?" I asked pointing at the bed. Whenever he'd gotten it, he had for sure paid a pretty penny for it because it was gorgeous and looked like something from a magazine.

"A couple weeks ago," he said trying to be nonchalant about it as he looked at his mail, but I instantly felt bad again for ignoring him when he was doing all of this for me.

"Was there something wrong with your other bed?" I asked trying not to sound obvious as I took off my shoes.

"Nah I just wanted a new one."

"Are you sure you didn't get it for me?" I asked as I went to sit down on it, but it was so comfortable that I melted back into it and laid down.

"You know how much this shit cost me? You think I like you that much already?" he asked with an unconvincing scoff as he tossed the mail back on his coffee table.

"Yes so just admit it."

"Do you like it?" he asked as he laid down next to me and I nodded. "Good," he said as he went in for a kiss, but I turned my mouth away.

"Say it's mine first."

"You already know it's yours," he admitted as he put his lips on mine. "I prayed and bought it hoping that you would come back," he said, but I didn't believe him because of how stubborn he'd acted towards me earlier.

"Don't bring God into this because there was nothing holy about what we did on that other bed."

"I don't know. Something spiritual was going on."

"Stop trying to make me like you too because it's not gonna work." He laughed.

"You already do," he said as he unzipped my dress and kissed my neck. "Lay back."

I sighed because it was a little true and I hated feeling like this. Situations like this one were always so cute in the beginning, but before long things would take a nosedive and I already saw my future with him flashing before my eyes. He would keep up this act just long enough for me to fall for him, I'd end up staying here for the relationship, then he would fuck up everything by cheating with somebody like Lauren.

"What's wrong?" he asked when he realized that I wasn't really into the kiss he'd initiated.

"I'm still trying to get myself over my last relationship and I have a lot on my shoulders right now so if you're not really the thoughtful guy that you're coming off as, just tell me now, okay?"

"What you see is what you get with me, Tillar," he claimed sincerely, but I still wasn't sure if I bought the act because I had heard it all before.

"Spoken like a man that's gonna break my heart. Are you gonna break my heart, Cam?" I asked him directly hoping that I would somehow be able to see the truth on his face, but it seemed just as genuine as it had been all night.

"Not even if you break mine," he promised as he kissed me again then suddenly stopped. "But please don't break mine. I like you a lot and it's been a long ass time since I could say that. And it's really fucking me up because the other day I was thinking that I might not ever see you again and now you're back here with me. Prayer works again, huh?"

"Mm hm. You better pray that you don't fuck anybody else on my bed then," I casually threatened him.

"Oh so now you want the strings too?" he teased me.

"Maybe just one or two strings for now," I bargained.

"No. All or nothing. I don't just want you in my bed, Tillar. I want you around period," he challenged me, but I already knew that he would accept whatever I wanted for now. And more than likely he would turn out to be just as trash as every other man out there, but for now I had him hooked and it was written all over his face. All caps again.

"Drive slow, homie. I literally just found out your last name tonight. Which reminds me..." I said as I got up to get my phone from my purse then he asked what I was doing. "Googling you before I sleep with you again and officially get sprung. My Auntie Diane always said men with two first names are crazy," I said playfully but immediately noticed the same panicked look he had from the last time I was here. Of course the timing of it was more appropriate before.

He quickly got up and took my phone out of my hands before I could even read what it said. And in two seconds tops he managed to mess up what had been a perfectly good evening and I was pissed off.

"What the hell are you doing? Give me my damn phone back!"

"Tillar, wait. Just let me explain everything first."

"No. Fuck an explanation, Cam. You didn't pay for my shit so don't put your fucking hands on it," I said as I held out my hand for him to return it. He sighed before reluctantly giving it back to me, but I didn't even bother reading what it said because me and my hoe bag were about to hightail it out of there. "Enjoy the rest of your night Mr. Logan," I said as I dramatically slammed the door shut after me.

I knew whatever he'd done was pretty bad because he didn't even try to come out after me. I stupidly let my curiosity get the best of me while I waited for the elevator and zipped myself back up. I looked at the search intently because I was expecting him to be some kind of serial rapist or pedophile ex-con with the way he was behaving.

A minute later the elevator came and opened its doors for me, but I was too fixated on what was on the small screen to move an inch.

Cameron Allister Logan Jr. was a murderer.

I stood there for a while going over a news article and had to make myself stay focused because every other line I was finding out something new that was exclaim worthy since he had omitted a lot of details about his life. Apparently his victim was the boyfriend of his estranged wife Summer Logan. I gasped out loud when I read minutes before being shot by Cam that the boyfriend had used the same gun to kill Summer and the eight year-old daughter named Cree that she shared with Cam.

The police report claimed that Cam was coming to pick Cree up for his weekend when he found her and her mother lying dead in their house and the boyfriend was about to kill himself before Cam wrestled with him for the gun. He'd tried to shoot Cam, but the bullet just grazed his stomach before Cam overpowered then shot him in the chest. The prosecutors decided not to charge him for the man's death because it was considered self-defense and it was deemed a reasonable response to finding his wife and daughter in that manner.

After reading all of the gory details about his past, I could have just left and never looked back. In fact I probably should have done that, but instead I let the elevator doors shut then slowly walked back over and knocked on his door. I guess I had been out there longer than I thought because he was already shirtless and seemed to be getting ready for bed when he opened up. There was a sadness in his eyes that I hadn't bothered to notice before, but now there was no getting away from it and it was all I saw. My eyes immediately fell to the scar that I'd asked him about the last time I was here and now it made sense why he wanted to avoid talking about it. I reached out and touched it with my fingertips before he put his hand on top of mine and walked us back inside.

"That's why I came here. He took my family from me and I couldn't live there without them anymore," he said as he sat back on the bed, but I chose to remain standing.

"Why didn't you just tell me that?"

"When did you give me a chance to? Between that half-assed first date and tonight, there was nowhere to even fit something like this in," he said defensively before he saw me about to dispute it. "I swear I was gonna tell you eventually, but experience has taught me that this is just not the type of shit you bring up on a first or second date."

"Which date would it have been then?" I challenged him.

"I don't know. But I meant what I said before. I like you and I hope you don't hold what happened then against me now," he said before bringing me to stand in front of him. "There's something about you that's drawing me to you, Tillar. I'm sorry for not telling you the whole truth, but I knew I wanted you to be mine when I first saw you and I guess I just didn't want anything to get in the way of that. And I promise I'll never keep anything else from you ever again. I don't even know how my feelings for you got this strong so fast because I still don't know shit about you either."

"Well I've never killed anybody," I said in bad taste because I was still flustered about what I'd just found out, but luckily it didn't seem to bother him. I shook off those feelings of uncertainty because despite the little amount of common sense I had, I wanted to start over with him. I took his hands from my waist so that I could reach out and shake one. "Hi. I'm Tillar Isley Reed. I live in Atlanta, Georgia and--" I began before he interrupted.

"Wait. Isley? Like Ronald Isley? Mr. Biggs? And you had the nerve to laugh at me about Cam'Ron," he cracked already ruining the moment I was trying to create.

"Whatever. My daddy was really on one, okay? And TJ is just lucky that they made him a junior otherwise his middle name would have been Pendergrass," I said honestly and he laughed until I made fun of his dorky full name that I'd seen in the google search.

I was glad that we'd found a quick moment of levity, but continuing the theme of sharing I decided to tell him something that I'd been keeping from everybody around me.

"My family and friends think I left my ex-fiancé because of his overbearing mother. I'm sure I would have eventually left him for that because she really was way too much, but the truth is I left him because he gave me an STI a month before our wedding day. It was curable and I was treated very fast, but I was humiliated and I couldn't get over it so I called the whole thing off. That is why we will always use protection and I won't ever jeopardize my health to prove that I trust a man again. So there, now you know my deep dark secret too."

By the time I was done talking a couple tears had managed to trickle down, but he got a tissue from his nightstand and expertly blot dried them for me.

"I'm so sorry you were hurt, Tillar, but I am glad that he messed up because now you're here and you can know what it's like to be with somebody who would never hurt you or make you cry."

"That's cute to say in the beginning, but you can't predict the future, Cam."

"That's true, but I can control my actions and I've never been a cheater."

"C'mon. Every man says that."

"Yeah, but I mean it. My dad told me the story of my Gram crying tears of joy at my grandfather's funeral because of all the running around he did on her and he vowed never to treat a woman like that. He taught me and my brothers that men who fuck everything moving are insecure. It didn't sink in for them, but as the oldest I took having not just his first name, but also our last name seriously. The Logan men are honorable. My dad decided and I decided too," he said with conviction and for the first time since I'd met him I knew for sure that he was being honest and I wished that TJ took having our daddy's name half as serious.

"So why were you separated from your wife then if there was no cheating?" I asked and immediately noticed that there were no more pauses before speaking because he was being free and open with me now.

"We had been together since we were kids. We were each other's first and only everything and after years of being a boring, old young couple with our daughter, she wanted to live different and I had no choice but to let her even though I was happy with our life. My only regret is not doing more to make sure she was happy too because if I did maybe they might still be here."

We ended up in bed because I wanted to know everything about him before I decided to proceed. He told me how he had worked through dealing with what he had done to that man even though he didn't regret it. I appreciated his honesty about that because he could have easily lied, but he assured me that despite the obvious he was not a violent person and that he had never hurt anybody else before or after that situation. I chose to believe him for now because I had been thorough with that search and I could always give his name to one of Nicole's PIs just to be sure.

"Tonight was almost perfect, wasn't it?" he asked with his lips to my head as I comfortably laid in his arms like I had done it a thousand times before. "You think we could try one more time for the perfect date?"

"This is already the second attempt. How many do overs are we gonna do?"

"As many as it takes to get it right. I'm up for it if you are."

I agreed to his challenge then got up to take off my dress and change for bed because I felt myself finally getting sleepy. He watched me closely, but instead of making a move he just did the same then got back cozy under the covers with me. Earlier I thought for sure that we would be having bed-shaking sex again, but instead we started talking about the book he'd given me as we held onto each other and listened to Sade on the record player until we fell victim to the Sandman. It was weird too because that was even more satisfying than his last performance in bed or at least it was in a more meaningful way.

The walk down the next morning was even different this time. He didn't have to ask if I would call him later or when I was free again because we both knew that I would be coming back and probably sooner than later.

5

A KING'S RANSOM

Feelings between Cam and I came lightning fast so we spent the next several weeks really trying to get to know each other and so far I really liked what I was seeing. Outside of the incident from his past he was perfect for me in every way.

He fucked like he was broke and needed a place to stay even though he had already shown me that he was very generous. He'd definitely been holding back the first time because once we got more comfortable with each other, he really let loose and had me letting him do things that I thought I would never do. But at the same time he was so gentle with me. My dark skin didn't bruise very easily and I looked sturdy so other men took that as a license to be rough, but he always took his time and put my comfort first.

Our compatibility went far beyond just sex though. Usually I wouldn't consider dating a man without at least one degree, but he was becoming the exception of all exceptions. He was well-read and could keep up with me far better than any man from my past and even intellectually challenged me at times. On top of that he had no student loan debt and I was sure he had a nice savings because he lived pretty simply and didn't have any credit cards. Yes, I had gone through his wallet when he was in the shower once.

I even had to admit that I was wrong about him putting on about being such a gentleman because he literally never let me carry anything except for my purse. He wouldn't even let me pay for or pump my own gas anymore whether I was with him or not.

"You know you can't just stop doing all of this once you get comfortable, right?" I warned him one day when we were out and he insisted on carrying a light bag, but he just smiled then kissed my lips.

"I've been comfortable and I promise not to ever stop, Tills." He had also started calling me Tills and it was so corny but cute.

Besides all of that though, I just liked getting to know who he was. He was basic in a good way because all he wanted was good food and company. And speaking of food, he really wasn't lying about being able to cook. He was a true homebody and was always whipping up something for me, but he still made sure to take me out a few times a week just to show me off. And when we were out he always held my hand or had a hand on my back when he was opening doors, simple things that I had overlooked in previous relationships.

He and I were almost always under and overdressed respectively and we hardly ever looked like we were going to the same event unless it was somewhere really nice, but I liked how he didn't try to change me and I didn't try to change him. And even with him looking as good as he did in a suit, admittedly he was at his best in clothes that he picked out. His fly, comfy chic style worked for him because it was an extension of his laid-back personality which was his biggest plus. He wasn't too extra or flashy or trying to put on a show for anybody. I'd seen his jewelry on one of my snooping missions, but he only wore some of it on date nights and none of it was gaudy because he didn't feel like he had anything to prove.

Most importantly though I felt like I could relax around him. He looked at me the same way even when I wasn't wearing any makeup. I felt safe with him and he never made me feel like he was trying to break me down because of my size or height. In fact, he always rubbed my feet when I came over because he liked me in heels unlike other guys that I'd dated. He complimented me literally every time he saw me no matter how simple or elaborate the look was and I could really get used to hearing my name replaced with the word beautiful.

I was over so much that I wasn't even surprised when he gave me a key a few days ago. I stayed with him a lot because his place was much closer to work and had become like a getaway for me. Plus he knew that I would crash after work and be dead to the world sometimes so he wanted to make sure he got to see me even if it was just while I slept. And waking up to him in the middle of the night only to be put right back to sleep was always a welcome treat.

But the biggest benefit to our situation was that I barely had to see Michelle at all these days because we always seemed to miss each other although her "wet ass" comment was still lingering in the back of my head. But little did she know he had been helping out a lot. It started when he mentioned that he wanted to take me somewhere and I told him that I would have to order something to wear. He offered to pay for it and ever since he'd randomly been sending me money. And I knew I should've been sticking to my guns about keeping it casual, but that was impossible to do when he was so good to me.

Today he was making me a big Sunday dinner so I was stopping by to drop off vanilla extract for his dessert. He had been bragging about his sweet potato pies for weeks now so I was eager to try it even though I didn't think that anybody could touch Diane's pie.

"Something smells really good," I complimented him as I let myself in and as expected he was lying across his bed with his nose in a book.

"Why didn't you tell me you were coming over so early?" he asked because he always met me at my car to carry my bags in. I didn't have much with me today though so I came right up. "I would've gotten started on the pies."

"I didn't want to give you time to sneak another girl out."

"Yeah that was a close one. You might've passed her coming up," he said playing along as he got up and walked over to me.

"Maybe. What did she look like?"

"Just like you," he said before planting a sweet kiss on my lips and sitting his book down on the stand by the door.

He'd asked if I wanted him to buy a TV for when I came over, but I didn't even really miss it much when I was with him. His aversion came from his grandmother not letting him and his brothers watch too much TV as kids and it was a habit that stuck well into adulthood. He had been reading less lately because of me, but I'd been reading more than I had in years since he took me to his favorite local bookstore and let me pick some out. Cutting down on TV had already been benefitting me because besides picking up more books, I also had more time to sketch and I was even being more creative at work.

Before bed sometimes I'd lay in his arms and we'd read the same book together. I read much faster than him so I would always annoy him when I reacted to exciting parts before he got there. It had quickly become our thing when I wasn't too tired from other pre-sleeping activities. And realizing that none of this cute stuff we'd been doing would have even happened if TJ had just been on time for work that day was wild.

"What are you reading today?" I asked because I hadn't seen him in over a day so I was sure he'd finished *Beloved* by now.

"*The Beautiful Struggle*," he said holding it up for me to see and I frowned because there was nothing cute or noble about struggling.

"Sum it up in a sentence."

"I can't. You should read it when I'm done. You would like it."

"I'll try to get to it when I have time."

"Make time."

"That's so easy to say when you work for yourself. Besides I'm only halfway through *The Count of Monte Cristo*."

"It's just the abridged version though," he remarked, waving off my plight like the true book snob I'd been realizing he was.

"Whatever. I don't need to read the full twelve hundred pages to get the gist that this guy means business and is serious about his revenge," I said making him laugh before I noticed he had yet another small paper cut from the crisp pages of the new book. "You need to come join the rest of us in this century," I quipped because I preferred my e-reader for convenience, but he loved physical books.

"Never!" he exclaimed getting play offended before grabbing an older book from his shelf then holding up the pages to my nose. "Smell that," he instructed as I closed my eyes and inhaled. I was instantly transported back to middle school when I used reading to escape the reality of losing my dad and feeling alone all the time. "See that has nothing on this," he said, tapping my iPad and jostling me back to the present.

"Yeah yeah. I can carry thousands of books in this thing without breaking a sweat meanwhile your scrawny arms would buckle with maybe ten," I teased him because he was anything but scrawny.

He didn't care to continue our ongoing debate though because his hands were already all over me saying that he wanted to have a different type of conversation. I was too sweaty from being outside though so I backed off and went to the bathroom to freshen up.

"Later. I'm already late meeting Jordan and Sofia. I just came to give you the vanilla extract and to soak up some of your air real quick. It feels like a sauna out there," I complained as I fanned my blouse. It was just over a hundred degrees outside, but this was the only day that Sofia could meet to begin planning Tiffa's birthday party next month so I had to grin and bear it.

"That's why I'm staying in today. You didn't have on your air in the car?"

"It broke yesterday and I need to take it to get looked at."

"Why didn't you tell me?" he asked after coming to lean on the bathroom's archway.

"Because it's my problem. Not yours," I replied as I carefully blotted my damp skin because this bottle of Fenty Body Lava was the last of my haul and I knew I would never be able to replace just one item without going overboard on new products.

"How much do you need for it?" he asked like he always did when an expense of mine came up around him. He'd taken spoiling me to a new level though and it made me think about being careful what I wished for because I just might get it.

"No, Cam. I'll figure this out on my own. We haven't even defined what this is yet and you're already doing way too much for me."

"No *you* haven't defined what we are, Tills. *My* definition is clear. And I'mma just google it and send you double if you choose to make this complicated."

"Then I'm gonna send it right back."

"You better not. I'm the only thing that's supposed to have you wet and sweating like this," he said before pulling out his phone then getting a peculiar look on his face. I didn't have to wait long to figure out what it was for. "Speaking of google, I finally got around to looking you up earlier."

"And?" I asked trying to play it cooler than I was currently feeling.

"And LinkedIn told me all your business. Why didn't you tell me how big of a deal you are at work?"

"I don't know. I guess it never came up."

"Nah. I asked you and you made it seem like you were just drawing shit for the company not leading an advertising team and," he began before reading a direct quote from my online resume off of his phone.

"That's such an exaggeration. I just tell them when they're being racist and sexist and they pay me extra for it," I said trying to downplay how integral my role had become since creating it.

"You don't have to hide shit from me. I don't care how much you make. That's your money and I always take care of mine regardless," he bragged and his cockiness made his accent come through more.

"Am I really yours though?" I teased him.

"You better be."

"We'll see. But you really don't have to worry about the money. I've been looking into getting another job while I'm here anyway."

"Another job? Like at night?" he asked with a frown.

"Yeah, but nothing too hard. My Auntie Diane has a friend who owns a lounge and I used to bartend on the weekends back in college so I'm gonna see if I still got it." Lord knows those tips got me through my graphic design program and I was hoping for them to come through dripping to get me out of this jam too.

"But I already barely see you now," he exaggerated and I laughed at him.

"Why are you lying? You see me nearly every day."

"But only for a little while before we go to bed sometimes and now that's about to be cut because you'll be working at a bar? Nah. I'll just give you what you need. How much extra are you trying to make a month?" he asked like it was nothing to just supplement another possible stream of income.

Jordan calling him a drug dealer quickly popped into my head and I hoped that it wasn't true because I wasn't cut out for that ride or die life. I would be singing like a canary on the stand before the judge even asked me anything because while I looked good in orange, those jail jumpsuits weren't cut to flatter anybody.

"It's too much to ask somebody for every month."

"But you're not asking me. I'm offering," he corrected me with a small grin.

"Well then you couldn't afford it," I said not even trying to offend him, but it was clear that I had.

"You know how much I can afford?" he asked with knitted brows.

"No, but I know you must be paying an arm and a leg just to live here. How much is your rent?" I asked using the opportunity to find out because I'd been dying to know anyway.

"Uh...it's supposed to be somewhere around two stacks, but I don't pay rent."

"And just how did you swing that?"

"I own this building," he said nonchalantly, but I was currently mentally rummaging all up and through his pockets and counting his money. I knew that he and his brothers split the profits from the original Fade in Harlem and the two other locations since their dad passed, but he was the sole owner of the shop here. Then I estimated rent from the tenants in a building this size and in this part of town and God knew what else he was hiding.

I could have fainted, but I kept my composure because regardless I would still have to say no. And I knew I was doing the right thing because I would feel like shit if I turned down this job opportunity then in a month or two Cam just up and decided that he didn't want to help me out anymore.

"I really appreciate the offer, but I can't accept it. Gifts and things are fine of course, but I was raised to not ever have to depend on a man because men are too fickle. "

"I'm not even gonna argue with that because it's true and I see that shit every day. But I can show you better than I can tell you. Give me a number," he all but demanded. I chewed my lip before reluctantly telling him the figure I'd come up with that would have me leaving in six months instead of the full year.

"That's it?" he asked like it was chump change when it was actually far from it. My phone vibrated in my hand and I was sure he had gone crazy when I saw the amount he'd sent. "There goes three months right there. Stop playing with me like I ain't got it, Tills," he bragged even though I could tell he was just being silly.

"Cameron Logan! No. This is too much."

"You're good. I've been meaning to get a sugar baby anyway."

"I'm not a sugar baby and you're not even old enough to have one," I reminded him because he loved to act like he was so much older than he was.

"Maybe I can't tell because you're so sweet," he remarked before putting his face in my neck and sighing.

"Are you sure about this? Because it'll just help me leave quicker and I know you don't want that," I warned just to give him one last opportunity to back out before I started expecting anything from him. It was weird because while I enjoyed him giving me money, *money just because* was different from it being a set number and time. I wasn't a child and I didn't need an allowance. I preferred things to be spontaneous because a schedule might have this feeling a little transactional. "What?" I asked after he'd groaned into my skin.

"Nothing. I just hate thinking about you leaving. You just got here," he said softly. I thought it was cute so I slid my hands inside his shirt to rub his back. "But I still want to help you even if it means you leave me sooner because I don't want to see you stressed out about anything."

"So why would you get involved with me at all when you knew that I was leaving from the start?" I asked before he picked his face up and firmly stood over me to look me in the eyes.

"Because I couldn't *not* get involved once I met you," he said simply but the words held more and more weight as I replayed them in my head.

"Well you have me now so enjoy me while you can. And maybe I'll play hooky and stay an extra week in bed with you before I go back," I told him and that seemed to satisfy him for the time being.

Behind him his phone began to ring with a FaceTime call and I knew that it was his grandmother because she was the only person besides me that he did that with. I'd only been around when he talked to her a few times, but I always pretended to be asleep because I was usually in bed with a scarf on and looking a mess. I was extra cute today though so I was finally ready to "meet" her. He had a huge smile on his face as he told her that somebody wanted to say hi.

When I laid eyes on her, I couldn't believe that he'd had the audacity to say that *I* looked expensive when we met when he was related to somebody who could pass for royalty. Her gorgeous brown skin was holding up well and she gave off that classic Diahann Carroll vibe effortlessly. And Miss Thang was in her late eighties using the latest iPhone with ease.

"Oh she's so pretty Cameron and by the look of those baby-making hips I might just get me a great-grandson before I go home to Jesus," she said and I couldn't help but laugh at her sweet bluntness.

"Don't worry. You've got plenty of time, Gram. You're gonna live forever."

We had friendly chitchat for a few minutes before they changed the subject to the meal he was cooking for Sunday dinner so I used it as an opportunity to slip out. I knew how some older women were and I didn't want to hear anything funny about him still having to do all of his own cooking because I didn't know how to.

He was better off though because even when I followed recipes exactly they would come out looking alright, but they were always lacking in flavor and soul. Like most men he'd always said he wanted a woman who could throw down in the kitchen, but when he didn't feel like cooking we would order in and he was fine with it. Men had lists too and just like women all that stuff went right out the window when somebody special caught your gaze.

On the drive to the mall I thought back to

my broke college days because that was the last time I'd been so strapped for cash. It was a good learning experience though because it taught me how to make money stretch. But this situation with Michelle and the house was different because it was the first time that I was responsible for basically carrying two households on my shoulders.

After paying bills I had just enough for gas to work so the money Cam had already been giving me was helping out a lot. These new zeroes in my account, however, were like manna from heaven, but I still knew better than to tell him that. I would show that I appreciated him in other ways because I didn't know if he was one of those men who threw things back in a woman's face when he got angry. I decided not to look a gift horse in the mouth for now though because the big sense of relief was all I could feel at the moment.

I'd been spending so much time with Cam that I was neglecting everybody else around me. I had been back for nearly three months now and I still hadn't found time to hang out with Sofia since she worked overnight and we had opposite schedules which was why I'd purposely double booked her and Jordan early in the day so I could still get back to him for dinner. Yep I was officially one of *those* women, but I couldn't help it. We were having fun and even Reese complained that she hardly ever got to see Cam either.

"You've been working really hard, huh?" Jordan asked me once we'd settled down at the food court. None of us were hungry yet, but little Miss Bailey was showing us how strong her lungs were as she hollered and tugged on Jordan's shirt. Jordan was immune to it and kept conversing over her while she got settled. "You're never around when I stop by Auntie Michelle's to visit her."

"That's not work. It's Cam hitting it out the park every night," Sofia joked trying to hold Bailey, but Jordan was snippy and insisted that she could handle her. I hadn't spoken to anybody but Nicole about Cam yet so I knew Sofia had to have heard it from TJ probably complaining about me. Jordan's ears instantly perked up at the mention of a man.

"Who's Cam and why am I just hearing about him? I didn't even know you were trying to date while you're here."

"I wasn't. I mean I'm not. It's just a thing that sort of happened," I said vaguely.

"Well what's he like? What does he do? Is he cute? Is he tall?" Jordan fired off questions trying to determine if he met her standards.

"You actually kinda know him or rather you saw him the day we did lunch at Wells on Wells."

"Wait you're dating that barber, Tilly?" she said dismissively as she waved me and the thought of him off. "I didn't think you went for blue collar men. I swear if you would just drop some weight, you could get someone better like Bryan again."

Before I could say anything Sofia was inserting herself on my behalf.

"You're talking as if your BMI is within a normal range," she said letting medical jargon drip all over her shade.

"First of all those standards are for white people and second, this is obviously baby weight," Jordan said defensively because she was fluffier than usual. I could tell that the comment really stung her because Sofia was naturally thin and always had been. She loved to compare herself to me in that department, but she never could with Sofia.

"Please I had a baby too and I know donuts and fries weight when I see it," she said aiming for Jordan, but I laughed to myself even though I got hit in her verbal drive-by as well.

"Well I guess it is much easier to snap back at sixteen, huh, Sof?" Jordan retorted going low. "And if anybody has donuts and fries weight it's Tillar. No offense," she said turning to me, but I stayed out of it because I wouldn't choose a side even though Jordan was being a bitch.

"And yet look at her and look at you," Sofia said pointedly about our appearances while obviously complimenting me.

"What is that supposed to mean? And why are you getting funky with me over some low-class barber? Is it because of TJ?"

"This ain't got nothing to do with TJ. You're always talking shit and looking down on people. Clearly Cam loves her size and he's a barber in the shop that he owns," Sofia said jumping in to defend him as well as me. No doubt she was his biggest fan because he was the only thing keeping TJ employed for the time being and she really depended on her child support checks to keep her head above water.

"You're judging him meanwhile your man hasn't had a job in a year," she added letting it be known that TJ still pillow-talked with her about our family's business. At the mention of her husband, Jordan's eyes nearly doubled in size and her face turned beet red.

"My *husband*'s company relocated and he was smart enough to have a plan in place for his family before it happened, but you wouldn't know anything about that, would you?"

"Girl bye tell me anything. I know you not doing all of that couponing for nothing. Y'all are broke just like everybody else. Don't try to dress it up," Sofia said.

And even though Jordan was much taller than Sofia's little petite self, I imagined her being dragged all over this mall so I stepped in before it came to that and promised myself never to double book them again. It had been years since we were all together so I figured their teenaged rivalry had burned out by now, but boy was I wrong.

"Jordan, Cam's finances are fine and I'm pretty sure he makes even more than I do."

"Pretty sure? You don't know how much he makes, but you're already sleeping with him?" she said with an absurd amount of judgement in her voice now turning her attitude back on me. And it was funny coming from her because I remembered how she used to wild out in high school and I had covered for her for years with Diane.

Still she had touched a nerve though since I'd just found out he had rental property before coming here. It was just more confirmation that I didn't know him as well as I was beginning to think I did. But I'd already had enough of this sweltering heat, Jordan and crying ass Bailey for the day so I decided to be done with the conversation because she was sounding too much like Michelle and I wanted to at least enjoy my time with Sofia while I had her.

"He makes sure to leave enough on the nightstand for me to know he's doing alright for himself," I said sarcastically as I got up from the table since love wasn't being served.

"Where are you going? I'm sorry if I offended you, okay? I just want to look out for you, Tilly," she offered with fabricated remorse.

"Well thanks, but it's really none of your concern. And for your information Cam treats me like a princess and I sincerely hope that you can find the same someday," I said upping my shade to show that her husband wasn't off limits with me either.

"And you better not go tell your mama on us because I like Diane," Sofia said to Jordan, making me laugh as we left her sitting there still trying to calm Bailey. When we got far enough away from the chaos, she stopped me. "You better not listen to her about Cam 'cause he really is a solid dude. He keeps to himself, stays out of nonsense, and I've never seen any hoes around him. And you know he could have plenty of hoes around him," she said like she was more familiar with him that I'd realized and I couldn't imagine how she had found the time to get to know him.

She told me how she first met him when Tiffa had been sick at school and she couldn't leave work to get her. TJ was supposed to be at work but wasn't answering so she called the shop looking for him. Cam was nice enough to get Lauren to pick Tiffa up then he let her sleep in his office undisturbed until she got off work.

I smiled to myself because he had never told me that. And it wasn't until then when I realized that I was no longer falling for him. I was already on the damn ground. All this time I'd been holding back a little just waiting for him to switch up on me, but he wouldn't because he really was one of those rare, good guys.

On our way out we passed a shoe store and I wanted to pop in to get him thicker socks since he loved putting his cold feet on me in bed.

"I know those big things aren't for you. He's got you sprung enough to be buying him stuff?"

"With his money. I know TJ told you how Michelle cleaned me out for the house."

"You know he did and you are a better woman than me because your mama is something else." Sofia was one of the few people who saw Michelle for who she really was, but she played nice with her because she was still holding out hope that she would be her mother-in-law one day. "But you definitely need to go ahead and trap that pretty nigga. You're just gonna have to move back up here for good because those women in Atlanta are no joke and would be all over him."

"No. I'm not bringing him home with me nor will I be staying here. And enough about him already. Are you dating anybody?" I asked, but she sighed heavily then complained about how she had no time with her long hours. "Well you better start flirting with the cute male nurses and doctors at the hospital."

"No, they just want to fuck the CNAs. I just work and bring my black ass back home."

"There's not even one who seems to be about something?"

"Just the ones who ain't black honestly," she said like it pained her to admit it. "But I am not trying to swirl and be some white man's fetish so I ignore them too."

"I don't see the problem dating any man as long as there's chemistry there and he treats you how you want. I've dated the rainbow and there's good and bad in all of them. Mostly bad," I said trying to get a smile out of her so she would let her guard down and actually listen to my advice. "Of course black love is beautiful and if you find it it's amazing, but it's not the only kind of love out there."

"I guess, but I'm not into pink dick," she said definitively so I dropped the subject altogether. No man of any race could've done her worse than my brother, but she was still holding out hope for him.

It made me glad that I'd never been afraid to explore my options. Diane always said that it was easy to fall in love when you were being loved right. She also said that we were all black when we turned off the lights, but I didn't want to think about her doing the do so I didn't mention that one to Sofia.

The sun had set by the time we finished running around in stores for party stuff and my stomach was officially growling so I took Sofia to get dinner for her and Tiffa before I headed back to Cam. He was shirtless and standing over the stove when I came in so I went over and kissed his bare back. I sang along with the music playing because it was finally a song that I knew the lyrics to.

"You don't know nothing about this," he said because he was a wannabe music snob too.

"You don't either. I swear you wanna be an old man so bad with your young butt."

He had all of his dad and grandmother's old records stored in the chest that he used for his coffee table. Like me, he liked rap too but only certain artists and I found out that he only played the newer stuff in the shop because it's what the mostly male customers wanted. He'd told me a funny story about his first review here being something along the lines of how nobody wanted to listen to the Commodores while they got lined up and I laughed for days.

"You really shouldn't be dancing that close to the stove. It's dangerous."

"Maybe for a novice like you, but I know

what I'm doing," he bragged before karma decided to pay him a swift visit in the form of bacon popping him on his chest and I nearly cried cackling at how fast he moved away.

"Told you. Trying to show off got you popped. And why are you making bacon anyway?"

"I use the fat for the cornbread," he said teaching me something that I didn't know.

After putting the heavy cast iron skillet in the oven, he finally gave me his undivided attention and came over to give me a hug. He must've been psychic because he always did this when I was trying to act like I wasn't in a bad mood.

"What's wrong?" he asked worriedly and I groaned into his chest.

"I think I'm starting to want all the strings too," I said honestly and I felt his cheeks turning upright above me.

"I was right. From the moment I saw you, I knew I could buy your love," he joked or at least I hoped he was joking.

"That's really what your first impression of me was?"

"Nah. I told you I just thought you looked mad expensive," he repeated and I asked him to elaborate because it was an adjective that I hadn't heard used by a man to describe me. "You know what I mean. You looked like you were well taken care of so I wanted to up the ante," he said with a crooked grin as he looked down at me.

"Well that has nothing to do with me wanting more strings," I corrected him because it was actually the conversation with Sofia. "I just really like you and I'm ready to admit that I only want to see you while I'm here."

"Took you long enough," he said then pointed to the pie that was cooling on the counter behind me. It could wait though because while we were on the subject of possibly taking this thing a little seriously, I wanted to bring up something that had been in the back of my mind since the beginning. It wasn't my place before because I wasn't exactly claiming him, but now I wanted to know for sure.

"Cam, have you ever had something with Lauren?" I asked him directly. He'd been cutting my hair at his place lately so I hadn't ran into her to see if she still had a problem with me. I didn't plan on going back any time soon to find out either because I preferred the extra personal treatment and tipping meant something completely different here.

"Lo? Nah. That's Reese's work. She's been trying to get her for years. That's why I hired her," he said chuckling.

"She likes you."

"She's just Fade Family Gang and rule number one is no fraternization with the customers or support staff."

"Well what about me?"

"You gotta pay to be a customer, Tills." He laughed then kissed me when he saw I was serious. "You don't ever have to worry about her or anybody else, okay?" he assured me and I had no choice but to take his word for it for now. "Now come get a slice of this last pie before I eat it all. I already finished the other one waiting for you to get here."

"Oh my god. Where does it all go?" I asked because he ate more than anybody I'd ever met but because of his height he never seemed to gain a pound. He just grinned and answered my question by looking down at his crotch. "You're disgusting."

Just like everything else he'd made the entire meal was delicious, but there was something different about that pie and I would be letting Diane know she had competition. I was a pretty picky eater so once I got a few staple meals down I bounced between them, but he always made me try new stuff and whatever I didn't like he would finish. It was a good system so I couldn't complain.

After eating we laid on the couch and got settled on opposite ends. I was reading, but I noticed that he was on Instagram when he clicked a rowdy sounding video so I got nosy and moved to see what he was looking at. So far the only social media that I'd seen him use was for the barber shop and he only followed other barbers on that page. I wasn't stupid though and I was sure he had private accounts somewhere so Nicole and I had put on our detective hats and searched for weeks before finally giving up. I decided to finally ask him about his clean digital footprint tonight since I'd already gotten a straightforward answer about Lauren.

"I used to have all that stuff. Before," he answered simply and I knew what he meant so I didn't inquire further, but he felt like he needed to explain. "I knew I didn't want to see my friends with their kids still growing up and not stuck at the same age like Cree."

"What was she like?" I asked before watching his eyes instantly fill with love as he talked about her distinct little laugh and how he used to let her pretend to give him haircuts. He said that he even still had her toy clippers on a shelf in his office. I'd seen them and just figured they were from his childhood because they were wooden.

I'd been curious about that part of his life, but I always treaded lightly since it was a sensitive topic and we were still so new. But that one question was all that was needed to get the ball rolling. He got up and pulled out a box from his closet. I'd seen it when I was looking around, but when I realized what it was I immediately left it alone. The fact that he was finally choosing to share it with me said a lot about how he felt.

He explained that the box had all of her favorite things that he couldn't just donate like he'd done for everything else. I looked at the old pictures of them together and smiled. The family photos with him, Summer and Cree looked so perfect and wholesome that it was weird knowing their story had ended in such a tragic way. And I felt really shallow for my final thoughts being that I was relieved to see that he wasn't a beardfish.

"Do you still want more kids?" I asked him as he put everything back in the box.

"I want it all again. I'm the best version of myself when I'm taking care of my family. After my mother passed my old man never remarried because he said he knew he would never be lucky enough to find the same thing twice, but I think he was just scared of losing somebody else too."

"He must've really loved her."

"He did. And I always wondered if he regretted his decision because I know he got lonely," he said like he could relate before he went on. "Summer was my first love, but I'm not gonna make the same mistake as my dad. She won't be my last. She's not my last," he said definitively while looking at me. "I know I'm not supposed to say this so soon, but I really can't wait to marry you and have some giant, Goliath ass kids," he said under the guise of a joke, but I could see the honesty on his face.

"And the truth finally comes out," I said dramatically trying to ignore that sudden tension in the air from his passionate words. "At first I thought it was just your affinity for my boobs, but I see now that you only like me because I'm tall!" I playfully accused him.

"It's both and that wagon behind you, but I do especially love that I don't have to bend down that far to kiss you," he said before I turned my head away from his incoming lips. "C'mon. If I'm gonna raise the next big stars in the NBA and WNBA then I need a woman like you, Tills."

"Nothing is guaranteed because genes are funny. My dad was only a few inches shorter than you, but look how small TJ is in comparison."

"Nah. Trust me, I read about this. We are gonna have some dunking, designer babies. I'm speaking it into existence," he said without a hint of humor in his voice and it sent a chill down my spine.

I let him have his fun and continue postulating about what our kids would be like meanwhile I was just trying to live in the moment and focus on what we had now. Talking about kids and marriage was a bad idea and we both knew it because he had rebuilt a life here and I had done the same in Atlanta. And we hadn't even bothered to bring up one of us moving like Sofia had suggested because even with as much as we liked each other, it just wasn't smart.

I'd heard that experience was the best teacher, but it was also the cruelest. I just hoped that it would be kind to us this once because he had already been driving too fast and telling him how I felt seemed to only add more weight to his leadfoot.

6

A ROYAL PAIN

I t had been just over four months of being back in Chicago and even I had to admit that things weren't as bad as I initially thought they'd be. There had been a few hiccups here and there, but lately everything was falling into place and I was right on schedule to be leaving in October. I was currently on cloud nine leaving Cam's place after spending my umpteenth weekend there. I spent most weekdays there now too, but there was something special about the weekends especially Sundays because we got to lazily lie around in bed until we heard the loud church bells from St. Michael's then do something fun in the afternoon. I was already into him a little too much now so I couldn't imagine how strong my feelings might be in the next few months, but I would just cross that bridge when I got to it.

What I thought would be a typical Monday at work ended up being anything but because the second I got in my car that morning I felt my stomach churning in a familiar but very unwelcome manner. Simply put, I had to go. But I knew if I went back inside that I would be late so I pushed through and figured that I could hold it until I made it to the office.

Generally I had a rule against pooping in public, but since my body hadn't gotten the message today I would just have to make an exception. My commute was shortened by a lot because I was leaving from Cam's place, but it still seemed like it took eons before I finally pulled into the office parking lot. I didn't let my heels slow me down one bit as I hustled over to the elevator and did a little jig to keep my mind off of what was happening to my insides.

All I could think of was how I had foolishly let Cam talk me into eating at Taco Bell after we museum hopped all day yesterday. I literally hadn't stepped foot in one in years and the reason why was suddenly coming back to me. I chose the biggest stall in hopes of nobody spotting my shoes as I let it rip then prayed that nobody came in after me. I made sure to flush as I went and I sprayed my little bottle of Poo-Pouri to make sure I didn't offend anybody's sensibilities because getting hit in the face with old Chalupa funk was no way to begin the day.

I figured that Cam would still be asleep since he had another couple hours of rest after I left, but he almost instantly replied with a toilet selfie of a deep frown on his face when I texted to find out if he was experiencing the same upset stomach. We'd already gotten passed the TMI phase of our relationship so I sent him one back and chuckled at the predicament that we were both in until I heard heels click-clacking and approaching the restroom. Whoever it was didn't enter a stall and just washed their hands at the sink. Not long after more click-clacking brought in even more ladies and I was now forced to remain on my porcelain throne until they all left.

"I think she's sending them to herself," I heard somebody say as they went into the stall beside me. "This generation of women will do anything for attention. Have you seen her Instagram?"

"No way. I saw one of the cards and they're from the same florist that my sister used for her wedding. No one is spending that much money at A New Leaf to fake it. Not even a cow like her," a second woman said and I suddenly realized who the voices belonged to and that little ol' shitty me was the topic of discussion for today.

Ever since I'd mentioned missing gardening with my dad, Cam had been sending me flowers from the flower shop next to the barbershop every Friday. And because I wasn't partial to a specific kind, he said that he would send a different arrangement each week until I found a favorite. It had only been a few weeks so far, but I guess that was enough to raise the antennas of the 'I Hate Tillar' club.

"Stranger things have happened. What's the name of the florist again? We could call to see if she's placed an order for this week," she suggested and a third woman instantly burst into laughter. "What's so funny? Do you think that's too far?"

"I think it costs nothing to be happy for somebody, *sistah*," I heard the third woman say and it dawned on me that it had been Erica in there with me the whole time. She usually kept to herself so I was surprised that she had even spoken up on my behalf.

As expected they said a few not so kind words about Erica once she left, but I had a feeling that none of it would have even bothered her especially because they weren't bold enough to say it to her directly when they had the chance.

Once the restroom was cleared of ninnies and my stomach felt relatively normal again, I was finally ready to get to work, but first I stopped by Erica's cubicle to ask her if I could have a minute with her in my office. I saw the confusion on her face because outside of cordial greetings and farewells we had never spoken to one another.

"I just heard what you said about me in there and I wanted to say thanks."

"You were in there for that?" she asked with a face full of surprise and I nodded. "You got a lot of self-control because I would have lost my job today."

"Please. I've heard worse from my mother," I told her with a smile, but she didn't know how to respond. There I went again making people uncomfortable. "Forget I said that. Just thanks again, girl."

"It was nothing. I jump at any opportunity to remind that Corporate Coon Cathy that no matter how much white ass she kisses, she's still one of us negroes. You expect the hating from the Beckies, but not from our own," she said candidly and I was stunned because I would've never known that she was so feisty underneath her usually sweet demeanor. "And really she's just mad that nobody has sent her nothing here but a court summons for unpaid child support," she quipped and I oop'd.

"She doesn't have custody of her kids? Spill," I demanded before going to get comfortable in my chair then I invited her to do the same. And just like that I'd officially made a work friend.

By the time I got home that evening I just wanted to take a nap before going back to Cam's house later, but first I had to do laundry and run errands. I felt drained for the first time in a while and I wasn't sure if it was because it was a

Monday or my reoccurring diarrhea throughout the day. I was surprised to see Michelle awake and watching TV in the living room because she usually slept until the time she had to get up for work.

"What's got you frowning walking in here? You've been smiling so much lately I was starting to get worried," she said as if me being happy was a crime, but I guess that it was in this family.

"Work was pretty tough today," I said as I walked past her and headed for the kitchen to get a bottle of water, but she must've really wanted to continue the conversation because she followed after me.

"Whatever it is, you'll figure it out. Now how are things between you and Cameron going?" she asked skipping right over an opportunity to get to know me and what I did a little better and jumped right into asking about him.

"Really good actually. I'm headed back over there in a little while."

"Hm. I thought you were staying home and giving your little cat a break for a change. I feel like you're never here anymore."

"First of all, ew please never say that again. And second I'm here all the time. Just not when you are." And if I was being honest, it was probably best that way. Sofia had told her about an open night position at the home for the elderly that she used to work for. It was overnights and since we were on different shifts we hardly ever saw each other, but most of all I was just glad that the new job was working out so well because it meant she was on her way to not needing me anymore after I got her caught up.

"I know you're grown and you don't need my two cents, but if you ask me fewer visits would make for better friends. Make him miss you some. You see him too much."

"No, he practically begs me to come over every time I'm away from him. I would agree for any other man, but not Cam."

"Oh so you think you found the one perfect man on earth, huh? Let me get Jesus on the line and tell him he's being shown up down here."

"Don't be ridiculous. I stopped holding my breath for the perfect man years ago, Ma, but I do think he's in a league of his own."

"A man better than Bryan?" she asked and I rolled my eyes at how he would always be the bar that they held my suitors to because he was supposed to be so unattainable for a woman like me even though if we looked passed how good he was on paper he was clearly terrible and wasn't fit to shine my shoes.

"He's light years ahead of Bryan. I mean really, what more could I ask for? He takes care of me in every way that I need. He respects me. He listens to me. He's the most considerate person I've ever met. He's gentle with me, Ma. And what I'm sure is the most important thing to you, I've never had to go in my purse to pay for anything."

"Never?" she asked in disbelief and I reassured her that I was being honest. "Well that may be, but listen to your mama on this one. He might be good now, but eventually you'll come to find that good things don't last forever. Just keep on living, Tilly. And if he's as good as you say he is then you're messing it up for the next woman when you leave him here high and dry when you go home. Unless you're planning on staying up here for him?"

"I'm not. I really like him, but Atlanta has my heart now and the first chance I get I'm going back."

"Then you need to keep that in mind while you're over there playing house with him," she said before sauntering off with her cup of coffee and as much as I hated to admit it, she did have a point. While I enjoyed spending time with Cam and my feelings for him seemed to be growing by the second, I still didn't feel like we were solid enough to uproot my whole life for him.

Oblivious to all of the angsty thoughts I'd been having all day, he texted me a little while later to see if I wanted to go out for dinner or stay in. I quickly responded *neither* because I was tired and planned on catching up on sleep at home. That must have thrown him for a loop because my phone began ringing in my hand and sure enough it was him sounding like he was in a playful mood and I wished that some of it could rub off on me.

"You can't sleep here?" he asked as a greeting. "I promise I aired the bathroom out after this morning."

"No it's not that. I'm just *tired* tired. Like not really in the mood," I lied because I still hadn't been able to get enough of him yet and I considered myself to have a pretty average sex drive usually.

"Oh that's cool. We don't always have to get into that when you stay here. I can give you the night off sometimes," he joked then the line went silent. "I just want to see you, Tills."

"I want to see you too, but it's just been one of those days, you know? I haven't really had a night to myself in a while and I think I need to be alone for a little bit, but don't take it personal okay?"

"Okay. Get some rest and I'll call you later. Let me know if you need something."

"Thanks for understanding," I said and he assured me that he did. That is until I stayed away for two more days then made up a bullshit excuse for a third.

After that he wanted to know if something was going on, but I convinced him it wasn't because there wasn't just one specific thing that I could pinpoint. I just needed some time to put things into perspective and to keep myself grounded in the fact that despite how good it was, this wasn't a situation that was made to last.

For the first time ever it seemed like Michelle was happy to see me at home, but I was sure that it was only because she thought that she'd successfully planted seeds of doubt in my relationship. For that reason alone I was ready to spend the whole upcoming weekend with him just to rub it in her face that we were still good. At least I was sure things were still good on his end until I made it to work Friday morning.

Usually I would get to smell my beautiful flowers before leaving for lunch, but today they were nowhere to be found. I had spoken to him the other day and he sounded fine, but it wasn't until then that I realized we had played phone tag yesterday and only texted. I stalled and read over the messages trying to detect a tone before finally admitting to myself that I was stupid for listening to Michelle of all people about any man especially one like Cam.

Right when I was considering taking a long lunch and swinging by the shop to see him, I was notified by phone that the delivery man was about to bring my flowers up.

"Somebody's in a good mood all of a sudden," Erica said as she let herself into my office. I didn't mind though because we'd been having lunch together all week and she'd already cemented her status as my work bestie especially when we saw that the bitties were mad we'd finally linked up. "Are you ready to go?" she asked and I remembered that she'd invited me to grab a bite with her then search a nearby department store for a new date night dress.

"Yep just give me a sec." I still had some paperwork to go over and fax back to headquarters before the day was over and I wanted to get it done because my head had been in the clouds all day. I'd already forgotten to pick up the soda, ice, and cups for Tiffa's party tonight, but luckily Michelle was off work and didn't fuss too much about having to get it for me. "Hey could you grab my flowers from the delivery guy while I send these off?"

"Sure thing. I wonder what kind you're getting this week. The roses and sunflower arrangement still hasn't been beat yet," she said before opening the door only to quickly close it back. "Damn this delivery dude is scrumptious. And he's tall! Quick, how do I look?" she asked hurriedly as she smoothed out her clothes then jumped in surprise when there was a knock on the door. I laughed at her before telling her that she looked fine and signing off on my form.

"Hi. I'll take those," she said in a professional but sultry voice.

"Hey actually let me give them to her," I heard Cam's voice say before I peered up at him. He smiled big when he saw the look of surprise on my face. "Hey Beetlejuice," he joked about my pinstriped pantsuit even though it was a much more stylish version.

"Shut up."

"I'm playing. You look beautiful," he said as he came over and bent to kiss my lips. From my peripheral I saw Erica's face and she looked pleased.

"So I take it that this is Mr. Cam?"

"She talks about me here?" he asked her but kept his eyes on me.

"Constantly," she said exaggerating because it had only been once or twice.

"Don't lie. And can I get a rain check on lunch?" I asked when I noticed the bag from my favorite Chinese takeout restaurant in the hand opposite the flowers.

"Looks like I don't have a choice, do I?"

"Sorry. But make sure to get something colorful and to avoid blends and trends if you can. And send me pictures," I reminded her about her dress because I wanted her to be cute even if I couldn't be there to personally veto some of her picks.

"I will. Enjoy your *meal*," she said suggestively then let herself out.

He locked the door behind her then came and sat across from me like he was a client.

"So what brings you here today Mr. Logan? You took a day off for this when you could've just sent me Uber Eats?"

"Just a couple hours. I gotta get back soon," he said and I figured because he was super devoted to the shop. "I wanted to come tell you face-to-face that I'm sorry."

"Sorry for what?" I asked with a wrinkled brow.

"For whatever I did to make you not want to see me," he said sincerely before inquiring about what it was that he had done.

"You didn't do anything. In fact, I was just getting ready to come by and apologize to you because it really was me and not you." He frowned at that classic line and I laughed. "I mean it. I'm getting too attached to you, Cam, and I might be in my head too much about us, but I'm not looking for any reason to stay here any longer than I have to. I should've just told you that instead of being distant though so I apologize."

"It's cool. I missed you too much to even be mad."

"Good because I was supposed to be making you miss me too," I admitted even though I didn't want to tell him about how what Michelle said had rattled me as well.

"What are you talking about? I always miss you. I miss you when you're here at work. When you're out getting your nails done. I even miss you when you're in the bathroom taking forever to put on your makeup so where did that come from?" he asked and I felt silly having to say it out loud because it sounded even more ridiculous after hearing how he felt.

"My mama told me that I might be smothering you by being around you too much."

"That's because she doesn't know me. If she knew me she would know that I like being smothered by you. Not that you're smothering me. If anything I'm smothering you. I mean look at me now harassing you at work," he said before getting more serious. "Alright, I think it's about time that we met so ask her if we can all go to dinner tonight. We can go to her favorite restaurant and I'll charm her just like I charmed you. Well not *just* like I charmed you, but she'll like me by the end of the night," he said confidently and despite my better judgement I couldn't say no to him.

"Okay, but we can't tonight. We've got Tiffa's party, remember?"

"Right. Well can I at least stop by for a minute just to meet her then?"

"Yeah I guess, but it's your funeral," I warned him then reminded him that Michelle wasn't like other mothers and that she was more stubborn than she was sweet. Still he insisted that he could handle her. I hoped that he was right because if he could survive her then maybe we had long-term potential after all. She didn't like anybody, but if there was anybody to like then it would definitely be Cam.

"Are you coming home with me after the party?" he asked after we'd finally started eating the food he'd brought for me.

"I've got to restock my *hoe bag* first. It doesn't just magically replenish itself, you know?" I ribbed him.

"You can finally retire it if you want. I can give you a drawer. Maybe two. Maybe even some closet space if you do that thing I like tonight because that's what I missed the most," he joked as he stole a piece of broccoli from my plate.

"I'll think about it," I said simply because I'd never left stuff behind at a man's house. I never felt secure enough in a relationship to so everything always left when I did. Even with Bryan, I never so much as left a sock at his place until we got engaged and moved in together. Besides this relationship obviously had an expiration date and we both knew it so I wasn't sure if I wanted to muddy those waters just yet.

Time was running fast today because what felt like a little while of catching up on the last few days and talking about a book by Octavia Butler that we'd both been reading, I'd gone over my break by about ten minutes. I'd been glad that he came in after most people had already left for lunch, but I was certain that they were back at their stations now. I dreaded opening the door because I didn't want to be the topic at the water cooler again, but sure enough all the cubicles were back filled and all eyes were on me and my visitor.

Cam either didn't notice or didn't care about our audience because he still gave me a few sweet goodbye nicks on the lips then headed back over to the elevator. Erica looked proud because the group of women who were known to gossip about me were clearly seething at me nabbing the fine specimen that was Cam. I could care less though because I'd already figured that the new gossip would be that I was his sugar mama or something like that. They could continue letting me live rent free in their heads though because I didn't care either way.

I was happy.

By the time I'd gotten off work, he'd gone to pick out a present from him because he didn't want to show up emptyhanded. It was just a gift card for Amazon, but it was the thought that counted and Tiffa would probably jump for joy when he gave it to her.

I gave him a quick house tour before going to the backyard to find Sofia, Tiffa, and a couple of her friends putting the finishing touches on the decorations. The yard was already filled with balloons and blown up pool furniture so there wasn't much left to do. They even had a section for one of her little friends who was DJing. It looked like a professional set up and everything was going as planned except for one thing.

"Tiffa, you talked to your daddy today?" I asked because I didn't smell any charcoal burning or any food on the grill and I hoped that he didn't flake on her big day. I had been telling him for over a week about a couple good deals on meat at the store near the house, but he kept saying that he knew where to get a better price.

"Yeah a minute ago. He said he had to take Cassie to the hospital and that we would do something together on Sunday," she said and the unconvinced look on Sofia's face said it all. I knew that the boys' mama Cassie wasn't very fond of Tiffa and Sofia or me for that matter, but I hoped that he didn't skip out on this because of her and if he did he was somehow an even weaker man that I'd been thinking all these years.

"He didn't say anything about dropping off

any food?" I asked trying to give him the benefit of the doubt.

"Nope," she said oblivious to the situation because she was already on Amazon trying to find something to buy after she saw how much Cam had put on the card. I left her to it because I didn't want her to think that her day would be anything less than perfect, but the second we stepped inside the house and out of earshot I let it all out.

"I hate him. I literally fucking hate him. It's like every time I start to have a little bit of respect for him, he goes out of his way to be the biggest fucking disappointment ever. I mean he had one job! Now I have to deal with a bunch of hungry teenagers that'll be in the backyard any minute now. And I'm even more mad at myself because I know better and I should've had a backup plan," I said feeling like I wanted to cry.

I was glad that I had Cam there to vent to because he just gave me one of his world famous hugs and let me get it out into his chest. I was probably overreacting, but it wasn't fair. TJ had the best example of a father but still insisted on letting his kids down every chance he got with his messed up priorities.

"It's okay," he said rubbing my back to soothe me. "I'll handle it."

The first call he made was to Lauren at the shop to get the phone number of a customer of his that owned a BBQ joint. The second call had him negotiating free haircuts for the owner and his three sons for the rest of the year if he could get enough food to feed a crowd here as soon as possible. Diane came in on the tail end of the conversation and stopped in her tracks when she saw Cam standing there. She mouthed her approval of his looks behind his back before sitting down the beautiful cake she'd picked out for Tiffa.

Sensing the previous tension, she asked me what was wrong and I explained how TJ had been a no show and we were scrambling to find food for the kids.

"It's done. He said that they're gonna bring what they have now then come back with more as soon as they can," Cam said as he poked my side and told me that I could relax now before introducing himself to Diane.

"You're a good man to have around in an emergency, Cameron," Diane complimented him and I smiled to myself because I knew he wouldn't correct her even though he didn't allow anybody but his grandmother to call him by his full name. "Did he let you know how much the total is? I may have to go to an ATM unless he has a card reader."

"It's already taken care of, ma'am," he said simply.

"Oh no. It's enough that you got your

friends to take the job," she said before they got into a back-and-forth insisting that they pay. I just took a seat because I knew how persuasive they both could be when it came to money, but after a minute it was clear that Diane had met her match because Cam could do this all day.

"Please just give up Auntie Dee. You're never gonna win this game with him."

"Win what game with who?" Michelle asked as she came inside with a couple bags of ice. I was surprised that she had actually done what I'd asked her to do which was just to pick up the sodas, cups and ice from the store that I'd ordered this morning. Cam skipped filling her in on the conversation and instead introduced himself the same way he'd done to Diane, but he wasn't received as well with Michelle.

"Tilly says you met at your barbershop. Is that what you do at your place of business, date the customers?" she asked as she looked up to him like she smelled something foul.

"No ma'am. That's actually the number one rule at my shop that I broke for her."

"And what's so special about her that you just had to break the rules?" she asked like she couldn't fathom somebody being interested in me for non-nefarious reasons.

"Well I don't mean to sound shallow, but your daughter is very pretty and she took my breath away when I saw her. Of course since then I've gotten to know just how beautiful she is on the inside too," he said sweetly as he looked over at me and Diane seemed impressed.

"I'm sure you have with as much time as you spend with her. Especially on all those overnight visits," she said and he nervously chuckled before asking for her car keys to bring everything inside for her, but she declined his offer. "Tilly, go tell some of them freeloading boys from out back to come help," she said, but Cam volunteered to do it again.

"It's no problem. They came to have fun, not work," he said nobly, but by his fourth trip to the car I could tell that it was more than he thought it'd be. Watching him work up a sweat was nice to look at though and I knew I would pay him back generously tonight for being so helpful with everything.

He finished right when the guys from the restaurant were arriving to drop off the first round of food so he went to greet them then show them where to set things up in the yard before rejoining us in the kitchen. Michelle immediately scolded me for not making him a plate before it was all gone.

"I can wait til the next round. Kids eat first anyway where I'm from."

"Just don't let Tillar go first or there won't

be nothing left," Michelle warned him before heading in the direction of her room. I turned to Cam who looked confused about why Michelle was being so pissy with me.

"Ignore that old bat," Diane said loud enough for Michelle to hear and I did just that. "Thank you again for saving the day, Cameron."

"It's nothing. I don't mind helping out since TJ couldn't be here."

"Didn't want to be here," I said under my breath, but Diane caught it.

"That boy can be selfish sometimes, but I don't know where he got that from. My brother would give anybody the shirt off of his back," she said as if she hadn't seen Michelle raise him to be exactly that way. I didn't have anything nice to say about him at the moment so I just changed the subject altogether.

"So Cam, you are gonna stay? Because I could use some company while I'm on lifeguard duty. Sofia takes it too seriously and refuses to even talk to anybody." We had worked together as junior lifeguards back in the day and she was always at the top of our class. Meanwhile I just volunteered today because I had a red, *Baywatch*-esque swimsuit that I had been dying to flex in but not get wet.

"Yeah I'll stay, but I really just want to finish the last few chapters of *Kindred* before you end up spoiling it for me," he said because I read faster than him and I always wanted to talk about it right after. "Where's your iPad?"

"Ebooks win again," I teased him as I went and fished it out of my purse. "And you better not move my bookmark either."

I excused us from Diane then led him back to my room because I wanted to shower and start getting ready for the party. He predictably clowned my Usher posters while I got a few things to take with me to his house for later.

"I can't believe you really sleep in this thing," he said as he laid back on the bed and it was cute how his long legs stretched way over the end. It was a tight fit for me too, but it wasn't nearly as uncomfortable as it looked for him. "But I might as well have one of these the way you sleep on top of me."

"I'll just stay here tonight then and you can have the bed to yourself again," I bluffed before he immediately started backpedaling.

"You know I wouldn't have it any other way. And I'm relieved to see that some other nigga couldn't fit in here with you these past few days when I was thinking the worst," he admitted vulnerably, but I still had to mess with him a little.

"Please. College made me crafty and you would be surprised at what I can get done in a twin bed." I winked at him before he closed his eyes and put his hands over his ears. "You know I had a life before you, Cam."

"I don't care. I just don't want to picture it."

He could be so innocent sometimes and despite how good he was in bed, he often said things that made me wonder just how experienced he really was. Of course I knew he was with Summer since high school, but it suddenly hit me that he had never mentioned anybody else.

"Cam, how many women have you slept with?" I asked trying to make the question sound as natural as possible.

"Two," he said without skipping a beat.

"Just two?" I asked not believing him because I was expecting at least ten.

"Wait three including you," he said before sitting up to nick my lips then getting a curious look on his face and flipping the question on me. I instantly froze because I was so focused on setting him up for a joke that I hadn't realized he would ask for my number.

"More than five?" he prodded after seeing me hesitate. "I told you I don't care. Whatever number I am will be the last one anyway," he said confidently enough to lure me into answering even though I knew this was a big nono. Seriously don't try this at home.

"Seven," I said just low enough to qualify as a whisper before he angrily repeated the number. He couldn't even fake it for a few seconds before he started laughing at my reaction.

"I'm lucky number seven, huh?"

"Yes, and if you've really only been with three women then how are you so good? I just laid there until number five," I said candidly, but he shrugged.

"I've had a lot of sex. It just wasn't with a lot of women."

After I showered and threw a dress on over my swimsuit, we rejoined Diane and Michelle in the kitchen where my mother decided to beat a dead horse about my hair for the umpteenth time.

"I still can't believe you want to run around looking like a man with no hair," she exaggerated because I had plenty up top and a little on the sides. She then turned to Cam, "Tilly always had long pretty hair growing up. It was nappy as hell, but it was long because I took care of it." She always took credit for my hair even though me wearing buns every day until college and my low-maintenance routine was what actually kept it healthy. "I know you're a barber, but men like long hair on women so tell her to grow it back. Maybe she'll listen to you."

"Actually I like her hair how it is, but I bet she's not thinking about me or you when she decides how she wants to wear it," he said causing Michelle to cut her eyes at him.

"Well I just think she should let it grow because short hair and her weight is aging her. People always mistake us for sisters because I look so young," she said, but she was a damn lie. Baby faces ran in the family, but she was clearly decades older than me.

"What blind fool thought you two were sisters?" Diane asked calling her out on her lie before Michelle went into a made up story about the new mailman asking her about me.

I just looked past her and peeked through the window at the yard. The tension in here was the complete opposite of the fun lights and music out there. Tiffa was on a floatie in the middle of the pool looking like she was enjoying herself and that made me smile because her having a good time was all that mattered to me tonight.

When I checked back into the conversation Michelle was still taking digs at my expense even more so than usual, like she was trying to goad Cam into saying something. I saw him about to take the bait when we were saved by the horn of the second round of food from the delivery truck. Diane must have seen it too because she stepped in.

"Cameron, let's go and see about these fresh rib tips. I don't know about you, but Auntie wants a plate now. Those kids had their turn," she said and managed to put a small smile on his face. He leaned over and kissed my cheek before he went with her to let them in.

When they were out of earshot, I begged Michelle to stop this little humiliation ritual that she was putting me through.

"Ma, I don't ask you for much, but can you please just not do this today?"

"Do what? Tell the truth," she said dismissively then began cleaning off the table because we were about to eat. "As long as there is breath in my body I'm gon' tell the truth, Tilly. I'm not wasting my sins to lie for nobody. Where did these flowers come from?" she asked after noticing the arrangement that I'd brought home from work. Usually I took them to Cam's house with me so I guess she hadn't seen me with them before.

"I send them to her every Friday," Cam answered as he brought in a couple trays of food for the chaperone crew. As expected Diane wasn't carrying anything because he wouldn't let her.

"Tilly's daddy used to spend hours growing them right out front and the damn things would die 'bout as soon as he cut them. Flowers are a waste of time and money."

"I used to think that too, but I know how much they remind her of working in the garden with your late husband and I'll do anything to put a smile on her face." Knowing all too well about my kiddie obsession with princesses, Diane made a comment about how I'd finally found my Prince Charming. "I'm trying hard to be."

Before Michelle could ask me to, I got off my butt and made everybody a plate before sitting down with one of my own. I'd never tried the food from this restaurant so I didn't get much since there was more than enough for seconds if I wanted more later. It wasn't because of Michelle's comments because Cam and I had definitely seen each other get busy on food before, but of course she had to make a big deal out of my small portion.

"Tilly, I know you're not trying to impress Mr. Man here. He knows you didn't get that big eating like a bird," she said and I saw the rib Cam had in his hand fall to his plate before he angrily reached for a napkin like he was finally fed up. An emboldened Michelle asked him if he had something to say.

"Yeah I do. What the hell is wrong with you? Your daughter is good to you. If my mother was like you I damn sure wouldn't be here handing over whole paychecks to bail you out while you talked to me how you do."

"If your mama was like me she would have raised you not to back talk elders," she said matching his energy, but I had to say something considering his mother wasn't alive.

"Ma, don't say that. Cam's mama passed when he was young," I pleaded with her even though it didn't seem to make a difference.

"That makes sense," she retorted, refusing to back down. Cam just got up from his seat and headed for the door before any harsher words could be exchanged.

"It was nice meeting you, Diane," he said before I followed after him.

"Where do you think you're going, Tilly? You gotta watch these kids while I go to bible study," she said reminding me that the only reason she'd agreed to let Tiffa have the party here was because I said I would take care of everything.

"It's not doing you much good so you can miss one class, ma'am," Cam said before pulling me out the door with him, but as much as I appreciated him standing up for me I wouldn't let him be disrespectful to her.

"Cam, I know she was being mean, but you were out of line. That's still my mama."

"Tell her to act like it then!" he said raising his voice at me before quickly calming himself down. "I would give anything to have my daughter here with me and she's mistreating hers like it's nothing. Go get your shit and let's get out of here."

"You can just go without me. I'll call you later."

"You're staying here after all she just said to you?" he asked me incredulously.

"I have to. She's gonna make them all leave if I don't and I don't want to ruin Tiffa's day. I promise I'll come over if it's not too late, okay? Don't be mad."

"Fine. Go back in there then and spend your night being talked down to instead of being with somebody who actually loves you," he said as he struggled to press the right app for an Uber on his phone because of his big fingers combined with the smoke coming from his ears.

"I told you how she was--Wait what did you just say?" I asked because I just knew I had mistakenly heard him use the L word.

"Just go back inside, Tills. I'm upset and I don't want to take it out on you," he said so I followed his instructions and left him there.

Diane and Michelle were arguing when I came back in, but they stopped talking when I closed the door. I didn't say anything to either of them. I just grabbed a big trash bag and began preemptively cleaning up. Before I could halfway fill one bag Michelle said that Cam was no longer welcome in her house and that I was stupid if I would be with a man who would talk to my mother like that. I could have told her that Cam was part of the reason why she even still had a house now, but I didn't say anything and just focused on cleaning because it was the one thing I was good at in her eyes. She just kept pushing though and asking if I would continue seeing him after he had disrespected her.

"Yes I will because you were wrong too, Ma! I know you haven't heard that too much, but you're actually wrong about a lot of shit!" I snapped at her before throwing the bag down.

"Who the hell do you think you're talking to?" she asked angrily as she stood up from her seat. Even though she was much smaller than me, I felt like I was the size of a tick as she walked up and demanded that I look at her. "Oh so because he gave you a little money and his little dick you're taking his side? You're choosing him over me?!" she shouted in my face.

"No it's not like that. It's just--" I began, but she insisted on drowning me out by shouting.

"I raised you by my-damn-self! I didn't have no help putting food on the table for your big ass, but the first chance you get you're putting a man before me," she yelled and continued trying to lay a guilt trip on me. "I bet he's taking care of every woman that comes in that barbershop, but he got you thinking you all that, huh?"

Diane usually stayed out of our arguments

and told Michelle about herself when they were alone, but she stepped in between us when Michelle pushed me against the counter. We had never gotten into a physical altercation before, but it wasn't from a lack of her trying. I just always refused to respond to the shoving and clothes grabbing when I was younger because I knew she was looking for any excuse to beat me and I did everything I could not to give her one.

"Michelle, you're like a sister to me and I love you, but you know as well as I know that you're as wrong as two left shoes here. You're always picking with that girl about everything and I'm glad she has somebody besides me who sees it," Diane said in a rarely used tone as she checked Michelle.

"Don't tell me how to talk to my child, Dee. Not in my house or anywhere!"

"I'll tell you whatever the hell I feel like telling you. Last time I checked I was grown and I'm not Tillar. I don't have to bite my tongue for you 'cause I will whip your little ass tonight then come pick you up for church on Sunday like usual," she casually threatened and Michelle and I both knew she was serious.

Like any other bully, once she was faced with a formidable opponent all of a sudden Michelle came to her senses and backed off before grabbing her purse and storming out of the house.

"Y'all need to be coming to bible study with me. And when I get back I want all of these funny looking kids out of my *clean* house, Tillar!" she said before slamming the door so hard I thought it would come off the hinges.

Despite me telling her that I wanted to be alone, Diane came to comfort me after I went back to my room. I'd ruined my makeup because the tears wouldn't stop coming down so she handed me my wipes before sitting on the bed. I just held onto them until I felt like speaking.

"You know she's never gonna get over this, Auntie Dee. I'm literally gonna hear about this for the rest of my life just like that bottle of perfume I spilled when I was five."

"Who cares? You have got to live your life for you, Tilly. Not her. Cameron had a point. You're already going above and beyond for her financially. She doesn't get to control your love life too. And if you ask me, she's just jealous she doesn't have one since Ronald ran off and left her. Not that he was worth having anyway," she joked before continuing. "Don't let this come between you and Cameron. He seems like a good man and I happen to like him."

"Why? Because he paid for the food?"

"Because he's not a pervert," she said definitively.

"What? How do you know that?" I asked

because you could never be too sure with men and she hadn't even been around him for that long yet.

"Because there's a backyard full of half-naked sixteen year old girls running around and he only wanted to sit in your room and read a book."

"Wow I didn't think of it like that."

"Most women don't or they do and just look the other way. That's why I got rid of my first husband. He always looked a second too long even at the little girls in his family. I knew what he was thinking and it turned my stomach."

Diane was always good for dropping unexpected jewels and since she thought I was too good for everybody, having her stamp of approval went much further than Michelle's. Especially since Jordan had told her that she thought Cam was some kind of scammer a few weeks ago, but luckily she knew I would never be involved with somebody like that.

"Why couldn't you be my mother?" I finally asked her a question I had been asking the lord my whole life.

"Because God knew there wouldn't be enough room for you, Jordan, and me to fit on the same couch," she cracked about all of our wide hips. "But I still love you as if you were my own Tilly. And I'll let the professor know he'll have to woo me some other time. You go and fix things with Cameron and I'll take care of everything here."

"Thank you so much," I said getting up before she realized how much work it would be and changed her mind.

"But you might want to go fix your face first," she said redirecting me to the bathroom.

I stopped by Cam's place, but he wasn't there so I went by the shop to find him. Reese and Lauren were the last two leaving out as I came in so I flipped over the *Open* sign to the *Closed* side then locked the door behind me.

"We're closed," Cam said before craning his neck backwards from his booth and seeing that it was just me and not a customer. "Did Cruella ruin the party already?" he asked me neutrally, but I cracked a smile at him referring to Michelle as the iconic villain.

"No. Diane is holding down the fort so I could come and make up with you."

"That was nice of her, but we don't have shit to make up about. I'm not mad at you," he said letting it be known that all of his animosity was towards Michelle.

"Good," I said as I walked over and hugged him. "Because I could really use a few orgasms to mellow out after the week I've had without you." Sex wasn't on his mind though.

"Is that how she talks to you all the time?" he asked and I sighed hard because being reckless with her mouth had become normalized in the family especially towards me. Him being an outsider only intensified what was already there. My lack of a response to his question made him pull me over to the mirror and stand behind me. "Look at yourself, Tillar. You're the closest thing to perfect on this earth so don't let nobody, not even your mother, make you feel less than because of a fucking number on a scale."

"I won't. I promise," I said thinking that it would be the end of the conversation so I turned around to bless the lips that spoke so highly of me.

"I want you to come stay with me," he said through the kiss. "And not just for the weekend but for good."

"Cam, it's okay. That's just how she is. I've learned to live with it and I swear it doesn't even bother me that much anymore," I reasoned because I was getting closer and closer to paying off the balance anyway so there was no need to rock the boat now.

"That don't make it right. I wanted to ask you anyway because I miss waking up next to you and not just because I don't know what kind of surprise might be waiting for me when I roll over," he meant about my breasts spilling out from the camisoles that I usually wore to bed.

"Seeing you is the best way to start my day and I just can't let you go back there and get treated like that."

"Why because you think you love me?" I hadn't intended on bringing it up, but his little slip did need to be addressed sooner than later.

"Because I know I love you, Tills," he said definitively and with my hands on his neck, I felt his heartrate increase as he looked down at me for my reaction.

"Didn't I tell you from the beginning not to make too much of this?" I asked him even though I hadn't taken heed to my own warning either. He just shrugged.

"You know I'm hard-headed, but do you think you might love me too?"

"Cam," I whined out his name because I just wanted things to go back to how they were before when we acknowledged our feelings but didn't have to use the L word. Those four little letters always complicated things and this situation was difficult enough without them.

"Okay then if you weren't going back to Atlanta, could you see yourself being with me long-term?" he asked instead probably because he already knew the answer.

"Of course I could."

"And you're definitely still going back?" he asked and I nodded because as much as I cared for him, after Bryan I decided never to make life-altering decisions with a man in mind again. "What if I come with you then? I've been looking at commercial real estate around Buckhead for a new shop and there's a few places that I like. What do you think?"

"I think that's crazy. Why would you move your whole life for me when you've only known me for four months?"

"Because when you know, you know. And I thought you liked spontaneous fairytale shit. Don't they all have love at first sight in them?"

"Yes, but you were not in love with me at first sight."

"I was. I swear I heard a Luther Vandross song playing in the background and everything," he said and I couldn't help but laugh at his silliness.

"Which song?"

"'Never Too Much'," he said as he let his hands fall down to my behind then squeezed it. "And next time your mother gets out of pocket, you tell her I said to kiss this."

"How about you kiss it instead?" I dared him after feeling myself get aroused from the way he was touching me. He immediately accepted before reaching over for his keys. "No. Do it right here," I said before loosening the knot on my dress and letting it fall to the floor.

It would have been more of a statement if I was naked, but I was still wearing the swimsuit that I'd been wanting to show him earlier. His eyes went to the front of the shop because even though the storefront windows had a slight tint to them, anybody strolling by or stopping at the intersection's traffic light would be able to see me. The exhibitionist in me was getting off on it.

"You know we can't do that in here," he said like he was trying to convince himself before biting down on his bottom lip.

"Are you sure? Because you already broke one rule for me so why not break them all?" I asked as I rubbed him through his jeans. It didn't take long to wake him up and I could see his shop related morals wavering as I sat in his chair. I was proven right when I went to take off my heels and he told me to leave them on because he had been wanting to fuck me in them for a while. I celebrated my corruption of him then instructed him to stand behind me like he did when I was getting a cut.

"Do you remember the first day that I sat here and I caught you looking down my dress?" I asked as I made eye contact with him in the mirror the same way I'd done then.

"How could I forget?"

"Tell me what you were thinking about doing to me."

He thought for a second before using his foot to raise the chair higher. He then slowly tilted my head back and planted a sweet upside down Spider-Man kiss on my lips.

"Is that it?" I asked ungratefully before he chuckled then ran his hands down to my breasts and squeezed them too.

"You sure you didn't get in the pool?" he teased me after letting his hand snake down to part my thighs. He wasted no time finding my sweet spot and strumming on it like a guitar that played his favorite song.

Watching him in the mirror while he kissed my neck and stroked me with his fingers had me coming with record speed, but he must've decided that I wasn't satisfied enough as he walked in front of me then got down on his knees where he ferociously licked me until I finished again, effectively taking his customer service skills to another level. I sat there in total bliss and blind to the world until I heard him groan in frustration. I opened my eyes to see him grabbing his keys and heading for the door in a hurry before I asked where he was going.

"I'll be right back. All my condoms are at home."

"You don't carry any with you?" I asked mirroring his angst because I had seen enough to protect a small army in his medicine cabinet.

"What for? We usually only do this there," he said hurriedly because I was holding him up without realizing that he was confirming his fidelity to me.

"How about we just go together and stay there then?" I suggested while laughing at his ridiculous plans.

"Nah. You got yours here so I want mine here," he demanded before coming back over and putting my hand where his face had been. "Don't stop. Keep it hot for me."

He kissed me with purpose and I felt the hunger for me coming from inside of him. I could tell from his erection and the pace that he left that he wanted nothing more than to finally enjoy me with nothing between us, but he respected me and my wishes and knew that doing the right thing was the only option here. He probably had no idea how much wetter I got realizing that I had hit the jackpot in so many different ways with him, but he would feel it for himself soon enough.

For a minute I felt silly just sitting alone in front of his mirror with my hand where it was. Don't get me wrong, I was a major proponent of getting it done yourself even if you had somebody to do it for you. But still, I'd never watched myself do it and for the first time I got to see everything how he did and the sight before me turned me on something fierce. I liked watching how I couldn't keep my lips together because of the low moans that were coming from me, but I loved seeing my full breasts straining against the apple red fabric of my suit, the bottoms of which were pulled to the side as I caressed myself the way he instructed me to. After a few minutes my hips were thrusting themselves upward because the only person who knew how to get me off quicker than Cam was me, myself, and I.

He must've ran the three blocks there and back because in no time I heard the door opening right as I was almost ready to call out my own name. He was barely able to lock the door again before he was in front of me, breathless and pulling his shirt off and anxiously stepping out of his jeans. He ripped my bathing suit clean off of me and I swear I had never seen a man want a woman more than he did in that moment. I came hard watching him suit up for what would be the final act of our sex play.

"I want you on top," he growled as he pulled the chair's lever hard and lowered me in it, but my capacity to stand on my own two feet was nonexistent at the moment. Without warning, he lifted me into the air and stole my seat, musical chairs style. Before I could even allow myself to be impressed once again at his strength, he was lowering me onto him.

"Mm. This chair was not made for this," I

moaned and laughed as I struggled to ride him, but he quickly had his hands filled as he helped me to get steady and maneuver up there.

I looked over my shoulder in the mirror and watched as he held on tightly to all of my curves and perfect imperfections. He was so obviously enthralled that he wasn't even speaking like usual and I couldn't believe I was seeing a side of him that I hadn't experienced before. I shifted so that I wouldn't block his mirror view anymore, but it was the wrong thing to do. The second he saw the reflection of me bouncing up and down on him, his legs got shaky and I knew he was about to come soon. I was right and he grunted so loudly that I was sure he'd woken the dead, but when he recovered he rubbed my clit like the gentleman he always was to help me finish once more even though I'd already had enough.

When we were done and just kissing and catching our breaths, the chair suddenly gave out underneath us and we hit the floor. We laughed like mischievous kids as we accused each other of being the culprit.

"You broke it!"

"No you broke it! This chair ain't used to all of this," he said as he caressed my butt.

"I've sat here plenty of times with all of this with no problem."

"Yeah, but you wasn't throwing it around

like that," he said sounding extra impressed at my performance.

"I did show out a little, didn't I?"

"Hell yeah. You gotta remind me to buy better chairs for the new shop if we're gonna be doing this in Atlanta," he said looking in my eyes as he sneakily went back to the topic that I thought was put to bed for the night especially since he was still nestled inside of me.

I sighed then lifted myself off of him and went to the bathroom in his office. He came in a minute later holding my dress and the scraps of the swimsuit.

"So you're just gonna pretend like you didn't hear me?"

"Cam, you can't just pack up and leave everything here. You already have your shit together. I thought I did too, but I see I still have a lot to sort out when I get back home."

"Sort it out with me then. I'm not finished with my life yet either. There's still a lot of shit I want to do," he explained, but I was still firmly against the idea until he went on, "Think about it like this. I have a new adventure every few days with a different book, right? But nothing compares to the adventure I've been on since you first walked through that door, Tills," he said with conviction as he pointed to the entrance of the shop. "Now why would I give that up just because you live in a different state? I mean I can cut hair anywhere. I've cut it on the east coast and in the Midwest. Maybe it's time I see how down south is looking. I know it's plenty of heads to cut down there."

"Yeah starting with mine!" I said as I pulled his neck down so that I could reach his lips. Logically it would've been much easier if I just stayed and worked here, but I loved how that wasn't even an option for him because he knew how much I loved Atlanta and he truly just wanted to be wherever I was. Hearing him talk like that cleared away all the doubt I'd been feeling over the last few days and immediately made room for a new emotion. "I love you too."

"So does this mean that you're moving in with me in the meantime because you'll get a big bed and me?"

"No I already have both of those. You shouldn't have let me milk the cow for free."

"C'mon. Just because you're helping out doesn't mean you gotta stay there since it's stressing you out. What, you want a bigger place or something? Because it's plenty of two and three bedroom apartments in my building. You know that old couple you speak to all the time? I'll put them out on their asses for you, Tills. Just say the word and gramps and his old girl are history," he joked, but I was really starting to believe that he would do anything for me.

"Please don't. And it's not about space. You know you're my escape from all the craziness, Cam, but when I decided to come here I said I would really try to build a relationship with my mama and TJ."

"And how is that working out for you?" he asked with plenty of sarcasm.

"Fuck you," I laughed out as I hit him then slipped back into my dress. "Look they're the last family I have so I still have to try."

"Yeah well you shouldn't be the only one trying. They need to be trying too," he said as he rubbed the side of my face. "How come you know you're the shit everywhere except for in your family? Everywhere you go you're the most beautiful woman in the room. Your job is bending over backwards to keep you happy. Just let them go because Tiffa and Diane are the only family worth holding onto."

"What about Bailey and Blake?" I joked about Jordan's kids because he'd left them out.

"They're a package deal with Jordan so they're cut too," he joked. I had never told him what Jordan thought of him so I asked why he didn't like her when he'd only technically met her once in passing when we ran into her and the kids at a farmer's market. "I don't just read books. I can read people too and I can tell that she's not for you."

"Why don't you read me then?"

"I already did and that's why I'm here. There's not a million Tillars running around so I'm holding on with everything I've got," he said sincerely before connecting our foreheads. "And they're not the only family you have anymore because you got me now, okay?"

"Okay. And I'll try to put some serious thought into moving in this weekend."

"Good. Now do you think you might want to do that again before we get out of here?" he asked as he rubbed his hardening penis on me and I nodded as I bit my lip. "I thought so. You don't have to be scared to ask for seconds with me," he teased me with plenty of innuendo as he turned me around and let my dress hit the floor again. "You ready to show me how bad you want the closet?"

7

DRAMA QUEEN

After everything was said and done Cam was respectful and didn't bring up Michelle to me anymore. I wished that I could've said the same for her because every chance she got she was bad mouthing him and telling me how he was no good for me. But it was futile because it just made me want to spend even more time away from her.

She made plenty of baseless accusations to anybody who would listen that Cam was brainwashing me against her when really I was just finally waking up to the fact that it was actually her who was always manipulating me into helping her. I had seen the signs of emotional incest so clearly with Bryan and his mother and even with Michelle and TJ, but it never occurred to me that I was susceptible to it as well. Michelle had used TJ as a replacement man in the house, but since his earning potential was so limited, she'd made me replace my father financially. I figured it out a little too late though because I only had a couple more payments to make before she would be back in good standing with the bank.

I felt like I could finally breathe again and the great sense of relief I had knowing it was almost over made me realize just how big of a burden it was that'd been placed on me. It made me decide that when this situation with the house was settled that I would no longer allow myself to be guilted by my mother. I had gone above and beyond anything she'd ever done for me so for her sake I hoped it was the last favor she would ever need from me.

Looking back, I still felt so blessed that I'd somehow been able to keep my head above water these last five months because I never missed a single payment on one of the many bills that I had between Chicago and Atlanta. With my salary, my Airbnb money, Michelle and TJ chipping in a little, and of course the bank of Cameron Logan, I saw the light at the end of the tunnel and I was almost free.

Months ago when I'd envisioned this moment, I was sure that I would be celebrating and packing to leave soon, but instead I had just been bringing more and more stuff to Cam's place. Sure I was nearly free to go and I really did want to get back to my routine at home, but I took advantage of the fact that I didn't have to rush. I'd been approved to stay for the full year and since things were going better in the office lately I didn't mind as much. After Cam's surprise visit, the men suddenly stopped being so helpful when they saw that I was in a relationship which in turn made the women like me more. If I'd known it would be so simple I would have brought him in myself much sooner.

But even as peaceful as things had been at work for the last few weeks, I took a mental health day and stayed in bed sketching all morning so I could have a little me time. I'd spent every night since the disastrous clash of the titans between Cam and Michelle here with him, but I still didn't think of myself as living with him because how things were set up felt more like residential purgatory. He loved every minute of it though and did everything to make it feel like home for me. He gave me the entire closet and built shelves for all of my shoes. It still wasn't enough space though so he bought me clothing racks to at least make all of my ensembles palatable to the décor if they insisted on taking up so much space.

I was worried that I was doing too much since he had to put a lot of his things in the storage space in the basement, but he assured me that he didn't care where his clothes were as long as I was next to him. And overall I thought it was a positive thing that we were getting this little practice run at sharing space in because it was true that you never knew somebody until you lived with them. I had already seen how tidy he was when I was just a guest, but he continued cleaning up after himself all the time. Hell, he even cleaned up my messes as I was making them. He wasn't a little boy that I had to teach to put the toilet seat down. He came fully trained and I really appreciated his father and grandmother raising him right because now that I was older I didn't have the patience to try to raise a grown son.

I'd forgotten that it was Friday until I saw an arrangement of daisies in Cam's hand when he came in from work. I'd read somewhere that fresh flowers helped to reduce stress, but I didn't know if I could solely attribute my recently lowered levels to all the plants in his place when just being around him so much elevated my mood. He kissed me as he handed them to me, but I noticed his eyes wandering to the place settings at the kitchen island.

"Ay whoa. Who are you and what did you do with my Tillar?" he asked as he took in the delicious scent in the air. He wasn't exaggerating much because it rarely happened and even when it did it was usually just from takeout that I'd brought in after work.

"Is that what I think it is?" he asked as he

finally recognized the smell then speed walked over to get one of the professionally wrapped sandwiches. I watched him as he took a big bite then closed his eyes how he always did when something tasted really good to him. "How did you get this sent from New York?" he asked with his mouth full.

"No silly. I made it."

I knew he was coming straight in from work so I decided to do something nice for him because he had earned it. I'd relentlessly teased him about his Harlem chopped cheese sandwich all the time because I felt that Chicago Italian beefs were better, but I had never actually tried his to compare until now. I spent an hour on YouTube watching different videos until I found the simplest, unfuckupable recipe then ran out to get what I needed. When I was done, I couldn't believe that I'd let myself get intimidated by what was basically a loose meat hamburger on hoagie bread.

"You really made this from scratch?" he asked again in disbelief as he inspected it to make sure it was authentic.

"Well of course I bought the bread, but yeah. Do you really like it?" I had to ask because he literally hyped me up about everything. He knew I couldn't cook worth a damn so even after he'd slaved away on a meal all day for dinner, he would act like my basic bacon and eggs was the best thing he'd ever eaten at breakfast the next morning and would swear that he could taste the love in it.

"It's just like I had at home. Shit better. Hajji's ain't got nothing on you, Tills," he bragged on me before he suddenly put the sandwich down. "I hate to look a gift horse in the mouth, but what's all this for? Did you break something while I was gone?" he asked playfully as he looked around the room.

"No. It's nothing really. Just that I wanted to celebrate Michelle getting to the ninety day mark at her job. And since I make the final payments to the bank soon, you won't have to give me my allowance anymore. Well at least not so much," I half-heartedly joked as I kissed his cheek because again while I wasn't selling anything, I wasn't exactly free either.

"Word? That's wassup," he said clearly not interested in anything I had to say about her, but I didn't blame him because I wouldn't care much about somebody who mistreated him either.

"Look I know you hate her, but you could try to sound a little more enthusiastic. This is good news for everybody."

"I don't hate her. She hates me," he said sounding like a stubborn little kid.

"She doesn't hate you. She hates the fact

that you stood up to her. Nobody but Diane ever does, but she only keeps her around because she's in competition with her."

"That's not why she hates me, Tills. She sees how good I am to you and she knows that if you get used to receiving then that means maybe you won't be so giving to her anymore," he said unaware of the weight that his simple observation carried.

His theory perfectly explained why she always made me feel like I was forever indebted to her even though if I was looking at things objectively, I could see that our whole relationship was tipped in her favor when she wasn't half the mother that she thought she was. At least not to me she wasn't.

"So I guess this means that you'll be getting up out of here pretty soon then, huh?" Cam asked after finally taking in what I'd said about paying off her balance for the house.

"I don't know. I'm not really in a rush. I mean I just started getting settled here with you and I really don't feel like taking that long drive yet, you know, so I think I'll stay a little while longer," I said being picky with my words, but it didn't matter because his neutral face slowly turned into a cocky smile by the time I'd finished speaking. "What? It's not because of you!" I swore even though he knew it was a lie.

"This is the best day ever. I got my chopped cheese and now I know for sure that you really love me because there's nothing that could keep you from Atlanta except real love."

"I didn't say that."

"So why aren't you leaving then, Tills?" he asked smugly and I shrugged like he always did. "Because I know Miss 'No Strings Attached' isn't staying just for me? I thought you caught flights not feelings," he asked and I couldn't help but laugh at how silly he was being.

"Now you're adding stuff. I never said that and you can think whatever you want," I said as I got up to clear the dishes, but he grabbed my hand and pulled me on his lap.

"Are you really staying for me?" he asked finally being serious.

"I refuse to answer that question without my lawyer present."

"Yeah you're deep in love with a nigga. I'm talking that ocean floor, Keith Sweat deep love. It's down there with the Titanic, ain't it Tills?" he bragged.

"You know what? Now I'm definitely leaving you here by yourself with your jokes."

"Nope. You're staying right here with me to trip over all of this stuff until I open the new shop and then we're going back together," he said officially setting our plans in stone and it sounded like a dream.

He got up to help me clean the kitchen because I'd made a big mess in there even though the people on YouTube made it look so simple.

"So about your allowance," he began as he handed me the last plate to dry, "I'm not cutting it." He looked down at me to see my reaction as he dried his hands.

"You're serious? Why?"

"Why not? You're already in the budget so you can spend it on yourself now or finally run Sallie Mae the rest of her money," he teased me about how I only paid the minimum payment on my student loans.

I thought for a second and realized that if I put the same energy into my student loans that I'd put into Michelle's house then I could be done in a little over a year then I could get back to saving up for my boutique plans with Nicole.

"And just what category did you put me under in your budget? It better not be something misogynistic."

"It's not. Wait is 'best pussy ever' misogynistic or a compliment?" he asked mannishly and I couldn't tell if he was being serious or not.

"Cam! Now I want to see what it says. Show me," I demanded even after he told me he was kidding. I was nosy so of course I glanced over the whole thing before seeing that he just had a category called Tillar. I had already estimated the total before, but seeing all the numbers in front of me at once was astonishing. I slid his phone back into his pocket then hugged him tightly.

"Thank you for everything you've done for me. I can't even begin to tell you how much I appreciate you," I told him before I felt myself getting teary-eyed when I realized that no one since my dad had ever taken care of me the way he had.

"For somebody who claims to be spoiled, you sure are grateful for everything," he said amused at how emotional I was getting when I fanned my eyes.

"That's like my defense mechanism. Growing up I got so used to not being spoiled that I decided anybody not willing to do it didn't really love me."

"Well I'm glad that you appreciate the things I do for you, but you don't have to overdo it with the thank yous. I'm not doing nothing that I'm not supposed to be doing. I was raised to treat women right especially the woman that I'm in love with. I like being appreciated, but I would love it if you knew you deserved even more than what I give you."

"I know. I deserve the moon and the stars too, right?" I asked thinking that his sweet words were about to become predictable.

"Nah you're still thinking too small. Fuck this solar system. My girl deserves all the galaxies even the ones scientists can't see yet," he said sprinkling a little nerdiness on his game before I pulled him over to the bed.

Even though today was supposed to be a day for myself, I'd missed the hell out of him while he was gone and I didn't want to wait until it was time to sleep to express how I felt about him. By the end of the night he'd asked me to make him two more chopped cheese sandwiches and I was starting to feel like I had created a monster, but I didn't mind at all. If I was deserving of a billion or more galaxies then he at least deserved the little piece of Harlem that he was now claiming only I could give to him.

♛

"Don't say anything. I promise this is the last of it," I said to Cam as I let myself in despite having my arms full.

Just when I thought I had collected the last of my belongings from Michelle's house, I remembered that I'd left about eight garment bags in the guest room's closet. I'd expected to find him lying on the bed with his nose in a book, but I got the surprise of a lifetime when instead I

244

saw Lauren sitting comfortably on the couch. I didn't have to look far for him because he was in the kitchen getting bottles of water from the fridge.

"You said that last time," he said as he tossed a bottle over to her. I looked around for any signs of Reese, but it quickly became clear that they were here alone.

Since Cam had announced that he would be leaving Reese in charge of the shop because he was moving to Atlanta with me, Lauren had actually been somewhat nicer, like she had finally given up on him. Until now.

"Hey Tillar. That's a really cute dress. In fact, I love all your clothes, girl," she complimented me as she picked up a floral blazer from my rack. "It's too bad that they're too big for me or else I would be sneaking some stuff home. I'll see you tomorrow, Cam."

Before I could utter a word she was out the door because her spirit must've felt the hurting that I wanted to put on her. The door closing loudly from behind startled me. I still hadn't spoken or put anything down because I was stuck looking at the perfectly made bed and wondering if he had just fixed it before I walked in. He was watching me wondering what was wrong, but when he realized what it was he threw the bottle down and used his long legs to get to me in just a few steps.

"We're not even about to do that, Tillar. Have I ever given you a reason not to trust me?" he asked as he peered down at me. I didn't answer him, but I sat my things on the floor and he sighed with relief because he thought the conversation was over. It wasn't. I just needed my hands free to focus on taking his keys off of my ring, but I was so angry that I broke a nail instead. "Ay stop. Fuck. Let me call her to come back and tell you that nothing happened."

"Don't. No bitch will ever think she had me bothered. Fade Family Gang, my ass," I said as I threw the keys at his chest. I knew I'd be crying soon so I left him standing there then went to the bathroom before any real tears could fall. It hurt even more knowing that Michelle was right about him and how I would have to go crawling right back to her with everything I'd just brought from her house.

"Look I wanted it to be a surprise to thank you for all the chopped cheeses the other day," he spoke to me through the door. "I bought you a projector so we could finally watch that Cinderella musical together. It was supposed to come tomorrow so I had it delivered at the shop and Lauren dropped it off because they just left it on the sidewalk. I swear to you on my mother and my daughter that I wouldn't do no grimy shit like that, Tills. I ain't never been no mutt ass nigga and I'm not about to start now. I love you. Please open the door," he begged.

I had to admit that he sounded believable and to my knowledge he had never lied to me, but I stayed quiet and let him sweat while I continued touching up my makeup. If we were breaking up then I wanted the last time he saw me to leave him with nothing but regrets. When I finally opened up a few minutes later, he was still standing in the doorway looking anxious about what I would do next.

"That's all that happened?"

"That's it. I promise."

"Where's your phone?" I asked him and before I could even finish getting the words out, he'd went over and snatched it from the wall charger then placed it in my hand. Only an incredibly stupid man would do that. Or an incredibly honest man. "What's the passcode?"

"Zero-four-zero-four," he told me without missing a beat, but I rolled my eyes at it being my birthday. He just leaned on the arch as I unlocked it like he knew I wouldn't find anything incriminating, but I would be the judge of that.

I'd never gone through a man's phone before so I didn't know where to start first, but I figured that his text messages would be my best bet for finding out the true nature of their friendship. Even if he was smart enough to have deleted stuff over time, there would still be subtext or something that inadvertently told on them.

The most recent exchange seemed to check out. Lauren had texted him about the package and said that she could bring it to him. He said thanks then gave her the address which meant that she had never been here before. Okay one point for honesty, but it was also deducted because he could have just met her downstairs to get it. But on the other hand, he knew that I was on my way home from work so if he was trying to cheat then he certainly wouldn't have scheduled it for now. And I actually should've been here much sooner since I got here before him most days, but he didn't know that I was going to get more stuff from Michelle's house.

It seemed liked he was telling the truth and I had even spied with my little eye the alleged Amazon box sitting in front of the bookshelf, but I fought the urge to sigh with relief because I didn't want him to know that he was in the clear yet. I prolonged it by reading all of their old messages which weren't anything except for her requesting a day off here and there.

I briefly looked up at him to find him still coolly hovering over me as I searched my name in his texts. He'd told his brother Chris that he missed his call because we were hiking a couple weeks ago then he defended me in a group chat with the other barbers from the shop. They'd playfully accused him of giving TJ even more special treatment than usual because of me and one of them even offered up his sister to take my place if he could come in late too. Cam's last message on the subject was what ultimately decided his fate today though.

Save your sister for Reese's Fade reign. I'm happily cuffed for good.

"Do you believe me?" he asked after I handed him back his phone. I looked down at my feet because I was embarrassed that I'd overreacted when he hadn't actually done anything wrong, but I also didn't want him to think that having another woman in his space, in our space, was appropriate if I wasn't there. Still, I didn't necessarily want to apologize for my part so I played it off.

"I don't know. I guess I do."

"Nah. It's either a yes or a no, Tills. Do you believe me?" he repeated sternly with a quick lick of his lips as he closed the space between us.

"It depends. Are you really 'happily cuffed'?"

"Yeah. Of course I am," he remarked while gesturing at how cramped his space was now with all of my belongings in it.

"Then act like it. And don't let anything like this happen again if you want to stay cuffed," I warned him before he pulled me into a soul crushing hug and began apologizing for the optics.

"I won't and I'm sorry about this. I was OD proud of myself for never doing anything to make you cry, but I fucked it up today."

"Well technically I didn't cry. My eyes just got a little watery," I said before embracing him back so we could begin putting this little incident behind us.

"So is that it then?" he asked trying to see where things would go from here. Admittedly I was a little confused too because this was our first real fight as a couple.

"That's it, but I'm gonna go. I need to be by myself for a while, alright?" He quickly nodded in understanding as he bent to pick up his keys to put them back on my ring then handed my purse to me. I took a step away from him towards the door but stopped myself when I saw that he wasn't going to. "You're really just gonna let me leave, Cam?"

"Yeah I know you're just going to get your nail fixed," he said with a cute smile before coming over to kiss my temple. "I'mma try to have all of this set up for you by the time you get back. I love you."

"I love you too," I said then quickly slipped out after telling him that he was responsible for finding somewhere to put my garment bags. He just laughed then locked the door after me.

Those couple hours away pampering myself did me some good and it allowed me to put things in perspective. I'd been in and out of love more times than I could count, but it wasn't until now that I felt loved all the way through. Cam was a good dude. Like a genuinely good, integrity-having, loyal man and he was nothing like any of the other men I'd had in my life before him. So from this point on I wouldn't allow myself to second guess us anymore because we were solid. Waiting for the other shoe to drop was pointless because at this point it seemed like it never would.

He must've heard me getting off the elevator on our floor because when I came back, he was standing guard in front of the door.

"What's the password?" he teased, making fun of me for going through his phone, but it was still too soon.

"M-O-V-E."

"Access granted," he said before stepping aside and letting me see that along with the new projector, he'd also bought and decorated with fairy lights.

"Since you're staying for a while, I thought you could use a little something to make this place feel more like home," he said because I had them up all over my place and my terrace at home. I always felt like they were the last bit of magic that adults were allowed to have so I'd gone a little overboard with them.

I thought back to a few days ago when he all of a sudden really wanted to see how my condo looked. He'd joked about wanting to make sure that I didn't have any posters of Usher up there too, but now I saw that the real reason he requested to see my AirBnB listing was because he had this up his sleeve.

The lights framing the bed looked especially beautiful and I couldn't wait to make love to him underneath them, but first we had a movie date to get to. I showered then changed for bed because I had a feeling that we would be turning in early tonight. When I came out of the bathroom he had yet another surprise waiting for me. I felt like I'd walked into a cozy drive in because he had tons of movie snacks delivered for the occasion and an endless supply of popcorn on the bed. I thanked him for planning such a cute date night in for me then got comfortable in his arms and waited for the real magic to begin.

"So what did you think?" I asked when the credits rolled because I didn't take my eyes off the screen once even when I heard him laughing at some parts. It was like I'd been in a world of my own falling in love with the story all over again.

Despite owning the film in every form that it came in, I hadn't actually watched it in years so this whole thing was a much welcome surprise. Especially when I realized how much had changed and surprisingly stayed the same since my first watch. Seven year-old me had witnessed something so grand that it still somehow felt new even for the nearly thirty-year-old me.

"It would've been perfect if they had a black prince," he said and I rolled my eyes. "What? Other than that it was pretty good. I liked it."

"Pretty good? Just liked it? No, it's literally the best musical of all time," I corrected him as I sat up in bed.

"Don't get me wrong. It's good, but I think the real reason you connect with it so much is because your life is just like hers."

"How is my life like hers?" I asked even though I'd noted the parallels since I was a teen. I just didn't think anybody else would ever see them since my peasant girl days were over and done with.

"Well from what you told me about her, Diane is definitely your fairy godmother. Your mother and TJ are checking off the evil stepfamily boxes. And of course I'm your Prince Charming coming to save you from them," he bragged before nicking my lips. "Wait I thought there was supposed to be magic rats in there somewhere."

"That's the original cartoon version."

"Was that one based in Harlem?" he quipped just to make me laugh. "So I've been thinking long and hard about this for the last sixty seconds," he joked. "You should let me throw you a ball because you can't *really* be Cinderella without having one."

"No, I can't be Cinderella with my ugly stepsister sized feet," I said putting my leg in the air for him to really take a look at my big foot. "You let me know when you come across some glass slippers that'll fit these Lil' Yachtys," I joked and he cracked up at my boat feet pun.

"If I can find you some, will you let me throw it?"

"No, because there has to be a reason for a ball. People don't just have balls."

"Because little Princess Tillar wanted one. That's the only reason you really need."

"I wanted a pony too back then. You gonna get me one of those?" I asked sarcastically, but he agreed to that too just to win. "It's a really sweet idea, Cam, but I'm grown. Tonight was an adorable trip down memory lane, but I'm too old for fairytales now."

"I don't think you'll ever get too old to be treated like a princess, Tills," he said convincingly before leaning over and kissing the top of my head.

And I wasn't sure if it was the pretty white lights flickering above our heads while he was on top of me or if it was just the spellbinding way that he used his magic wand tonight, but by the end of making love he'd gotten me to agree to it. Princess Tillar was having a ball.

8

BATTLE ROYALE

Cam had been super secretive about planning the ball for the last few weeks. He refused to include me even a little bit because he reasoned that Cinderella's only job was to show up looking beautiful. The only thing that I knew was the location which would be the courtyard of the big flower shop next door to the shop. I'd never actually been inside, but the view from Cam's office windows was unbelievable and I couldn't wait to dance the night away surrounded by exotic plants and tropical looking shrubbery.

The date he'd chosen just so happened to fall on Halloween so it was only natural that we would go as Cinderella and Prince Charming for the occasion. And of course I didn't want any of the badly designed costumes that I'd come across online so I decided to design them myself and have Nicole bring them to life. That decision had been made weeks ago though and she was still waiting around for his measurements before she could really get to work. Nicole worked pretty fast though so I was sure that it wouldn't be a problem, but I knew no matter what we had to get everything back to her tonight since the ball was just a little over a week away.

Cam had been a little stuffy and wasn't feeling very well when he went to work that morning so I wasn't surprised when I pulled up from work and saw him about to go inside.

"What are you doing home so early?"

"I just sneezed and clipped this dude's ear so I knew it was time to go," he joked, but I saw how exhausted he looked and hugged him how he always did for me when I wasn't feeling my best.

"Aw you poor baby. Let's get you inside so you can get some rest. I'll order up some soup for dinner and I'll let you sleep for as long as you want after we do the measurements for Nic, okay?"

"We gotta do those right now?" he whined like a little kid as we got on the elevator.

"It'll just take a minute, Sneezy. I promise."

Despite the open window and the windy day we were having, the apartment still smelled just like the Vicks Vapor Rub that he'd smeared all over himself last night before bed. You would've thought he was dying by how much he used, but he swore that his grandmother covering him in it as a child always made him better. I let him go shower and do his little nighttime beard routine before we got started since he would likely be out for the evening after having his soup and being measured. I also decided to use that time to talk to Nicole before he came back out.

Even though I'd known for two months that Cam would be moving back south with me, I still hadn't told her yet because I was trying to wait for the right time. But with her officially deciding to come here for the ball I figured that there was no time like the present. I opened my laptop to FaceTime her since we would need a steady camera for the measuring and I wanted to see her face as I broke the news to her. I chewed my lip out of nervousness as her line rang because we were like a dynamic duo at home so I didn't want her to think that I was switching things up too much by bringing a man into the equation. I knew that I had stalled and made small talk for too long though when I heard Cam turning off the shower.

"So remember when I told you that I would probably be coming home sometime in January?" I asked her and she nodded. "Yeah there's been a slight change of plans."

"You're staying up there permanently, aren't you?" she asked and I could see her trying not to let her disappointment show on her face.

"No no no. I'm still coming back. It's just that I won't be coming by myself. Cam says he wants to come back with me," I told her before waiting for her to roll her eyes or wrinkle her nose, but I got nothing. "What? Say something."

"What can I say? I encouraged this," she joked. "You must really love him?" she asked me right when he opened the door from the bathroom and flung his underwear near my face.

"Ew. Stop it. I'm on camera," I playfully scolded him.

"They're clean," he defended as he made sure to stay out of frame since he was naked. He quickly put on basketball shorts and a t-shirt before climbing in bed with me.

"Did you hear me?" Nicole asked.

"I'm sorry. What did you say?"

"I said do you love him?" she repeated probably thinking that he couldn't hear her because I had my AirPods in. They weren't synced though and he waited with seemingly bated breath like he didn't already know the answer.

"I do," I said as I fussed around with his hair.

"Then I say the more the merrier. I'm really happy for you," she said and I could tell that it was genuine.

"Thanks. Now let's get this over with so

Cam can get to bed," I said before showing her that I'd found the exact same cloth measuring tape that she used on me at home.

"Wassup Nic?" Cam said as he stood to his feet.

"Wow you're dating Wizard Kelly," she joked as he finally came into frame because the top of his head was cut off. Of course he didn't get it because he barely watched TV as a kid so I had to explain that it was a very tall character from *The Proud Family*.

"Everybody's tall to her because she's so tiny. Wait til you see her in person. She barely reaches my boobs when I'm in heels."

"Alright. Alright. Let's get to his measurements, not mine," she said because she was sensitive about being so small. I stood up to get to it, but she stopped me. "Tillar, I think we might need to do yours too. You didn't tell me that you've been working out more up there."

"Just a little bit before bed," Cam answered for me and it sounded extra dirty because he was so congested. "I mean she hits the gym with me sometimes too," he unconvincingly corrected himself after I threw him a look. I just rolled my eyes as she instead instructed him where to do each measurement for my dress.

"I knew it. You lost a few inches all over."

"Guess I wasn't paying attention especially

living with Paula Deen the butter queen over here," I said because I really hadn't noticed a big difference in my clothes. I was just glad that she'd caught it though because I needed my dress to be perfect.

Nicole got a call as soon as I finished measuring his inseam so I let her go as I picked myself up off of my knees then got back comfortable on the bed. Cam plopped down next to me and inquired about why I looked so relieved now.

"It's nothing. I was just worried that she was gonna hate the idea of you coming back with me, but she's actually fine with it."

"Why would it matter to her?"

"Because she hates men. It's like her fuel. It keeps her going and gives her a reason to get out of bed every day," I joked even though she had said that verbatim before.

"Is she a lesbian?" he asked with furrowed brows.

"No, but she wishes she was. And FYI wanting to eat pussy is not a prerequisite to hating men. In general y'all are pretty terrible human beings, you know?"

"You're right. My bad. I know niggas ain't shit," he conceded with a smile and we high-fived in agreement.

"I bet you wouldn't say that in the shop

tomorrow," I playfully challenged him.

"Yeah I would. Oh wait not tomorrow because it's National Barbers Day and niggas' blades are gonna be extra sharp," he said chuckling too hard which made him cough a little.

"Didn't y'all just celebrate that last month?" I asked because I distinctly remembered his post on Instagram.

"That was *World* Barber Day. It's a big difference. And speaking of that, I'm still waiting on my present because you didn't get me anything to show that you appreciate my contributions to society," he said sarcastically even though he did do his part to bring a little joy to his customers' lives on every visit.

"What do you want?" I asked as he cuddled up next to me and I prayed that I'd taken enough vitamin C not to catch his cold.

"Nothing. You're already the best gift and I get to unwrap you every night," he said as he kissed my neck and slipped his fingers into my pants.

"Aht aht. I thought you were too sick to work so I know you're too sick to play."

"I'm sick, Tills, but he's not," he said looking down at his growing erection. "It's a big difference," he repeated mannishly.

"Okay, but first let me see something," I said before reaching over for the measuring tape because there was just one more part of him that I'd forgotten to use it on.

☖

I was running late to my early dinner date with Sofia because I'd forgotten to bring along Tiffa's dress for the ball which was the whole point of the meeting. Since volleyball season had come back around I hardly ever saw her unless I was able to make it to a game because I no longer stepped foot in Michelle's house unless I absolutely had to. I didn't even know that she'd want to come to something like this, but the minute she expressed interest, Nicole squeezed out one more beautiful gown for her. I thought I'd use tonight as another opportunity to try to get Sofia to come too, but she had used all of her sick days for the year and had nobody to cover for her.

Earlier when we were deciding where to meet for our meal, Sofia excitedly told me that she had some good news to share with me. I was expecting her to tell me she'd gotten a raise, had met someone, or even just decided to take a vacation or something, anything but what she actually let fly out of her mouth.

"We're finally gonna be family, Tilly! TJ proposed last night!" she exclaimed just after sitting down and despite knowing better I wasted my time looking down at her finger to find that it was still bare. She instantly started wringing her hands and explaining away the absence of a ring.

"We're gonna get them later for Christmas gifts or maybe at tax time. Well he said he might just get a watch because he doesn't like rings," she began rambling and I instantly tuned her out because I knew what time it was.

Diane had already told me weeks ago that Cassie finally got fed up of the back and forth and threw TJ out on his ass so the timing of this sudden proposal was certainly suspect. Either it was a way to get Cassie's attention or just to secure other housing that included pussy for the winter. Whichever way it was, it wasn't good enough for Sofia and I sat there with an empty smile trying to figure out how to tell her that without hurting her feelings.

Usually I wasn't arguing with any woman over what she thought she was worth. Sis knew her vagina better than me so whether she thought it deserved a Happy Meal or a Bentley, who was I to judge? But I knew I couldn't leave here without saying something to her when she asked me to be her maid of honor.

"Sof, you know I would be honored to be a part of your big day when it's the right time, but are you sure that time is now…with TJ?" I asked trying my best to be gentle because I really wanted to smack some self-esteem into her, but to my surprise she didn't even seem upset. She just lowered her head.

"He said he wants to try to be a real family again," she said lowly and I translated that to mean that he just wanted to possibly be let off the hook for child support.

"And you believe him?"

"Yeah I mean I kinda have to," she said barely trying not to sound defeated.

"No, you don't. You are so amazing in literally every way. And I know it's wrong to say this about family, but you're just too good for him. Hell a meth addict bum would be too good for TJ so you know you are," I said trying to build her up, but it just made her eyes water instead.

"It's okay, Tilly. I know that there ain't no balls and Prince Charming type of shit waiting for somebody like me. Marrying my baby daddy is as good as it's gonna get and it just is what it is."

"Says who? I used to think the same way about myself and look at me now right in the middle of everything I've ever wanted."

"But I'm not all fancy and glamorous and smart like you. What other options do I have? Ain't no good man trying to wife no ass-wiping CNA baby mama. That's just not real life," she said matter-of-factly and I thought it was so interesting hearing how she thought about herself because up until maybe the last five years of my life I'd wanted to be everything that women like her were: small, short, and skinny. But I pushed my own feelings to the backburner because I had to get her together before it was too late.

I reminded her how she was a great mother to Tiffa. How beautiful and bright she was. How much joy she brought to her patients and how she was the backbone of her job. And finally how if she wasn't satisfied with her life that she could improve her situation at any time by finally going back to school to be a nurse or even changing fields altogether. Tiffa was older now so there were no more excuses like when she was a baby. She could totally reinvent herself at any time just like I'd done when I went to college because it was never too late to adjust her crown then course correct.

I was glad that we were seated in a pretty empty corner of the restaurant because she cried like a baby on my shoulder for a while as I told her that I wasn't gonna let her settle on my brother any longer because she could do better. It had been seventeen years of back and forth and two "outside" kids. It was time to move on. I even suggested maybe moving and getting a new start in Atlanta or somewhere else with a lower cost of living because it could be good for her and Tiffa and I could help her more there.

"Are you gonna be okay?" I asked her after she'd finally pulled herself together.

"Yeah. I guess Tiffa will be the only frog kisser around here after all," she joked because her green dress was made in the style of Tiana from *The Princess and The Frog.*

"Not my baby. I wish I could guarantee her a life with no frogs, but we all had to go through it so she probably will too."

"Tilly, what do *you* know about kissing frogs?" she asked me like the idea that I had been less than lucky in love was absurd when that was far from the truth.

"I know that Bryan was the biggest, baddest, slimiest frog in the pond," I said and since I didn't want her putting me on some undeserved pedestal, I decided to come clean about some stuff to let her know she wasn't the first or the last woman to lose herself because of a man. Hell my whole life I had judged women for sleeping with dirty men with dirty nails then acting surprised when they got burned. Until the same thing happened to me by my clean cut and manicured Morehouse man who wore suits to work every day. That slice of humble pie tasted horrible, but I swallowed it then and swore I wouldn't be back for more.

Before she left for work, Sofia let me know

that she was going to tell TJ that the engagement was off and that he needed to take his belongings back to Michelle's house because they were over for good. She seemed confident in her decision and I was proud of her for getting out before things went too far.

When I was leaving the restaurant, I got a call from Tiffa saying that a few girls from her volleyball team were supposed to have a sleepover, but the friend whose house it was being held at had gotten in trouble so it was cancelled at the last minute. She went on to say that Michelle and Sofia had just agreed to let her host it at the house but only if I was there to keep an eye on them. While I wanted nothing more than to go home and mount Cam, I did a U-turn and told her that I was on my way because I felt guilty for not seeing her as much lately. I also needed to pick up some mail anyway so I planned on popping in for just a little bit because I trusted Tiffa not to let any little boys come over.

Apparently she had been talking about me a lot to her friends because upon arrival I was treated like a guest of honor then bombarded with questions galore. She'd told them all about Cam and the ball and her dress so of course they all wanted to come too. I ended up staying and indulging them a little with age appropriate answers to their boy questions. They were still so young so I knew that my advice wouldn't matter until they were older, but I just wished somebody would have given me some of their jewels at their age. Of course Diane had been amazing, but she was still old school and couldn't even fathom the tricks these new men and boys had up their sleeves.

Before we knew it it'd gotten pretty late and they were falling asleep one by one so I was preparing to sneak out on them after I texted Cam that I was finally on my way home. I tiptoed into the kitchen to grab my stack of mail then heard the front door opening in a huff. It was a foggy fall night and it'd gotten a little chilly outside so I figured it was just Michelle rushing in until I turned to see an angry TJ standing there.

"You told Sof to move to Atlanta with you?" he asked as he stepped to me like he had a problem.

"Excuse me?" I played dumb because I was not in the mood to argue with him about this tonight when I had a cute bookworm waiting to rub my feet at home.

"She said you told her to move on and get a new nigga. What, you tryna get her down there to be a dyke like you?" he spat at me as he sized me up. I just sighed before calmly sitting my things back down because there were empty glass bottles within my reach and I had no problem sending him to the ER if it came down to it.

"Fuck you! We both know you're just trying to get off of child support and you should be ashamed since she's barely making it *with* your little crumbs."

And I still loved Sofia like a sister, but I hated how some women couldn't just abide by girlcode for once in their lives. The conversation that we had was between us and none of his business, however I was glad that he'd finally heard the truth about himself even if the words were delivered secondhand.

"Mind your fucking business. You wouldn't appreciate it if I went and told Cam to stop fucking with you because you be fucking them old white men for promotions and shit," he baselessly accused me and I laughed at his poor attempt to shade my accomplishments.

"Even if that were true, it'd still make me smarter than you fucking women for a place to stay, you overgrown bum," I retorted and laughed in his face.

"You don't even know what you talking about. I swear I can't wait til Cam gets down to Atlanta and sees some real bad bitches so your fat ass can get humbled quick," he said raising the volume of his voice as if I would back down and be scared of his weak bark.

"What is all this commotion in here? I could

hear y'all all the way from down the block," Michelle slurred coming into the side door. From her attire and the purse she was carrying, I could tell that she had also been to the casino, but I ignored her because I had been waiting all my life for this moment.

"That's the best you got, TJ? You know I shouldn't even call you that anymore because you don't deserve to have the same name as my father. He's probably rolling around in his grave at the sorry excuse for a man and father that you turned out to be!" I yelled at him and hoped that every word hit him like a dagger.

I didn't realize that I had been slapped until I felt my head hitting the door to the fridge, but before I could even begin to process it my reflexes had already sprang into action and made me grab a bottle off the table. I swung and missed his head by centimeters before Michelle jumped in and wrestled me to the floor to get it out of my hands.

When TJ saw how Michelle was struggling to contain my rage, he knew he'd fucked up and quickly left before I could get my hands on something else because I was determined to complete the eye for an eye that he'd initiated here tonight. The only thing that started to calm me down and keep me from going after him was seeing a sleepy looking Tiffa come into the kitchen confused at all the yelling. Michelle shooed her back to bed then came after me.

"Where you going, Tilly?" Michelle yelled as I headed for the door. "You better not run go tell your little boyfriend about this. I don't want you messing up TJ's job."

"Fuck his job and his life! Your sorry ass son is dead to me. And he better not come by the shop anymore because when I see him it's on sight!" I threatened him, but she waved me off as if I was overreacting.

"Girl, hush and come clean up this mess you just made. I don't want to hear about this nonsense no more. I'm going to bed," she said before taking a few steps towards her room, but before she could get there I grabbed the other empty bottles and threw them on the floor until there were sharp green shards of glass covering her floor.

"I am not your maid anymore. You clean it up!" I demanded while she looked at me like I had lost my mind and a part of me felt like I had, but it was actually just me finally reaching my breaking point with being the punching bag of this family.

It wasn't until I parked in front of Cam's building that I felt the throbbing on the side of my head. I inspected it in my rearview mirror and almost cried seeing the thick handprint across my face and the little knot forming on the other side. TJ's shrimpy ass must have hit me harder than I'd thought because this looked like it would leave a bruise.

I prayed that Cam was sleeping because I didn't want to worry him if he saw me like this and I figured that I could probably explain things better in the morning when I felt better. He was predictably in bed with a book on his chest, but he must not have been asleep long because he immediately sat up when he heard the door close.

"What took you so long? I was getting worried," he yawned out into the darkness.

"You waited up for me even though I told you not to?" I asked trying to sound as normal as possible.

"I did. I was gonna meet you downstairs. There was a robbery a couple blocks over so for real start back calling me when you're close by so I can come down for you," he said thoughtfully even though it wasn't a stranger that I had to worry about bringing harm to me. It was my own blood.

I purposely faced the opposite direction as I changed then slipped into bed, but when he went to kiss my temple how he always did at night I groaned and recoiled in pain.

"What? What did I do?" he asked worriedly as he reached over and turned on his lamp. I tried to turn away, but he made me look at him as he inspected the big purple and red handprint on the side of my face. "Tillar, what the fuck? Who did this to you?" he shouted as he excitedly jumped up. I knew he didn't mean to scare me, but the angry tone in his voice was the last thing I needed to hear and the waterworks were soon in full effect.

"TJ," I sniffled out in between sobs.

"I'mma kill him," he announced calmly with the same look in his eyes that I'd just had only I knew he was serious because he was already headed for the door and he didn't even have any shoes on. I moved quicker than I ever had and stood in front of him to block his only exit. "You want me to climb down the fire escape then? Because this ain't gonna stop me from putting hands, feet, and elbows on him."

I wasn't above watching TJ get stomped out for what he had done to my face, but when Cam said that he would kill him he wasn't just talking shit. I knew he was really capable of it and even though he was an asshole, I didn't want my brother dead. And he wouldn't get off again because this time it wouldn't be self-defense. And I didn't want a life without Cam.

"No. He's still family and we'll deal with this ourselves. I really didn't want to get you involved in this, but I just couldn't stay there tonight after what happened."

"You're not going back there ever again.

And family or not, he don't have the right to put his fucking hands on you."

"I know, but--" He interrupted me as he took hold of my face and connected our foreheads. The first tear of his that fell down my face was unexpected, but the flood that followed lapped under my chin with my own.

"Tillar, don't ever make excuses for a man putting his hands on you." Before I knew it we had switched roles and I was now comforting him as he broke down in my arms. I knew he cared about me a lot, but I had a feeling that this was deeper than the current situation. When he finally calmed down after a few minutes he explained himself. "This is exactly how that shit started with Summer. She asked me not to get in it so I didn't. I minded my business because I knew if I did something to him it would just make shit worse and she would still go back to him anyway. And now her and Cree are both dead because of me and I regret it every day. I'm not losing you like this too, Tills. You're all I got."

"But if you hurt him, you are gonna lose me, Cam. TJ is a bitch, but shit just got out of hand tonight. He wouldn't do something like that to me. Hell, I would kill him before he got the chance to hurt me. You should have seen me an hour ago with my mama's bottle of Asti Spumante," I said because I knew that would get a cheap laugh out of him.

"Where do they even sell that shit anymore?"

"I don't know, but she's got the hookup because she keeps a couple bottles in the fridge," I said as I wiped the last of the tears from his face. "I don't want you getting in any trouble because of me. Promise me you'll let me handle this," I begged him, but he looked away until I forced him to make eye contact with me. He sighed hard.

"My only priority is making sure you're safe. Let me book you a flight home right now and I promise I won't lay a finger on him."

"No. I'm not leaving without you. And what about the ball and all the planning you did? I'm not letting him take this away from us."

"Tillar, if you stay and something happens to you, I could never forgive myself. You're leaving on the next flight so fuck that ball and pack your shit," he said with authority as he went in his closet and pulled out my suitcase. "I'm just gonna put some mismatched shit in here so you better come help me," he warned me showing that he wasn't backing down, but neither was I.

"Can you please stop it?! I'm not going anywhere."

"Why? Why would you want to stay here now? Because I know it's not just for some party."

"First of all it's a ball, not just a party. And

because…"

"Because what?!" he asked raising his voice at me.

"Because if I leave now then what's gonna happen to us?!" I shouted back as tears began to pour down my cheeks again. "You said you would move for me, but when I'm gone you'll come to your senses and realize that maybe I'm not worth all of this trouble you're going through and then you'll end up with somebody like Lauren." He sighed hard again before finally dropping the suitcase and walking back over to me.

"I don't know how I'm gonna get it in your head that I only love you, Tills. It's gotten so bad that I don't even see anybody but you."

"But why? What, you think fat girls don't cheat or that other men won't want me or something like that because it's not true?" I asked as that little unconfident chubby teen inside of me popped out for a minute.

"Tillar, I don't care who does or who doesn't want you. I want you. And I don't need a reason to love you. I just do," he said with pain in his voice and I swear I felt a small shock of electricity run through my body from his touch.

"I love you too, Cam. That's why the only way I'm leaving is if you come with me," I repeated even though I knew I was putting him in a sticky situation because he had obligations here that he couldn't leave just yet. I expected him to come up with an excuse for why it was impossible, but he just thought for a second then agreed to it. "You're sure?"

"Yeah I'll figure everything out when we get there. Reese knows what she needs to do here so the shop is taken care of."

"Okay then so why can't we just wait a couple more days and still go to the ball? Nothing is gonna happen before then," I said before reminding him that it had gotten bigger than just something for me since we had so many people looking forward to it with Nicole and even his grandmother coming from out of state.

"Alright. But after the ball, we're outta here," he told me sternly before touching the bruise on my face again and making me wince. "I'm sorry I wasn't there to protect you. I promise it'll never happen again."

After hugging it out I just wanted to crawl back into bed, but he made me go get checked out at the emergency room even though I told him that I was fine but just a little shaken up. Really I was more embarrassed than anything especially when the nurse took one look at Cam sitting next to me then made up an excuse for him to leave the room. I quickly explained to her that he didn't do this to me. The size of his hands was proof of that and she relaxed when she realized it.

She apologized to him for the implication, but he didn't even care. He just wanted to make sure I was fine. After being okayed to leave with a prescription for pain meds, I was asked if I wanted the police contacted, but against his wishes I declined. I really just wanted to sleep and pretend like this night never happened. Plus when TJ's probation officer found out that he'd been fired, he might've been heading back to jail without me even getting involved.

When we got back home, I still wasn't able to rest well at all and I knew it wasn't just because of how much my head hurt. It was because I was scared that Cam would sneak out and do something to TJ before I could stop him. He didn't sleep too well either because every time I moved, he moved just like that.

When I got up that morning and inspected my face again, I knew I would not be going back to work here. I contacted both offices and let them know that I had another sudden family emergency which required a couple weeks off but after that I would be back in the home office for good. I was so relieved to get an immediate response from my Atlanta boss wishing me and my family well and being thrilled to have me back home because finally something was going in my favor.

I kept the conversation brief when I talked

to both Sofia and Diane because I was already over the whole thing and just wanted to forget about it. Sofia kept apologizing on TJ's behalf and claimed that he had been drinking when she broke up with him, but I didn't care for that excuse. I'd gotten drunk before and the worst thing I did was piss myself and spill my own tea. TJ was a man-child who would never grow up because no one had ever made him and he simply lashed out when he saw he'd met his match in me.

Cam tried to play hooky with me, but I convinced him to go to work since it would now officially be his last day. He agreed but wouldn't let me out of his sight so I had to go with him. It wasn't so bad because after every few customers he would come check on me in his office to make sure that I didn't need anything. I didn't. I'd laid out on the comfortable couch with a good book and I had food delivered so I was better than fine considering everything that was going on.

On her break Lauren decided to be extra and go buy a cake for Cam so all the barbers congregated in the break room to say their goodbyes to him. I obviously wasn't in the mood to be social so I skipped it because I didn't want any more pity looks since everybody knew what'd happened between me and TJ. Plus I'd been a little dramatic with my autumn sun hat and big sunglasses when I came in because I knew this would be my only opportunity to dress like the women in one of those nineties Lifetime movies.

When it was almost time to go I was so thankful for the day to be over. I'd tried to use my time wisely and make arrangements for our moving day, but like everything else Cam told me to relax and let him worry about the details so I did. At the sound of the music being turned off, I knew that the last customer had left the building because it was replaced with the sounds of the barbers hurriedly cleaning up their booths to get out of there. I was in the middle of stretching and putting everything back just the way I'd found it when I noticed Cree's toy clippers on the shelf. I didn't know what all he was bringing with him, but I knew for sure that he wouldn't want to forget them amid all the chaos that was going on.

I was walking over to put them in my purse when I suddenly heard Michelle's very loud outside voice yelling at Cam. She was hysterical and speaking quickly so I couldn't decipher everything, but I definitely picked up something about him choosing sides when he didn't know our family's history.

"Tillar ain't no damn saint either! That girl is always meddling in business that ain't hers when she needs to be minding how much food she's eating. My son is a hard worker and you had no problems with him until her fat, worthless ass came to town. Now you're okay with knowing that he could be going back to jail over this nonsense?!" she shouted at him, not even caring that she was humiliating me by putting our family drama on display for the barbers.

"You're lucky that jail is all that's gonna happen to him. If I had it my way, you would be planning a funeral right now so you better thank your daughter for saving his life," he said in an even tone and an eerie chill ran through the shop because everybody could tell that it wasn't just an idle threat.

It didn't seem to shake her though because she continued her hypercritical rant on me then looked surprised to see me there when I finally opened the heavy office door. She still didn't take anything back though and instead doubled down on her stance of me ruining everything since I'd gotten here.

"Really? I gave up my whole life to come here and help you and this is the thanks I get. I'm glad I see now that nothing I do will ever be enough for you so I'm done trying. And when you leave here and go back to your house that *I* saved, know that I only did it because of my father. It was never about you," I said just to be hurtful because having a healthy relationship with her was all I'd ever wanted.

"Oh boo fucking hoo. You think somebody

owes you just because your daddy died. Don't nobody owe you shit, Tillar! You always were competing with me for his attention back then. That was my husband! Why don't you get you one and stop mourning mine?"

"She already has one," Cam said interjecting on my behalf, "and you'll never have another one because nobody will ever put up with your miserable ass again!" he barked at her.

She balled up her fist and her mouth as she walked towards me like she was about to set it off, but Cam immediately stood in front of me. He made it clear that while he didn't want to hit her, he wasn't gonna let me get hit again either and that she could take that however she wanted to. The door to the shop suddenly swung open and everybody's eyes landed on TJ who'd apparently been waiting outside watching everything.

"You got the balls to walk up in here after what you did, man? I should fuck you up on principle," Cam said taking a step in his direction.

"Cam, no you promised. Please, let's just go," I begged him trying to get through to him, but he kept on his intended path as TJ cleared his throat to speak. And it was worthy to note that my brother suddenly had all the manners and respect in the world now that he was talking to a man who was a foot taller than him.

"Cam, I don't want no problems with you,

but watch how you talk to my mama--" he began but was cut off by the sound of Cam's left hand slapping him so hard that there seemed to be an echo to it as he fell to the floor.

"You like slapping women, huh? Get back up!" Cam yelled, but TJ looked scared for his life and wouldn't move an inch which only seemed to anger him more. Cam lifted his heavy Timberland boot and used it to kick him in the side with so much force that it sounded like a rib may have cracked. TJ hollered out for Michelle and she ran to his side just as the other barbers surrounded Cam to break it up.

"This is your fault!" Michelle yelled at me as she rocked a seriously injured TJ in her arms like he was a baby. "I knew I should have aborted your ass when I had the chance. As far as I'm concerned I only have one child now!"

"She don't need your fucked up family anyway. I'm her family now!" Cam said from behind the guys who had formed something like a blockade around him. They were a little too late though and I could tell from the unsympathetic looks on their faces that they thought TJ deserved what he got.

"Oh you a real tough man, huh? Going after my son for that bitch," Michelle said about me like she was referring to a stranger and not her own daughter.

"Hell yeah. I'm always gonna protect her and you better watch how you talk about her before I aim for his neck next time," he warned her, but she seemed emboldened at the fact that the other men wouldn't let him through again.

"You couldn't even protect your own daughter. How you think you gonna protect mine?" she asked in a haughty tone and I gasped out loud. I had told Michelle about Cree after their big argument, hoping that she would have some sympathy towards Cam, but never in a million years did I think she would use the information like this.

I looked up at Cam and saw venom in his eyes before he suddenly charged through the guys towards Michelle. She quickly moved out of the way, but it became clear that he wasn't going after her when he struck TJ again then mounted him on the floor and repeatedly punched him. It seemed like since he couldn't put his hands on her that he decided to settle for the next best thing. I could tell from the drastic change in his demeanor that the Cam I knew had left the building because it looked like something else took over his body. I had never seen anything like this from him and it scared me to know he had this inside of him.

After what seemed like a long but difficult struggle the guys managed to pull him off of TJ and into his office, but his bloody and nearly raw knuckles clung to the door frame trying to finish what he'd started. Michelle's cries seemed even louder than the eventual police and ambulance sirens that came from outside, but soon enough my ears were numb to it all as I walked out of the shop and left all of the chaos behind me.

9

THE GRAND BALL

Yet another sleepless night had me feeling like a zombie by the time the sun came up, but with everything that was going on I knew I couldn't stay here any longer so I did the only thing that I could think of. I packed. I organized my clothes by fabric and color and season until everything looked just about the same as it did when I'd brought it from Atlanta months ago. The only piece that had no place to go was the beautiful blue gown that hung mockingly on the empty silver rack. It was much too heavy to sway from the breeze being brought in through the open window, but my slow calming rocking almost gave the same effect.

From the beginning I knew that this whole thing was too good to be true because just like Sofia, deep down I'd still felt that balls and happily ever afters weren't meant for women like me either. And I didn't know if Cam and I would be able to recover from something like this or how he would react to me leaving him the night before, but for now I was just waiting for Nicole's flight to get in. Even though I knew that no ball would be taking place tonight, I selfishly didn't call her to tell her to cancel it because I wanted her to accompany me back on my drive and I needed somebody to be here just for me.

Early that morning I'd gotten a text from Reese letting me know that she was going to bail Cam out and I'd heard his key turning in the lock behind me, but still when I turned to face him it was startling to see him standing there with TJ's blood still on his shirt. For a full minute we just looked at each other before he looked around then broke the painful silence.

"You only packed your stuff," he said simply as he took a seat on the edge of the bed.

"Yeah. I didn't know what all you wanted to take with you or if you were still going or…if I even still wanted you to go," I said honestly before he lowered his head in shame.

"I get it. And I'm sorry that I broke my promise to you, Tills, but if you can forgive me for this I swear I'll do whatever I have to do to make everything right. I'll cover TJ's medical bills. I'll apologize to him and to your mother. Just please don't let this be the end of us. Please," he begged me from his seated position while I stood to my feet.

"Cam, what happened last night wasn't

okay. I know you just wanted to make TJ pay for what he did to me, but there's still a line and you crossed it big time. I mean roughing him up and maybe giving him a black eye would've been one thing, but what you did was unacceptable."

"I know and I promise I'm gonna get help for the part of me that's capable of doing what I did to him. But just for right now, I need you to tell me we're not over."

I sighed as I walked over and stood in front of his open legs. He reached out and pulled me close until our bodies melded into one with me cradling his head on my chest and his arms wrapped around me so tightly that it was hard to breathe.

"We're not over because you were right. We should've left the other night and none of this would've even happened. I'm just so ready to leave this city for good and never look back again. I hate it here."

"Well what about tonight?" he asked and I shrugged.

"We don't have to do it anymore. My only plans now involve getting you packed and getting us both to Georgia in one piece, not going to some stupid party."

"But I thought it was a ball," he said lightheartedly, but instead it aggravated me because I was starting to see that Michelle wasn't completely wrong about me ruining lives while I was here. I hadn't even begun to think about how all of this would affect Tiffa and the boys let alone Cam's future.

"I'm glad you think that me fucking up your life is funny," I said as I tried to step away from him, but he held onto me even tighter.

"What are you talking about? How have you fucked up my life?"

"Look at this whole mess of a situation that you're in. I know how much it meant that you had always stayed out of trouble and now you're gonna have an assault charge following you everywhere you go."

"It's nothing. The cops around here know me and they know why I did that and they're on my side. One of them even already told Reese that they're trying to get it dropped to a Class C misdemeanor since it's my first time and then I'll just have to pay a fine," he said thinking that it would make things better, but it didn't. "Last night wasn't your fault, Tills. I let my temper get the best of me, but I'm not letting you take responsibility for my actions. Not when you've added so much to my life in comparison to one bad night," he explained, but I just scoffed.

"What have I added? I've literally only taken from you since we got together."

"No. You gave me everything. Shit I forgot

that I even knew how to love somebody because I didn't want to again until I met you," he said as he put his mouth close to mine then looked down at my body. "Look at all of these curves. I knew the job would be dangerous when I took it," he teased me and I playfully bit his lip.

"I guess you did tell me that you were Superman when we met so I shouldn't be too surprised that you keep trying to save me." He smiled then asked again if we would still have the ball. I thought it over for a second then agreed because I figured things couldn't possibly get any worse than they were now.

"Good because nobody deserves what I planned for tonight more than you," he said sincerely as he kissed my lips and I could tell that it wasn't just because he'd spent so much time and money on the event. He just genuinely wanted to see me happy and enjoying myself.

"Are you hungry?" I asked when his growling stomach interrupted our smooch.

"Yeah, but I just got out of prison so right now all I want is you," he said making me laugh for the first time in days and it was much needed after how difficult and emotionally draining things had been.

"Cam, you were not in prison and I am not about to let you use being in a holding cell overnight as street credit."

"Why not? I could finally start rapping and give Cam'Ron some competition."

"Please don't," I begged him as I pulled his soiled shirt over his head to get him ready to go shower. I still had to pick up Nicole soon and I didn't want him meeting her wearing my brother's blood.

"Wait. Check this out. Straight off the dome, Tills," he said being silly and I was glad to see him in such good spirits so fast. "*Once upon a dime/There was a girl named Tillar/She was so fine/And wasn't nobody realer*'. What you think?"

"I think you should keep your day job. Now let's get you cleaned up ASAP, Rocky," I said throwing a double entendre his way about another rapper from Harlem and the *Rocky* movies since he'd been fighting.

"Yeah your bars are definitely better than mine," he admitted, but before he could get inside the bathroom he came back over to apologize for everything once more and to thank me for giving him another chance. The way his bare warm skin and lips felt against my body made me tingle inside, but I shooed him away to get ready.

We were a little late getting Nicole from the airport, but she didn't seem to mind too much because she smiled big when she spotted me. Things had been happening so fast that I didn't have time to catch her up on the last few days so when she saw Cam's bandaged hands reaching for her luggage and the bruises on my face she instantly thought the worst. Her expression let me know that she was about to go off so I quickly explained the situation to her before she could make a scene and believe me her little itty bitty self could make a scene.

Like magic, her anger disappeared before my eyes and she just held me and told me that she was glad I was finally going to be done with Michelle. She said she was always afraid to overstep boundaries by telling me the truth about her before especially since she was on a relentless search to find a mother that had given her up. We stood there hugging and crying for a minute not even caring that we were holding up cars behind us because this was long overdue. When she saw Cam rubbing my back for emotional support and getting teary-eyed at our moment, she just laughed to herself.

"You're perfect for her overly sensitive ass," she said looking up at him. "But I'm not a crier so this never happened, alright?"

"Same," he said before wiping his eyes then they shook on it and agreed. I smiled at how dramatic they were being about showing vulnerability in front of somebody besides me because from the start neither was ever afraid to show it to me.

Nicole was an expert at covering scars and her tattoos when she did cosplay so she volunteered to handle my makeup for the night before we dropped her off at her hotel which was just a couple blocks away from us.

When Cam and I got back in, I was glad to hear that his brother Chase was coming with their grandmother and getting a rental car because it meant that I could finally get some shut eye in. I hadn't slept well in days so that extended nap was right on time.

Cam was still snoring when I rolled over and looked at the time, but he woke up when he felt me get out of bed to find my sketchbook in my packed belongings. It was getting dark out and it was almost time to begin getting ready for the ball, but I had something I wanted to work on first. He laid there and watched me for a while before yawning and sitting up in bed. I quickly turned to a blank page because I'd never let him or anybody besides Nicole see my ideas and to my knowledge he had never peeked in it before.

Clearly in a playful mood, he swiped my pencil then began to draw stick figures of us on the new page. I thought it was cute how bad he was at this as he drew a big T and A on me.

"Is that really all you see when you look at me?" I asked trying to sound serious before he immediately looked over at me to say otherwise because he'd bought it.

"No. I was just kidding. You know I love your body and how confident you are, but that's not all I love about you," he assured me as he rubbed my leg.

"Is there some reason I shouldn't be confident about my body?" I asked to further test his response because obviously my weight wasn't an issue with him. He could barely keep his hands off of me even when it wasn't sexual, but he held onto me during sex and got lost in his admiration of me.

"Nah. You know what I'm saying. I hear guys talking about women always wanting the lights off and shit. They bring their insecurities to bed with them. You don't and I like that about you."

"Prove it then. Close your eyes and tell me something else that you love about me," I challenged him. He closed his eyes and accidentally touched my breasts before finding my heart and letting his hand rest there.

"I love how big your heart is. You love everybody even the people who don't deserve it from you and I wish I could be more like you," he said sincerely.

"Really?"

"Yeah. Now your turn." As a gag I closed my eyes then reached under the covers to touch his penis. "Be serious Tills," he demanded before I reached up and touched his mouth.

"I like how I can feel the love that you have for me in your words because it sets the tone for our relationship and you always back them up with your actions. I've been in situations before where that wasn't always the case and I never knew how much I needed it until I met you." By the time I'd finished talking, I decided that I would finally let him see the things that I'd been working on in the sketchbook. About half of it was for work, but the other half was fashion drawings so I told him about the boutique that me and Nicole had been saving for before I got here.

"These are really good," he complimented as he looked through it amazed that he'd actually seen me in some of the clothes. "You and Nic are mad talented. Let me know when y'all get to the investor stage because I'm in," he said pledging his support.

"Thanks, but we've been in the dreaming phase so long that it's looking like it's never gonna happen."

"Why not? If this is what you want to do, I think you should do it."

"I want to and it's a nice dream, but realistically I wouldn't even know where to start. It takes way more to run a boutique than just drawing and tailoring."

"Figure it out then," he said like it was so simple and I rolled my eyes. "So you're just gonna go back and live the same life you were living before?"

"Hey! I like my life."

"You should love it though."

"I'll love it more now since you'll be there with me," I said as I kissed him. "And thanks for the encouragement, but I like my job. It's stable. I have great benefits. They love me there and as you can see they're always willing to accommodate me so why would I leave that for something that may not even work out?"

"Because you have to at least try. And I think you only like your job so much because it gives you an excuse to pick out dope clothes every day." I smiled at his accusation.

"No, that's only part of it. If I did this, I would be starting completely over. I would have to go back to school for two years. The closest fashion program is about thirty minutes away from my condo which means at least an hour commute back and forth with traffic. I barely know how to sew as is. It would just take too much sacrifice."

"I thought you didn't know where to start," he challenged after I inadvertently let it slip that I'd looked into it before. "You sacrificed everything to come back here for your mother.

Why can't you do the same for yourself?"

"Because it's crazy and I have these little things called bills that come every month and they need to be paid or else I'll be out on my behind." He scoffed like what I was saying was completely ludicrous.

"You know I'm gonna handle the bills anyway so you can't use that as an excuse," he said sternly and it made me grateful for how complex he was compared to other men. He was old-fashioned enough to know that he was supposed to protect and provide but also new school enough to know that providing didn't mean he could control me and I appreciated it.

"For two whole years?"

"Forever because I just want to take care of you. You being in my life made my dreams come true so now I want to help you make yours become a reality too." It all sounded nice, but I was rightfully reluctant to let myself be financially vulnerable to anybody. He could walk away at any time and I would be screwed. He must've read my mind because he instantly added on, "Would putting your name on my accounts make you feel more secure?"

"Why would you do that? We're not getting married."

"At the rate we're going, we'll be there soon," he said casually, but my worst nightmare popped into my head.

"Cam, if tonight is one of those surprise weddings you better let me know now or I'm bringing tennis shoes to run away just like Julia Roberts did," I warned him and he laughed.

"It's not. Trust me this was hard enough to plan by myself so I'm letting you do the wedding shit on your own," he assured me before searching for his phone.

"What are you doing?"

"I gotta call the pastor and tell him not to come now," he joked until he saw that I wasn't amused. "I'm kidding. I've got something better in mind when the time comes, but hypothetically speaking would you have said yes if I did ask tonight?" he inquired sounding unsure of himself and for some reason his full, furrowed brows were really doing it for me now.

"Wow you're really taking this Prince Charming cosplay to heart, aren't you?" I teased him, but he wanted me to be for real.

"C'mon answer me. I don't want to be making forever plans with somebody who doesn't see forever when they look at me. Tell me that you see forever in me too, Tills."

"I do and it scares the shit out of me," I told him honestly before he chuckled.

"Don't be scared," he told me simply and I promised to try not to be.

"So what about you? What are you gonna do differently when we get to Atlanta? I mean I know you always wanted to be like your dad, but is being a barber all you ever wanted to be?"

"Yeah. I love being a barber. The customers. The trash talk. The energy. But I did always want to write a book. Just to see if I could do it, you know? To see if I could come up with something that would connect with people."

"With as many as you read I'm sure you could do it in your sleep. What kind of stuff do you want to write?"

"Maybe romance. I'm pretty good at it in real life sometimes," he bragged on himself.

"I think so too and I've got a great first story for you so how about after you get the new shop up and running, let's get you in a creative writing class or something like that?" I suggested and he nodded before kissing my shoulder. A quick look at the time had him climbing out of bed and bringing me along with him.

"We gotta get up, Tills. It's almost time to ball out."

♛

All day I'd ignored phone calls from Jordan, Sofia and Michelle because I didn't want to talk about what happened last night with TJ and Cam in any capacity. I did return Diane's text inquiring about if the ball was still on when I saw it, but after that I put my phone back down and started my transformation into the princess that Nicole had dubbed Thickerella. The moniker definitely suited me in this dress and I planned on wearing it out in hashtags when I eventually posted pictures to social media.

She had also hooked up my hair and had my makeup somehow looking light and natural even though it was caked on to cover my bruises. When I finally saw her finished product in the mirror, I couldn't believe that I was looking at a reflection of myself. I mean I was a stunner on any given day, but this was next level and honestly I felt that it was almost wasted on a Halloween costume because I was serving face and body from every direction as I spun around in the beautiful sparkly blue gown. Just as I'd predicted, I wasn't able to find any glass slippers in my size, but I threw on a pair of sparkly blue pumps that I already owned and it still completed the look perfectly.

I'd begged Nicole to wear something just as nice too, but she insisted on letting her little cheeks out and wearing her Chun-Li costume that she'd made for the event she was missing to be here. I respected it because this was the only time of year that the rest of us dressed as someone else since she cosplayed all year round.

Cam had left out much earlier than me to go see his grandmother and he took his costume with him because he would be getting ready with her and Chase. Really I knew he just wanted to see me for the first time with everybody else though because he was going overboard with the ball theme for what would end up being just a fancy Halloween party. I decided to humor him though and got into character as well, but it wasn't like I had much of a choice when I heard a little commotion outside.

His block was never very noisy, but it had never seemed so quiet before I heard what sounded like hooves hitting the pavement and loud whinnying through the window. Nicole and I exchanged looks before going over to get a look as a couple trick-or-treaters approached the white horse-drawn carriage that was now parked in front of Cam's building.

"You didn't?!" I exclaimed to him after he'd answered the phone with a telling hello.

"I did! Now hurry up and get here, Cinderella."

"That's Thickerella to you, Charming," I corrected him as I glanced at Nicole who was already halfway out the door because she wanted to see if the driver would let her ride the horse first. I told Cam that I'd see him soon and scooted after her to keep her wannabe daredevil behind from breaking her neck if he actually let her go through with it.

On the way over I found myself wishing that we lived further away than the three blocks from the venue because the ride seemed to be over just as quickly as it began. The ball was in full swing by the time we arrived and the music could be heard from the sidewalk. I could tell that Cam had spared no expense when I saw the beautiful fairy lights that lined the walls and even the nearly bare fall trees in the courtyard. It was breathtaking and even tough as nails Nicole told me that I had done well when I picked him because it was so beautiful that we actually should have been getting married here. It was a sweet thought, I mused to myself as I took in the sight before me.

I'd walked passed this place countless times over the last six months, but I had no idea that it could look like this or that he had something like this in him. But I guess it was just like how he'd seen something in me that first day because all this time I thought hanging around barbershops long enough just guaranteed me a haircut, not the man of my dreams.

The driver had went to help Nicole out on her side first so I was startled when I felt something touch my white gloved hand. I settled down when I saw that it was my very own, grinning from ear to ear, Prince Charming here to help me step out of the ornate buggy.

"This isn't canon, Cam. I'm supposed to be at the top of the stairs when you see me."

"So what? I had to see you in this thing. You look so beautiful, Tills," he said as my feet hit the ground. The second we were securely out of the carriage, the driver climbed back up and commanded the horse to go while there were no cars in the intersection. "Don't worry. He'll be back for us at midnight," he said before I could even think of our ride home then opened the door for Nicole to go inside and closed it after her.

"What are we waiting for? It's getting dark so I know it's almost past your grandmother's bedtime," I cracked because I knew that the elderly liked to be asleep early.

"I'm telling her you said that."

"You better not or else I'm telling Diane that you said your sweet potato pies are better than hers," I teased him as I adjusted his sash.

"But you said it first!" he exclaimed making me laugh out loud.

"So what? Who do you think she's gonna believe? Me or you?" I playfully warned him before we both agreed to keep our lips zipped. I headed for the door before he stopped me.

"Look at us, Tills. You and me...we're

classic," he said as he pointed at our reflections in the long window of the venue. Nicole had done such a good job with his costume as well because the gold epaulettes and accents on his ivory jacket and red pants looked so official and glitzy that I would have believed he was the real prince of some obscure country.

"No you're classic. I'm sexy," I said turning to the side to let him see the long revealing slit. I couldn't decide if I wanted to do a traditional or risqué Cinderella so I'd done a little of both and depending on which angle I was seen from, I could go from princess to pin-up girl in mere seconds.

"Damn right you are. I really lucked out because you're smart and have a good personality too, but I'm not gonna lie. I would've put up with you for a long time even if you were dumb because damn. Look at these legs," he said as he shamelessly felt me up then whispered in my ear. "And I came prepared just in case Thickerella wants to make one last stop in the shop after midnight."

"Doubt it. Princesses don't have quickies, Cam, and I'm not letting *you* break another chair before we leave. I saw Reese looking at me funny after the last one."

"You broke that chair," he accused for the millionth time as he finally opened the door for me, but I had no rebuttal because it was ball time.

There were some people scattered about inside, but the real party seemed to be in the courtyard like I knew it'd be because it was so gorgeous with all the lights and flowers. He let me take it all in and stop to speak to a few people before bringing me over to the table where Chase was. I'd extended invitations to a couple coworkers of mine including Erica who I saw was dressed as an adorable pink Power Ranger.

Even with the bad Jheri Curl wig on I could still see the resemblance between them because Chase looked like a slightly leaner version of Cam with less facial hair. When I got closer I realized that he was supposed to be Samuel L. Jackson's character in *Pulp Fiction* and it was a fitting costume choice because it didn't seem like he wanted to be here and old Sam was always angry about something.

He stood to his feet when he saw us and I stared for a second too long because it was always interesting to see siblings who looked so much alike but still had clear differences. Cam introduced us then helped me sit before I asked him to get me something to drink.

"Chase, keep an eye on her for me. I see the way Candyman keeps looking at my baby," Cam joked about one of the guys from the shop before leaving us alone.

I made small talk with Chase about his flight and the weather in Chicago before I inquired about their other brother Chris's whereabouts. I knew neither of them had the best relationship with Cam so he wasn't upset at his absence, but I still wanted to fish for clues about why they weren't very close. Before I'd figured that it was something personal that Cam would share when he was ready, but now I was back in snoop mode.

"This isn't his kind of thing. It's not mine either, but Gram wanted to come so we flipped for it and I lost. I really need to stop picking heads," Chase answered before chuckling bitterly.

"Well I'm sorry you got roped in, but I am glad to finally meet you and I hope you enjoy yourself tonight," I said sincerely because I didn't want to have the same discord with Cam's family that we'd had with mine.

"I will," he said distractedly as he watched Nicole walk by with her phone up filming for one of her accounts. "Isn't that Cosplay Bae?" he asked me calling her by her internet viral meme name before I nodded. He predictably followed up by asking if I knew her.

"Yep. She's my best friend so don't even think about it," I told him because Cam had already warned me all about him and Chris and their ways. It was obvious that he'd seen her cute little booty and thought since she'd worn a revealing costume that she would be open for sex when it couldn't have been further from the truth. There was nothing she loved more than to make men beg for something that they would never get to experience.

"Introduce me and I'll put in a good word for you with Gram," he said trying to bribe me, but I was as unbought and unbossed as my shero Shirley Chisholm.

"Your grandmother already adores me," I told him matter-of-factly.

"Not after Cam got arrested dealing with you," he countered and my smug smile fell to my feet because I didn't know he'd told them about the fight. I had already sensed that Cam didn't really like him so much and now I could see why. "Now about your friend…"

"Sure thing," I said sweetly as Cam came back over and sat a glass of wine down in front of me. I was just pretending to play nice with him because I couldn't wait to see Nicole get his hopes up then finish him just like the real Chun-Li.

"Gram has been in the bathroom for a while. Can you go check on her for me?" Cam asked after I'd taken a sip of wine. I agreed then gulped down the rest now that I knew she wasn't as fond of me as I'd thought before.

It took me a minute to track down the

bathroom in this big place, but when I found it I heard a woman's voice asking if anybody heard her coming from inside. The other people nearby probably couldn't because of the music playing.

"Is that you, Ms. Ida?" I asked as I entered and saw Cam's grandmother half wearing a conservative take on a Tina Turner costume. She had so much personality over the phone that I was surprised to see that she was just as small as Nicole and I was amazed at how her lineage had grown so tall after only one generation.

"Well thank heavens. I've been calling for help for fifteen minutes and I left my cellular phone in my pocketbook with Chasen," she said sounding ancient even though she didn't look it. I quickly came to her rescue and fixed the zipper issue she was having and had her looking as good as new in no time.

"There you go. And here I thought I would be the only one showing a little leg tonight," I teased her after she'd thanked me and I knew she was grateful that it was me who found her and not a complete stranger.

"Now that we've got that settled, let's see if I can get the truth out of you about Cameron's arrest," she said in a less than pleasant tone and I was taken aback at how fast she had switched up on me.

"What did he tell you?" I asked before I said

anything contradictory to his version of events.

"He said that the incident revolved around a misunderstanding with a relative of yours and that he was defending you from an attack."

"Honestly that about sums it all up," I said going along with it even though he had fibbed a little because I wasn't in any imminent danger when the fight happened.

"Oh I know my Cameron so I assumed as much. You know he never did lie to me as a child, but he loved to leave certain things out and I just don't want him involved in anything that could land him in serious trouble."

"I understand. And I know that Cam has been through a lot before me, but I give you my word that everything will be fine once we get settled in Atlanta. I'll take care of him just like he's always taking care of me."

"I'm happy to hear that and now we can begin moving on from this. You'll be a Logan in no time and us Logans let bygones be bygones so I want to welcome you to the family, Tillar," she said warmly as she hugged me and I appreciated it because she was his only mother figure and her approval meant everything.

"That means a lot coming from you because I know how close you two are," I told her as we separated.

"I'm not sure if Cameron told you this, but I

had a minor health scare after my son passed earlier this year," she shared with me and I offered her my condolences about Cam's dad. "Losing him made me realize that I'm not sure how much longer I have on this earth. But I would leave here just as happy as can be if I knew that my boys would stop feuding and recognize that they're all each other has now. Well Cameron has you and I'm praying that those other two grandsons of mine quit running around and get it together soon."

"I'm sure they will," I said even though I could see that Chase in particular was in no hurry to settle down. There was a knock on the ladies' room door.

"Is everything alright in there?" Cam asked while slightly peeking his head inside

"We're fine. Just having girl talk," I assured him before shooing him away because we were just on our way out. She just smiled at us then headed for the door.

"I'm glad he finally found somebody."

"Me too," I told her as we left the restroom with looped arms.

When we got back to the courtyard and spotted Chase hovering over Nicole, she mused to herself that he had found a princess too. I wanted to ask if we were looking at the same two people because Nicole was clearly not interested, but I let her have her dream as I went to get another drink.

Diane arrived fashionably late and made quite an entrance when I saw that she was dressed as Whitney Houston's version of the fairy godmother. I was disappointed to see her without Tiffa, but I understood her absence considering what'd happened. Without saying a word, we embraced for a long while before I brought her over to introduce her to Cam's family.

"This is so spectacular, Cameron," she complimented him and didn't seem to even be upset at the situation between him and TJ because it was mostly justified. "If I didn't know any better I would think you two were getting married here tonight."

"No ma'am. Not with all of these ghouls and goblins running around. Besides I'm leaving all of the real wedding planning to Tillar soon," he said looking down at me and the people around us began commenting on him not shying away from marriage talk. It didn't even faze me because he had made his intentions crystal clear long ago.

"Reese, you gonna make that trip down to the A to be my best woman? It might not be that long," he told her and I thought it was a little rude considering that Chase was standing there, but again I knew they weren't very close.

"Let me see what the bridesmaids are looking like and I'll let you know," Reese cracked and put me right back at ease.

After we got all of the important family stuff out of the way the real fun finally began. I went and stood at the top of the modern loft stairs for my picture to be taken because I knew I would be doing the ball a disservice by not having at least one iconic pose from the movie. By the time I was finished with my impromptu photoshoot I was starving and of course as the world's best Prince Charming, Cam fed me finger foods all night to keep my white gloves clean.

He thought he was slick by having the DJ sneak in little old school sets every now and then, but I thought it was cute how him and his grandmother enjoyed it more than anybody else. After getting one final dance in with her, he told her that it was passed her bedtime with a covert wink at me then sent her on her way. Cam and Chase gave each other a stiff hug before I suggested that Nicole get a ride with them as well since they were staying at the same hotel a few blocks over. She rolled her eyes at first but then followed them after we made plans to have breakfast before her flight home tomorrow.

It was getting close to midnight so almost everybody had left because Cam was adamant about the party ending at eleven-thirty. I thought it was just because of noise ordinances and him wanting to sneak next door for some late night royal love making so I sat and talked to the nice owner while the venue's clean-up crew got to work.

After everything was put back into place inside I wandered back out to the courtyard to search for Cam since it seemed like he'd disappeared. It was then that I noticed the DJ hadn't left yet and was obviously waiting around on something. I had been planning to kiss him at midnight so when my alarm went off and I still didn't see him I was disappointed until I heard the loud church bells from St. Michaels ringing off into the night. I didn't know how, but I knew he had something to do with it and I was sure that the whole neighborhood would be wondering what the hell was going on because they only rang on Sunday mornings. His secret was safe with me though because he'd remembered to get such a small but important detail about the movie right.

"Would you look at that?" he said from behind me and I turned to look at him. "The clock struck twelve and you're still a princess. And since you don't have anywhere to run off to, that means you've got time to have one more dance with me," he said with his hand out and I took it. With my hands around his neck and his at my waist, we had our final slow dance to The Whispers and he softly recited the words in my ear as he promised to make me his wife. I knew I had scoffed at the idea of a surprise wedding before, but in that instance I said "I do" to him in my heart because I knew that there was no better love for me than his.

He hadn't asked, but I wanted to let him know what I'd discussed with his grandmother while we were alone since she had officially welcomed me to the Logan clan.

"I think I'm good with her again. We had a nice talk," I assured him.

"You always were, Tills. I mean at first she was worried that we were moving too fast, but she was fine when I explained that this city didn't feel like home for me until you got here. That's how I know I'll be good wherever I go as long as we're together," he said sincerely and it wasn't until then that I realized everybody from the shop had shown up tonight except for Lauren and I knew that he had something to do with it.

"Did your little secret admirer Lauren have other plans tonight?" I asked as he spun me around, but he just shrugged. "C'mon Cam. I know she wouldn't miss this for the world."

"Alright. I told her to sit this one out."

"Why?" I asked and I hoped that I hadn't come off too crazy back when I'd wrongfully accused him of cheating with her.

"Because I don't know if you're picking up on some women's intuition thing that I'll never be able to understand, but I do know that she makes you uncomfortable and I didn't want you to feel like that tonight so I didn't invite her."

"How did you get like this?" I asked amazed that he was how he was at such a young age. Most men would have tried to make me feel like I was being difficult or even paraded her around to make me feel jealous and get under my skin, but not him. He acknowledged that something was a problem to me so he got rid of it and that was the end of it.

"It's simple. I know I'm gonna spend the rest of my life with you so I'll do whatever I have to do to make you feel secure."

"I swear you better keep this same mentality when we get to Atlanta," I warned him because I had seen firsthand the lengths that some of those women went to get a taken man.

"I'll keep it wherever we go as long as you tell Usher to watch his back," he promised and I smiled before we suddenly heard the horse begin to whinny. I thought it was just leftover jitters from maybe hearing the loud bells a couple minutes before, but it was something else this time because I heard someone yell fire.

Trouble had been sleeping all day, but somebody had clearly just woken it up.

When we got around to the front of the building to see what was going on, I saw that it wasn't the flower shop that'd caught on fire. Instead there were dark flames and smoke coming from the waiting area in the barbershop. The carriage driver was on the phone with the emergency dispatcher explaining that he'd just seen a man break the shop window then throw something inside. It didn't take a rocket scientist to deduce that my brother had something to do with this so I looked up at Cam ready to apologize for his pride and joy burning before our eyes, but he wasn't by my side anymore.

In an instant I watched him run over to the door to unlock it with his keys. There was a lot of smoke coming from the left side so he struggled to open it as he fanned the smoggy air away from his face.

"What the hell are you doing? You can't go in there!" I frantically yelled at him before I inhaled a little smoke from standing so close, but I coughed it out then stepped down wind to avoid it happening again.

"Tillar, stay back! I'm just going to get Cree's clippers and I'll be right back out," he assured me before disappearing inside because the smoke was so heavy I couldn't make out the shapes of anything in there. My instincts wanted to go in after him, but the carriage driver pulled me away from the growing flames.

I figuratively held my breath waiting for

him as long as I could until I felt like I'd turn as blue as my dress, but there were still no signs of Cam when I peered through the window again. I heard sirens blaring in the distance, but he had already been in there long enough so I knew something was wrong.

He must've been looking for the clippers on the shelf where he always kept them, but I suddenly remembered that I'd moved them the other night because I planned on bringing them with me. I knew going in would be dangerous for me too, but I felt responsible for him now so I remained hopeful as I tore off the train to my dress to cover my face then ran in after him.

The actual fire was still contained to one side, but the smoke was so thick in there that it easily covered the whole shop. I carefully shuffled through it all to make it back to his office where I found him lying on the floor with the clippers beside him just outside of his grasp. I wanted to panic, but I did my best to stay steady as I stuffed them between my breasts for safekeeping then began trying to pull him out.

He was so heavy to move, but I must've had a rush of adrenaline because I was able to drag him by his feet to Lauren's desk before I started feeling lightheaded myself. Right when I felt like I would be joining him on the floor soon I heard the firefighters out front and thanked my lucky stars because I couldn't go on any longer.

Cam and I were both brought over to the ambulance and the blue fabric was removed from my face so that I could be given oxygen. One of the paramedics tried her best to get me to relax, but I couldn't because I could see the others performing CPR on Cam only it didn't seem to be helping.

"Cam, please get up!" I begged him even though he lay seemingly lifeless on the stretcher.

"Listen Princess, I know you're scared, but you're going to have to take care of you first and let my friends here work on the Prince. Can you do that for me?" she asked as she placed the mask back over my nose and mouth.

They began talking in complicated medical jargon that even the most devoted *ER* fan wouldn't be able to understand, but finally after one last round of CPR he began coughing so harshly that it sounded like he'd smoked three packs a day for twenty years. After that they gave him oxygen as well through a mask and I could see the worry in his eyes as he looked around for me and tried to sit up.

"Calm down sir. You're going to be just fine thanks to Cinderella here," she assured him. I had never been so thankful for my long arms as I was now as I reached out for his hand and squeezed it.

"You saved me?" he asked in a very raspy

voice after they'd loaded us in the ambulance, but I was just so happy he was okay that I couldn't get words out. "I'm Superman. I'm supposed to save you."

"You already did, Cam. You already did."

10

HAPPILY EVER AFTER

Old Town had literally and figuratively been set ablaze after news of the fire spread all over the local news and social media. When Cam heard that the flames eventually spread to the flower shop, the first thing he wanted to do was make sure that the owner was alright because he knew she filled orders at night sometimes. I told him that she was fine and reminded him that she was at the ball with us since he'd clearly forgotten.

Even though he'd hit his head on his desk when he passed out, he didn't have amnesia or anything like that. He was just a little confused about everything that'd happened and honestly so was I and I was awake for everything. But along with his disorientation he was hoarse, short of breath and coughing up a lot of mucus, but luckily the small burn on his arm wasn't too bad and already seemed to be healing up nicely.

The police had already been to the hospital twice to get a statement from him, but since his speaking wasn't that clear and he was too weak to write, it'd yet to happen. But since the cause of the fire was arson they had been questioning everybody close to him.

"Do you know anyone who would want to cause Mr. Logan harm? A disgruntled customer that's capable of arson?" one officer asked me before another interrupted him.

"Might this have anything to do with the altercation we picked him up for involving your brother, a Timothy "TJ" Reed?" he asked and in that instant I knew that I had to choose between Cam and my family, but the decision wasn't as hard as I thought it would be because the choice would always be the person who had never hurt me.

"I believe he was involved. I was at the ball so obviously I didn't see him do it, but I'm positive that he was behind the whole thing."

"We think so too," he said before pulling out his phone to show me something. "Is there anything that you can identify from these photos or video?"

The surveillance tape from the bank across the street showed a limping man walking around the horse and carriage then struggling to start a fire out front. He had accidentally lit his arm when he tossed a bottle into the building, but he quickly patted it out before stumbling away out of frame. I couldn't see his face, but I could recognize those hips anywhere and knew that it was indeed my brother that I was watching. I didn't tell the officers that though and just pointed out the black Nike hoodie that I'd seen him in several times. That seemed to be all they needed to hear and they left shortly after.

I could tell that Cam's grandmother didn't want to leave his side, but she, Chase and Nicole had already stayed an extra day to be here with us and they were on the verge of missing their new flights if they didn't go soon. She was finally ready to go once the doctors told us that he would be fine after getting consistent rest and breathing treatments for a few days, but before she left she made me promise to take care of him as she hugged me with all the strength in her little body.

"I heard that you snitched for me," Cam said weakly when it was just us in his room later on when he was awake and feeling a little better. His voice was still really raspy though.

"I did and I've officially lost all of my street credit thanks to you so good thing we're leaving town soon," I said playfully even though I wasn't feeling up to it. "Cam, now do you see how I'm ruining your life?"

"This isn't your fault either. I put myself in danger and it was for nothing because I couldn't even get what I went in there for."

"Actually," I said before I remembered the embarrassing place that I'd stashed the clippers when I found them, "I smuggled them out for you after I dragged you out. They're waiting for you safely at home," I told him before he summoned all the strength that he could as he sat up in the bed and kissed me.

"I love you so fucking much, Tills!" he said excitedly and I knew that he meant it.

That night when we were watching the news in Cam's hospital room I found out with the rest of the world that my brother had been arrested for arson, resisting arrest, assaulting a police officer, and half a dozen other crimes that all sounded the same.

Cam wanted to know how I felt about everything, but I told him I was fine and was just concerned about his shop. He assured me that his insurance would cover repairing everything and it would be like this whole thing never happened. I listened as he talked, but I knew that wasn't true because this thing had rocked the whole neighborhood and my family. Buildings could get rebuilt anytime, but relationships were a lot harder to repair.

I was so relieved to see that Cam's recovery didn't take very long. It seemed like forever, but he had only inhaled smoke for a couple of minutes before I pulled him out. He was mainly still just a little hoarse, but he was sent home in a couple days with inhalers and antibiotics for extended treatment.

While he got better, I made him take a break from reading and we stayed in and watched some of my favorite old movies on the projector. We even watched Cinderella again and he was now claiming that his modern botany themed ball was even grander than the one in the movie.

"That's a reach, but it was really beautiful and I wish I could live in that courtyard," I said closing my eyes to imagine how perfect all the plants and lights looked that night.

"I guess I'll have to get you a house with a courtyard then, huh?" he said simply without a hint of sarcasm.

"You know one of these days you're gonna have to give me a breakdown on where you got all of this money from," I said even though I could tell from meeting his grandmother and Chase that the whole family was pretty well off. But Cam wasn't the bragging type and I knew he wanted to be known as a hard worker more than anything.

"It's not a secret. We weren't supposed to get our trusts until thirty, but my dad and Gram gave me an advance on mine when I got married so that I could buy a house. Chase and Chris have been hating me ever since," he joked with a hearty cough.

"So that's the big deal with you guys? Money?" I asked trying not to sound too judgmental since I had no room to talk about a dysfunctional sibling relationship, but I hated to hear that theirs was over something as silly as that.

"Nah. Gram moved theirs up to twenty-five because they kept complaining and everything was good for a while, but now they're mad that my old man left me the record collection knowing that they wouldn't even listen to them like I do."

"Still, maybe they wanted a piece of him too," I offered trying to see things from their points of view.

"That's not it. Before he passed he asked us all what we wanted. Chase picked the car. Chris got his jewelry. I chose the records so they're mine now fair and square."

"And you would rather be right than try to meet them in the middle?"

"Pretty much. If they need me for anything then I would be there in a second, but brothers or not, they're just not the type of dudes that I rock with anyway so it's no sweat off my back. Maybe when they get a little more mature we can try to fix shit, but until then this is how it's gonna be," he said evenly, but I could tell that their lack of closeness bothered him some. I decided to let it go for the time being though because we had a long day of driving south tomorrow so we both needed to get a full night's rest.

And even though he hadn't been going anywhere he still hadn't slacked on his little nighttime routine for his beard and I thought it was so cute. He was just about all better, but he'd come to enjoy me doing it for him since he loved it when I played in it anyway.

"You tryna get it wet first tonight?" he asked mannishly because we hadn't been intimate in nearly two weeks and we were both missing each other in that way, but I was more concerned that his lungs were healthy and strong again before I made him lose his breath.

"Not until you're all the way better."

"But Tills I am better. Listen," he told me before taking a few exaggerated deep breaths to prove it to me, but I just laughed at him. "And that's gonna give me that Popeye super strength that I need to get to one hundred percent," he begged as he tugged on my pants.

"Is that so?" I mocked him for a while before I ultimately decided to take him up on his offer then began preparing my seat on his face. And he was definitely right about one thing. He was all better now.

On our last morning I got him up early so he could get checked out once more to make sure that the long-term effects of the smoke damage would be minimal and that he would just have to use the inhaler for a little while longer. When we got back from the doctor's office Reese and the guys from the shop were already there waiting to pack up the little U-Haul car attachment that we had gotten to take our stuff back to Atlanta in.

Well Reese was there to unlock the door for them because after that she chilled with me as I sat on the couch and looked pretty because I had just gotten my nails done the other day, not that Cam would have let me help either way. When they were almost done, she told me that she would be paying us a visit when Cam got the new shop opened, but I told her she was welcome to come anytime because she was Fade Family Gang.

Diane was out of town for the weekend with the professor and we had already said our goodbyes so I was surprised to see her car pulling up in front of the building out the window. When I looked closer I saw that it was actually Jordan in the driver's seat and she looked so funny when she got out because she didn't have a crying baby on her hip. I saw her stop and talk to Cam for a second before he seemed to direct her to my whereabouts. Reese saw that Jordan had come to talk to me alone so she grabbed the lightest box she could find then closed the door behind her.

"You guys sure have a lot of stuff," Jordan remarked about the full load outside.

"It's mostly my heavy clothes and I feel so bad for not helping," I said lightheartedly because she was clearly here to make up with me since I was leaving.

"Yeah he really does treat you like a princess, huh?"

"He does. Where are the babies? I wanted to say goodbye to them."

"Sorry I left them with my unemployed husband so that I could have a break for a change," she ribbed herself then got serious. "I just came here to say that I'm sorry for how our relationship is and for all the ways that I used you as a punching bag over the years too. It wasn't just Auntie Michelle and TJ. I was kind of like an ugly but actually really cute stepsister to you too because I was jealous of you."

"You were jealous of me?" I asked in disbelief.

"I was because even though I've always thought that I should have something over you, you still always seemed so hopeful and it was the one thing I never had. But even though I didn't always show it, you were always my favorite girl cousin."

"That's because I'm your only girl cousin," I joked as we hugged it out.

"She wants to talk to you before you go," she said and I knew exactly who she was talking about without names being said.

"I'm sure she does, but I've been pretending she doesn't exist since she publicly disowned me."

"I think you'll want to hear what she has to say. I certainly appreciated it and it's the main reason why I'm here now."

"I'll think about it," I told her as Cam came back inside to make sure we had everything.

"We're good to go," he said before Jordan apologized for judging him too quickly then told him that he was the best thing that'd ever happened to me. "Where did that come from?" he asked confused after she'd exited, leaving us alone for the first time in hours.

"Some stuff is long overdue I guess," I said just above a whisper because I was internally fighting with myself about if I would actually go see my mother one last time.

"You ready?"

"Yeah, but I want to see Michelle first. I'm not just running away anymore."

Cam was immediately against the idea, but he knew he couldn't stop me so he just came with me. I drove over the speed limit, but the ride to her house still seemed to drag on longer than usual. I tried to prep myself as best as I could for the yelling and the tears that I knew would be falling from my eyes soon because I planned on finally confronting her about every horrible thing she had done to me.

Tiffa answered the door with the boys on her heels and I could see the look of joyous surprise on her face before she embraced me and told me how much she had missed me. It meant so much that she wasn't mad at me for what'd happened to her father because I did still feel a little responsible. I knew Sofia was still confused about how she felt about everything, but all I could give her was distance and time.

I asked everybody to give me a minute alone with Michelle in the living room. Tiffa and the boys left without a word, but Cam stood in the open doorway refusing to leave because he knew like I knew that things could turn physical in an instant.

My mother's eyes already looked like they should have been all cried out, but somehow more came down as she told me that she'd been sober since the fire and that she had finally gone to both Alcoholics and Gamblers Anonymous meetings through her church. I knew something was different because even the way that she spoke to me sounded like she had come out from underneath all the fog.

"Your problem is that you're too soft, Tilly," she said ironically in a baby soft tone that I'd never seen her use with anybody let alone me. "You always have been. When I was coming up, my mama used to say you had to make girls tough or else the world would break them in two," she began before admitting that she now realized that her way wasn't the right way. "And when I saw how much it hurt you when your daddy died, I didn't know how else to bring you up without him. Sometimes it was just easier putting everything on you instead of facing it myself. I just hope it didn't make me lose my only daughter because I believe that I'm ready to be a good mother to you now."

Cam's disbelieving scoff could be heard for miles.

"I know you're not buying this shit, Tills. She didn't know what she was doing, but somehow it was only with you and not TJ? She's just saying this because he's in jail and she's about to lose her last meal-ticket in you," he rightfully accused because it had been the pattern before, but something seemed different now. I wasn't sure if she was being genuine or not, but I at least wanted to finish hearing her out.

"Just let her finish first," I told him then calmed him down because this may have been my last chance to hear her acknowledge her wrongdoing and I needed it to ease my own guilt and pain about never feeling good enough so that I could finally heal too.

"Cameron, you don't have to believe me.

You loved my daughter better than anybody including me so there ain't no more bad blood between us coming from my way. I just want to thank you for opening my eyes to see how special my baby girl truly is," she told him before she broke down crying about being conflicted about helping TJ get a lawyer since our cousin Joseph had already refused to take his case.

"Mama, TJ made his own bed and now he has to lie in it," I said trying to sound tough even though I was on the verge of tears because of how bad I saw her hurting. "I know you're thinking about borrowing against the house again, but my name is on the paperwork now and I'm not gonna let you. He needs to be a man for once in his life and face his own consequences. You've coddled him for long enough."

"You're right and if your daddy was here right now he would tell you that you don't owe us anything. We've relied on you way too much as is so you go on back home now or else I'm putting you out of here," she said with a hint of humor as she reached out to hug me and I swear it felt like the first time when our bodies connected, but it felt right. I knew Cam was still a skeptic, but I knew there had been a real change in her even though I would still have to love her from afar from now on. "Will you call me when you get home?"

"Don't worry about me right now. Just be good to your grandkids but especially Tiffa because she's gonna need you now more than ever. You can still salvage your relationship with her if you try," I advised before getting up.

I almost felt bad for leaving her here all alone to deal with the broken pieces, but I was decidedly only thinking about myself now. I hugged Tiffa and the boys once more then told them I loved them before saying my goodbyes because it was time to go.

The second I got into the driver's seat I expected Cam to tell me that I was a fool for listening and believing her, but to my surprise he didn't. In fact he said the opposite.

"This is why I love you so much. You're just a good fucking person, Tills, and that's so hard to find these days," he said before kissing the back of my hand.

After starting up the car, he all of a sudden remembered leaving Cree's clippers next to the couch at his place. I could've sworn that I'd seen him put them in a box, but I headed back that way preferring to be safe than sorry. I was a little annoyed because we were already running late and I was ready to get this drive over with, but I didn't show it because he had been more than patient with me through everything.

For whatever reason he insisted that I come

back up with him to double check that I hadn't left anything either. We passed his nice elderly tenants getting off the elevator as we were getting on and they wished us well after Cam let them know that we were leaving for good.

As expected the clippers were nowhere to be found, but he still searched high and low for them before going over to the bed and reaching under it for what looked like a shoe box. I knew he was up to something because he couldn't hold in the smile anymore when he came over and handed it to me.

"I can't believe you didn't see Reese bring this in for me earlier," he said sounding proud that she hadn't accidentally ruined the surprise. "I told you I would find some for you."

"What is it?" I asked pointlessly because I could see that it was a Jimmy Choo box, but I just knew what I thought was inside could not be in there. I opened it to find literally the most beautiful pair of shoes that I'd ever seen in my life. I literally gasped when the glimmer from the Swarovski crystals caught my eye.

"You want to try them on?" he asked like this was just some regular degular pair of shoes and not *thee* best of the best of Jimmy Choo's Cinderella collection. Like every other budgetnista I had drooled over them when they debuted, but I knew that they would never be mine because of the outrageous price point. Until now.

He got down on one knee to put it on for me just like he'd seen in the movie so I took a seat on his ottoman and let him do the honors. He took my left foot in his hands and kissed the top of it before slowly sliding on the superior form of footwear.

"Does it fit?" he asked as I freely wiggled my toes inside.

"Yes. It fits perfectly, but you literally just spent enough to put a car on my feet. Like a used Nissan, but still a car nonetheless," I joked as I stared down at the right shoe and cooed at it like it was a baby.

"Well you deserve them. And since you're so impressed and I'm already down here, can this be my proposal too?" he asked suddenly and all the laughter from me immediately ceased. "C'mon. Don't look so surprised. I told you this would happen on day one so I gave you ample warning."

"You did," I said because I remembered being so turned off by what I thought were his shallow words about us getting married and having kids then.

I knew that I would always wonder why he had decided to invest so much into me from the beginning, but I also knew that I would never doubt his feelings being real anymore because there was an unmistakable passion behind his eyes that said he would burn the city down just to show me the lights.

"So is that a yes?" he asked after I'd been reminiscing in my head for a few seconds too long.

"It's a yes," I told him as I pointed to the other shoe and had him put it on as well. All smiles, he stood to his feet and spun me around. "But this is so non canon, Cam. I didn't leave this at the ball and you didn't have to go searching for me or anything," I playfully whined.

"Nah I've been searching for somebody like you for longer than I even knew. And who cares if we went off script a little? We're telling the story our way and none of that matters as long as I get my happily ever after with you," he said sweetly before laying an equally saccharine kiss on my lips.

"Now what kind of car will I be putting on your finger when we get home?" he asked about how much I wanted my engagement ring to cost, but I couldn't even think straight because I liked that he was already referring to Atlanta as his home. Our home.

I was so hype about the shoes that I refused to take them off and I wanted to wear them home. As cute as I thought they were hours ago, my sneakers just weren't cutting it anymore.

"You won't be able to drive in those, Tills," he warned me even though I knew I would. "Tell you what. How about you sit back and relax let me do it?"

"You want to drive?" I asked because he had finally confessed the real reason he hadn't driven and it had to do with not getting Cree to the hospital in time to save her.

"Yeah I think I'm finally ready," he said sounding sure of himself, but I still wasn't convinced. "Okay let's take a spin around the block first to make sure I remember what I'm doing," he joked.

"That's okay. I trust you," I said as I handed over the keys.

"And I love you." He nicked my lips one last time before closing the door to the apartment and it wasn't until then that I realized we'd had all of our firsts here.

We were leaving much later than we'd planned and the sun was beginning to set, but nothing was going to stop me from getting out of Illinois tonight. Cam put on a Sade album for the road and when the song about skin came through the speakers, I thought about how all this time that it wasn't just a man that I'd needed to wash away from my skin. It was also all of my family burdens and all the lingering self-doubt I'd had about myself. My weight hadn't weighed me down anywhere near as much as walking around feeling responsible for everybody's well-being and happiness except for my own did.

Fortunately my relationship with Cam had helped me realize that I was supposed to be put first because I was the prize. I guess deep down I always knew it and even acted like it, but it was hard to put into practice when the one person who was supposed to love me unconditionally always made me feel less than enough.

I thought back to my first night here in Chicago when I'd wished that this experience would end up a fairytale so that I could finally get something like a good ending and how it'd unexpectedly come true. And maybe finding someone to take care of his princess was the real reason why it seemed like my dad had wanted me back here. No, I didn't get to go live in a fancy castle and be waited on hand and foot, but with Cam's help I'd managed to get something even better than a typical Cinderella story, something she was never able to get. I received apologies and closure from the people who had wronged me and now it truly felt like I could finally have the life I'd always wanted for myself.

As the sun was finally beginning to fade into the darkness, Cam pulled up at a red light and reached over to run his big hand over the low hairs that just touched my neck. The adventure that was the past six months flashed before my eyes and I quickly closed them to imagine the next adventures that we were about to embark on as we headed home to begin living happily ever after.

THICKERELLA

FOLLOW ME

Thanks for reading! If you don't want to miss out on any updates about the next installments of this series (*Sleeping Cutie* and *Trapunzel*) or other works of mine then find me on all social media platforms as TanSaidWhat.

Visit www.tanzaniaglover.com

And if the cover art took your breath away as much as it did mine, check out the talented artist Bree Douthitt! Thank you so much for bringing Thickerella to life!

THANK YOUS

I said that I was done writing dissertations to my family and friends in this section so I'll try to keep this brief especially since my love for them has remained the same since the first time I did this. But I do want to say that I feel like the luckiest person in the world to be able to go on this journey with people who genuinely love and care for me. Because of the immense amount of love and support that I receive from them, I get to do the thing I love most in the world and I'm forever grateful for it.

www.ingramcontent.com/pod-product-compliance
Lightning Source LLC
Chambersburg PA
CBHW021215310726
48971CB00006B/1564